D1520363

*THE ARTIST'S HEALER*

Cover Design and Interior Format
© THE KILLION GROUP, INC.

GRACE
-BY-THE-
SEA

3

# The, Artist's Healer

# REGINA SCOTT

*To my mother, who doesn't always realize how wonderful she is, and to the Lord, who loves all of us, no matter our intelligence, beauty, or talents.*

# CHAPTER ONE

*Grace-by-the-Sea, Dorset, England, July 1804*

S HE WASN'T MADE TO LIE abed all day.
     Abigail Archer stared at the ceiling in her bedchamber. It wasn't a grand ceiling like those in Castle How on the headland above her shop or Lord Peverell's Lodge on the opposite headland across Grace Cove. The cream-colored plaster bore no coffering, no elaborate beams, no mosaic pattern or allegorical painting of mythical beings.

She could paint one. Perhaps Poseidon rising from the depths, waves crashing around him. But no, she didn't need the reminder of the autocratic fellows in her life.

The biggest autocrat at the moment wouldn't allow her to paint in any regard.

She carefully shrugged her right shoulder. Immediately, pain shot down her arm, causing her fingers to tighten. No, no painting. Not yet. But she would not be deterred.

Her mother bustled into the room. On the best of days, theirs was an uneasy truce. Now the carefully coiffed white curls around her mother's face, her neat and cheerful cream on spring green printed cotton gown gathered at her neck, and her purposefulness only served to remind Abigail of all she could not be at the moment.

"Let me fix your hair," her mother said, going to the walnut bureau on the opposite wall to fetch the tortoiseshell brush. "And help you change into something prettier. Miss Pierce the elder sent over a lovely bed jacket—green quilted satin. Can you imagine?"

"That was very kind of her," Abigail said as her mother came around the bed, brush in hand. "But I can't move my arm enough to don it, and I doubt this bandage would fit inside even if I could."

Her mother frowned at the swath of linen wrapped around Abigail's upper arm. "That is a problem."

It certainly was.

And it wasn't something she'd ever prepared for. Bullet wounds were unheard of in the village of Grace-by-the-Sea. She ought to know; she'd lived here for all her six and twenty years. She'd made cherished friends like Jesslyn Chance and now Eva Howland. She'd learned to read and write, learned to sail, learned to paint. She'd built her own business, provided for herself and her widowed mother. Now all that was threatened because she had been in the wrong place at the wrong time.

Her mother had nearly collapsed when two of Abigail's fellow shopkeepers, Mr. Carroll across the street and Mr. Lawrence, the jeweler, had half carried her down from the headland two nights ago.

"But what happened?" she kept repeating as Abigail curled up on her bed, holding her arm while the men went for the physician. "Why are you bleeding?"

"I was shot," Abigail managed, pausing to clench her teeth against the pain. "I was helping the magistrate up at the castle. He suspects the French have been using it to pass messages."

"Messages?" Even in Abigail's fog of shock, she could see her mother's face scrunching up. "But the French are still massing across the Channel. They haven't invaded."

Yet.

"There may be some in the area," Abigail said.

"How?" her mother protested. "Why?"

She would not lose patience. She tried so hard. Abigail drew in a breath, mustered the last of her energy to explain. "Mr. Howland hoped to catch one of them, so he and the militia surrounded the castle, hiding among the trees. Jesslyn and I were inside with Eva and Mrs. Tully, keeping an eye on things, when one of the Frenchmen slipped through their net and into the castle. I ran out to alert the magistrate, and a militiaman fired his musket, thinking me the enemy. Now, if you don't mind, I think I shall faint."

She'd woken in her nightgown, with her mother hovering over her. The bullet had carved a deep trough across her upper arm, and that physician had insisted she must rest to heal. After all that, they had caught only one of the French agents thought to be haunting their village.

"It's fine, Mother," she said now. "I don't need to dress. It isn't as if I have anywhere to go."

Her mother bit her lip a moment, then set about running the brush through Abigail's hair. Ginger-colored tendrils whipped past her eyes as if fleeing the vigorous strokes. She knew how they felt.

"Well, it's always wise to look your best," her mother said, avoiding her gaze. "You never know who might call."

A knock at the door to their flat attested to the fact.

"Oh!" her mother fumed. "I wasn't ready." She hurried to grab a handful of hairpins from the bureau and dropped them and the brush in Abigail's lap. "Here. Do what you can. I'll delay him a few moments." She hurried out.

Abigail shook her head. She couldn't raise her right arm, and she could hardly dress her hair one-handed. She set the brush on the table beside the bed, then scooped up the pins and let them slide down next to it. As the rattle subsided, she cocked her head and listened.

Through the door her mother had closed behind her

came voices, three of them. She couldn't make out words, only pitches and tones. One of the higher, excited ones belonged to her mother, but the other? A lady visitor, perhaps, though why she would sound so reluctant was beyond Abigail. And that deeper one…

She stiffened a moment before the door opened. Doctor Linus Bennett walked in, black leather medical bag in one hand. Not that she would admit it to anyone who asked, but the ladies at the spa must be in alt at the very sight of him. Warm brown hair waved back from a brow that spoke of intelligence. Grey eyes appeared to look upon the world with wisdom and compassion. The firm line of those pink lips promised no complaint. His color and physique attested to good health.

"Miss Archer," he said. "How are we today?"

"I have no idea how you are," Abigail told him. "But I'm ready to get out of this bed."

His brows rose ever so slightly, but he gave no other response to her testy comment. He came around the bed to her side and set his bag on the table, sending a few pins to the hardwood floor with a tinkle.

"No pain?" he asked, beginning to unwind her bandage.

Though his gaze was on his work, Abigail felt her cheeks heating. Where was her mother? Always before she had remained in the room while Doctor Bennett examined Abigail. It was bad enough that he must visit her in her bedchamber, with her in her nightgown, the sleeve cut away to make room for the bandage. In a moment, the bare skin of her arm would be in view.

He'd seen it two nights ago, of course, when he'd first attended her, and the other morning as well. But this time, alone with him, seemed too intimate.

Then the wound came into view, an ugly slash against her fair skin, red, raw, the gap closed with white stitches as good as her mother's embroidery. Abigail swallowed.

"The sutures are holding together nicely," he said, studying the wound. "No sign of an inflammation." His gaze met hers, and breathing became difficult. He frowned and laid a hand on her forehead, the touch cool and commanding.

"No sign of a fever, though your color is higher than I'd like. How much laudanum have you used?"

"None," Abigail said, pressing her back against the wood of the walnut headboard to remove herself from his distracting touch. "I'm fine."

As if he didn't believe her, he went to locate the bottle on the bureau, held it up, and peered at the liquid sloshing about inside.

"Do not bother prescribing more," she warned him. "I won't take it. It makes me nauseous."

He set down the bottle and came back to her. "Have you been eating?"

"Broth and toast, as you apparently dictated," Abigail told him. "I could do with something more substantial."

"Gruel, then," he said, taking a fresh bandage from his bag.

Abigail stared at him. "Gruel? What of mutton, sir? At least plaice."

"Tomorrow, if you have no more nausea," he said, beginning to cover the wound anew.

"I only have nausea if I take the needless medicine you ordered. I cannot stay in this bed. I have a business to tend to, the magistrate will need assistance locating those French spies, and I must help Jesslyn Chance prepare for her wedding."

His head was bowed enough she could only see the crown. The strands of brown looked far softer than his demands.

"I am assured Miss Chance can manage," he said. "Everyone has gone out of their way to praise her skills and organization. And as for your business, the visitors to the spa will simply have to shop elsewhere for the next fortnight."

Abigail jerked away, and the bandage slipped out of his grip. "A fortnight! You cannot expect me to lie here so long. I demand you let me up, immediately."

Linus Bennett had to clench his teeth a moment before responding. He'd dealt with difficult patients in the past, in Edinburgh, where he'd attended school, and Mayfair, where he'd had his last practice. But even his nine-year-old son, Ethan, when he had been ill and abed for weeks had been more receptive to his suggestions than Miss Archer, who seemed determined to thwart his care of her.

"You cannot get up immediately without risking a fever," he said, catching hold of the bandage to tie it off. "You could also break the sutures and reopen the wound. The bullet grazed your bicep, madam. Unless it heals properly, you will never lift your lower arm without pain. I imagine that would be rather inconvenient for a painter."

He leaned back to find her green eyes narrowed and her lips working as if she was piling up words to hurl at him. Her color had only gone higher, and this time he was fairly sure of the cause.

She was furious.

"It would be more than inconvenient, and you know it," she finally said. "But my paintings aren't the only things in the shop. Nearly every woman in the area helps support her family through the crafts I sell on commission. If I make no money, neither do they."

The workings of this village continued to amaze him. He'd visited the famous spas at Harrogate and Scarborough and knew of inland Bath and Lyme Regis along the coast. None had such a generous arrangement. At Grace-by-the-Sea, families lived from the income of the shops, the goods and services sold to the spa where he had been appointed physician, and the visitors it brought in. The Spa Corporation that paid his salary divided profits among the village families quarterly.

"Perhaps one of your ladies could watch the shop for you," he suggested, snapping shut his bag.

She started to cross her arms over her chest and seemed to think better of it. "I prefer to manage things myself."

That came as no surprise. "Unfortunately, this injury requires more attention than you can give. If you have any sign of a fever or swelling, you are to send for me immediately."

Her face settled into tight lines. Her cheekbones were high and firm, the maxilla and mandible of her jaw well defined. Sculptors must long for such a face to model.

"I do not appreciate being ordered about, sir," she informed him.

Neither had Catriona.

He shoved the thought aside. Miss Archer was nothing like his late wife. Catriona had been blond and buxom, with a focus on her own pleasures. Miss Archer had a slender physique and hair the color of the bruised ginger the apothecary used in Linus's preparations. It fell about her shoulders now in thick waves that seemed to beckon him closer.

All while the light in her green eyes warned him to keep his distance.

"Ordering my patients about is my duty," he said, picking up his bag. "So is helping them understand the ramifications of ignoring my counsel. Wounds that are not allowed to heal can turn gangrenous. I prefer not to perform amputations, but I understand there's a surgeon in Upper Grace who is delighted to pull out his saw."

The color that had concerned him fled, and she dropped her gaze to the quilt covering her lap.

He felt a twinge of guilt. He hadn't intended to frighten her, but she had to know what could happen if she didn't take care. Catriona had refused to listen to him. He would not lose another.

"No need to trouble him," Miss Archer murmured as if far more contrite. "I'll do what I must to heal."

Linus drew in a breath. "Good. Any other questions for me?"

Her gaze rose once more. Oh, but he'd been wrong. Not contrite. Merely gathering more ammunition.

"Have you reinstated Jesslyn Chance and Maudlyn Tully to their positions at the spa yet?" she asked.

He should have known she'd bring that up. Miss Chance and her aunt had managed the spa between the time the previous physician—Miss Chance's father—had passed last year and Linus had arrived. Was it only a week ago, now? The Spa Corporation president and his wife did not see the need for the ladies' services now that Linus had taken charge, but he began to think them indispensable. For one thing, many of the ongoing spa guests refused to set foot in the Grand Pump Room without them. For another, he was having trouble just getting the fountain that dispensed the mineral waters to operate correctly.

"I regret that I have been too busy to make Miss Chance's acquaintance," he said. "But I have asked everyone who mentioned her to have her visit me at the spa."

She puffed out a sigh. "When you intend to apologize, sir, you go to the person you have wronged. You do not demand that they go out of their way to find you." She narrowed her eyes. "You do intend to apologize, don't you?"

"I intend to correct the misperception that I insisted on their dismissal," Linus explained. "And begin discussions on how to reinstate some of their services."

Her chin edged higher. "Some?"

He met her gaze, hoping that his own held half that determination. She could not know how important this position was to him and to Ethan.

"I am the physician at the spa, Miss Archer," he told her. "There isn't a need for another."

She continued watching him a moment, then nodded slowly. "Very well. I'll endeavor to have Jesslyn here when you call tomorrow morning. But I warn you, sir. I have started a crusade against your despotism, and I will not cease until I have satisfaction."

# CHAPTER TWO

A S SOON AS DOCTOR BENNETT left, Abigail called for her mother. She took her time answering.

"Is something wrong?" Abigail asked as her mother ventured into the bedchamber. "I thought you'd join us when that physician was here."

She glanced back over her shoulder, then aimed a smile at Abigail. "Sorry. I was busy. What did you need, dear?"

Busy? The flat was small enough that they had little housework. They took their meals from the Mermaid and Mr. Ellison's bakery, so she had no need to cook outside a cup of tea brewed on the hob. She was gifted at needlework, but that could be set aside easily. What had her mother been so busy doing?

Abigail's stomach sank. "You weren't in the shop."

Her mother went to the bureau and began rearranging the few items that remained. "No, dear," she said, not even looking at Abigail. "The last time didn't go over well."

With anyone. It had been one of their busiest seasons, right before Easter, and Abigail had been needed at a meeting of the Spa Corporation Council, of which she was an elected member. She hadn't wanted to close the shop, so she'd accepted her mother's help in keeping it open. She'd learned her lesson that day.

Her mother had so enjoyed chatting with the customers

that little had been sold. When she had sold something, she hadn't been able to calculate change, so items had left for less or more than they should. And she hadn't written down what had been sold, requiring Abigail to conduct a full inventory to determine which of the people who supplied her with their handiwork should be paid and for what. She hadn't requested her mother's help in the shop since.

Her mother turned to her now with another bright smile, waiting patiently.

Abigail pasted on a smile as well. "Thank you for taking care of me, Mother. I need to speak with Jesslyn. Will you send word to ask her to visit before the spa opens tomorrow?"

Her round face bunched. "Oh, I wouldn't think so. That's when the physician calls."

Precisely. "I know," Abigail told her. "I'd like the two of them to meet."

Her mother's rosebud mouth tightened. "Jesslyn Chance is to be married next week. She has no need to meet our new physician. I was hoping him for you."

Abigail stiffened, and her arm protested. "Doctor Bennett and I will never suit."

She sighed. "You say that about all the gentlemen."

At least, most. She found Captain St. Claire, the retired naval officer recuperating at Dove Cottage up the hill from the spa, to be rather dashing. He'd never been anything less than charming to her, but, then, a handsome face and winning manner could still mask a cruel character. After seeing the damage her father had done to his family and home, she wasn't about to trust any fellow so easily.

"Be that as it may," Abigail said, "I would like to get word to Jesslyn."

"I can't," her mother said, turning for the door. "I'm busy."

"Doing what?" Abigail called after her. "You could at least wave out the shop door at Mr. Carroll. He might be persuaded to help."

The only answer was a thump from the sitting room, followed by voices.

Voices. Plural. Who was here now?

She ought to leave well enough alone. Her mother had any number of friends—Mrs. Mance, the vicar's house-keeper; Mrs. Ellison, the wife of the baker; even Jesslyn's aunt Maudlyn. One or more might have dropped in.

Before eight in the morning?

Something was going on. How could she simply sit in this bed and not find out? She wiggled forward, pushing back the quilt her mother had made from scrap pieces the Misses Pierce, of the linens and trimmings shop, had given her. The movement made her arm protest again. She bent it at the elbow, kept it protectively close to her body, leaned forward, and craned her neck.

Their chintz-covered sofa was empty. She could see all the rose-on-cream pattern from here. Were they in the dining room, then?

She leaned back and studied the floor beside the bed a moment. Doctor Bennett had never said she couldn't move her legs, just her arm. She swung her feet off the bed and levered herself upright. There. That hadn't been so bad. She shook her hips to settle her nightgown around her, then padded toward the door. Her mother's friends might be shocked at the sight of her in her night-clothes, but it would only be for a moment, and at least she would have had the luxury of movement.

But their little flat was silent now. She could see most of it from the doorway. Located behind her shop, between High Street and the hill that led up to the castle on the headland, it had two rooms front and back—sitting room, dining room, and two bedchambers—with a wide cen-tral corridor down the middle. The final room behind her bedchamber at the back of the shop she'd reserved for her studio. No use going in there. Her mother would never entertain guests among Abigail's paintings.

Would she?

Once more her stomach dropped, and she marched down the corridor. That was her space, her refuge. No one entered without her express permission.

But someone was exiting. A boy came out of her studio, arms laden with parchment and her charcoals.

"Ho, there," Abigail called. "Where do you think you're going with those?"

He stopped and stared at her. She stared back. Very likely he'd never seen a lady in a lawn nightgown. She'd never seen him. Why not? She knew everyone in the village, from the newborn to the aged. Few of the visitors to the spa brought young children with them.

He was dressed in a simple brown coat and trousers over half-boots. Difficult to guess his age. He was as short and slight as Mrs. Bascom's seven-year-old daughter, but those brown eyes looked far more knowing, as if the vicar, Mr. Wingate, was intent on examining her. They looked warily out of a narrow face under a crop of brown hair streaked with gold.

"Mrs. Archer said I could draw," he told Abigail.

So tempting to cross her arms over her chest, but impossible. She shifted on her feet instead. "Did she now? And who might you be?"

"Ethan Bennett. Who are you?"

Abigail frowned. "Mrs. Archer's daughter. Are you Doctor Bennett's son?"

He nodded.

"So, my mother must have agreed to watch you while your father is working," Abigail surmised.

"When I'm not taking lessons from the vicar," he said.

Well, that was interesting news. A few days ago, her mother had surprised her by answering an advertisement in the local newspaper about a widower seeking someone to care for his son. Her mother had said she had been lonely, and Abigail had felt a bit guilty about that. Between painting and running the shop, she hadn't had much time to spare. But she'd thought her mother happy with her friends in the village, her work at the church school. When they'd learned the lad in question was Doctor Bennett's son, Abigail had tried to dissuade her mother from pursuing the position. She'd thought the matter closed.

Well, apparently it was closed, just not the way she had thought.

"And where is my mother now?" she asked.

"She went across the street to see someone," he said. "She'll be right back. May I go draw?"

The parchment was already starting to slide from his grip. Abigail stepped aside to let him pass. "Certainly, sir. Forgive me for detaining you."

He did not smile at her tease but continued down the corridor for the flat. Abigail followed.

He went to the dining room, climbed up onto one of the lute-backed chairs, and dumped his finds on the butter yellow tablecloth. As she watched, he arranged one of the sheets of parchment before him, turning it this way and that as if trying to find the exact right position. Then he selected one of her charcoal pencils and considered the paper so carefully he might have been preparing to compose a symphony.

So like his father—solemn, calm. At his age, she'd been running all over the village with Jesslyn, learning to sail from her friend's father, doing anything to avoid her own father.

The main door clicked, and her mother hurried in. She caught sight of them through the arched doorway and stopped. "Oh, good. You've met."

"Young Mr. Bennett tells me you are watching him,"

Abigail said.

Color rose in her mother's cheeks as she continued toward them. "When he isn't taking lessons from the vicar. His father will bring him by every morning before eight and return for him when the spa closes." She smiled at the boy. "Such a well-mannered young man, just like his father."

So it seemed. And it also seemed that Abigail would be seeing even more of the physician, whether she wanted to or not.

Miss Archer was in bed when Linus came to retrieve his son that evening. Her mother was all for disturbing her, but Linus declined. She needed her rest if she was to recover. If he had ever doubted that, he had only to look at his son.

Ethan trudged along beside him as they headed down High Street toward the cove and the cottage the Spa Corporation had given them. The fishing boats bobbed on the waters, rocking with the incoming tide. Until coming here, the only harbors he'd seen had been clogged with massive sailing ships, loud with the sound of stevedores unloading, first mates rallying their crews. Here the only sound was the call of a gull soaring overhead.

"I understand sometimes spa visitors go bathing in the cove," he told his son as they turned down the path to the little stone cottage tucked into the bank. "Would you like to try it?"

"No, thank you, sir," Ethan said, gaze on the pebbled path.

Linus bit back a sigh. He'd been just as quiet a child. His mother had found ways to invite him closer, get him to share his thoughts and hopes. He didn't have the knack.

The best he could do right now was give Ethan some stability, some normalcy.

A shame he had not been able to settle on a schedule yet. He was to open the spa every morning except Sunday at eight, but new guests might appear at any time, from mid-morning until late in the afternoon. They arrived in the village by carriage, mail coach, horseback, or ship. Some wanted treatment, even if just a drink of the mineral waters for which the spa was famous. Others came for the society. He did well enough with the former, but entertainment had never been his forte. Unfortunately, without the social aspects of the spa, the number of guests had declined precipitously.

Perhaps that was why he could only be relieved when he found another woman with Abigail Archer the next morning.

"As promised," Miss Archer sang out from her place on the bed, hair about her shoulders in her lawn nightgown. "Jesslyn Chance, allow me to introduce Doctor Bennett."

The former spa hostess was not what he had expected. From all the comments made about her, he'd thought she might be a dark-haired, more athletic version of Miss Archer—no nonsense, determined, a veritable Amazon. Instead, her fashionable pink muslin gown showed off a slender figure. Her blue eyes seemed too large for her fine-boned face, which was surrounded by blond ringlets.

"Doctor Bennett," she said in a soft, high voice, "a pleasure to make your acquaintance. I've heard a great deal about you."

He could imagine she had. He refused to look at Miss Archer. "And I've heard a great deal about you," he countered. "Allow me to clear up a misperception. I did not request that you leave your position."

She blinked, lashes fluttering. "I did not think you had."

"I did," Miss Archer put in. "But I should have known

better than to accept anything Mr. Greer says without looking deeper."

Mr. Greer was the village apothecary and the Spa Corporation president. Linus wasn't sure why Miss Archer would not believe his word. He had never struck Linus as anything less than forthright.

"Nevertheless," Linus said, "I understand from Mr. Lawrence, the corporation treasurer, that the spa has been doing poorly recently."

Miss Chance nodded. "Since my father passed. Everyone assumed it was the lack of a physician that was keeping people away."

"Hence the need to hire you, sir," Miss Archer added.

Linus inclined his head. "Having worked at the spa a sennight now, I can see how medical care is necessary."

"Of course you would," Miss Archer muttered, look darkening.

"But I can also see why it isn't sufficient," he persisted. "The spa at Grace-by-the-Sea is known as much for its society as it is for its healing."

"True," Miss Archer allowed with a glance to her friend.

Miss Chance was watching him. "What are you suggesting, sir?"

"I propose a partnership," he said. "I will manage the medical aspects. You would manage the social."

Miss Archer beamed at him. How extraordinary. He felt as if the sun had burst into view on a cold winter's day. He wanted to bask in the warmth.

"I take it Mr. Greer has approved this arrangement?" Miss Chance asked in her sweet voice.

Linus brought himself back to the conversation with difficulty. "I have not broached the subject, but I believe funds can be made available."

"I'll make sure of it," Miss Archer promised. "You must start immediately, Jess. It's already July, and people will expect the Regatta to go on as planned."

The very air seemed to shimmer at the word. Linus glanced between them. "Regatta?"

"Grace-by-the-Sea hosts a race every August," Miss Chance explained. "We have a number of local ships, and guests come from up and down the coast and as far away as London to join us. We would have to check with Mrs. Kirby to see how many have arranged for houses, and Jack Hornswag at the Mermaid will have heard how many have requested moorage."

"Will you be taking out your father's boat?" Miss Archer asked eagerly, wiggling on the bed. Linus had to stop himself from moving forward to assist her. She would not welcome it, and he might do more damage to her arm.

"I'll leave that to Alex this year." Miss Chance nodded to Linus. "My brother. Though he may prefer to sail with Captain St. Claire instead."

Miss Archer slumped. "Well, I suppose I wouldn't be much use to you with this arm in any event."

Surely she didn't mean she sailed. With her injury, he could not allow it. "Depending on the date of this event," he told her, "you may still be confined to bed, Miss Archer."

She straightened. "Now, see here, sir…"

Miss Chance held up her hands, as if she were the one surrendering. "Please, Abby. You must heal. I want you with me when I walk down the aisle next week." The look she sent Linus dared him to argue.

"Congratulations on your marriage," Linus said instead. "Forgive me for not realizing it was so soon. Perhaps I should speak to your intended husband about my proposal for you to continue working at the spa."

Miss Chance's pretty face remained pleasant, but she seemed to have grown an inch or two. "No need, sir. I am fully capable of determining my future and will explain the matter to Larkin Denby, my betrothed. Now, I should allow you to see to Abigail. You are already late opening the spa."

He was, and that was a bit of a stumble, but he could not shake the feeling he had stumbled here as well. "Thank you, Miss Chance. Will I see you later at the spa, then?"

"Of course, Doctor Bennett. I merely have to alert our Regulars that it is safe to return."

He bowed, and she left.

"There, was that so difficult?" Miss Archer asked as he straightened.

"The only difficulty was finding a way to contact her," he said, moving to her side. "Thank you for making the arrangements."

"Thank you for seeing to reason," she replied, leaning back against the headboard. "I hope you will be as reasonable about letting me out of this bed."

She looked up at him, lashes fluttering as she obviously attempted to mimic her friend's sweet demeanor. He smiled but made no promises. He was removing the bandage when there was a knock at the open door. He glanced up to find Mrs. Howland in the doorway. The curly-haired brunette had been one of his few friends in the village so far. An heiress, she had married the magistrate a few days ago only to orchestrate the siege of Castle How against French agents.

"Oh, good," she said, coming into the room, her lavender skirts swirling about her. "You're both here. I bring news about our French spies."

# CHAPTER THREE

A BIGAIL PULLED AWAY FROM DOCTOR Bennett's touch to focus on her friend. "What's happened?"

Eva moved fully into the room, hugging her rose-patterned shawl close. As she stopped at the foot of the bed, her Saxon-blue eyes twinkled with mischief. "Mr. Denby was able to convince Mr. Harris to confess."

"Oh, well done," Abigail said.

Doctor Bennett nodded. "Well done indeed. The spa has been ablaze with gossip since you apprehended him. That was the night Miss Archer was shot." He looked to her as if she had somehow planned that.

"It certainly was," Eva agreed with a smile to Abigail. "And what a night! I'm simply glad our valiant Riding Surveyor was able to get through to Mr. Harris. Of course, at first, the miscreant denied any wrongdoing, but he eventually declared that a French invasion is imminent."

Abigail shivered at the very thought. "That was bravado talking, surely."

"So we hope," Eva assured her. "Before we remanded him into the custody of an agent from the War Office, however, he admitted that as many as four French agents may be lurking in the area."

Abigail stared at her. "But we can identify them."

Eva made a face. "Unfortunately, no. He never met

them in person. He only left messages at the castle. He received his orders that way too. So, we have no idea who they are, what they are doing. That's why James sent me to find you. We need your help. We must watch for strangers."

While Eva had been talking, Doctor Bennett had succeeded in unwrapping Abigail's bandage and now dropped it into his bag. "Easier said than done. Nearly everyone is a stranger to me."

Much as it pained her to admit it, he was right. "And, on any given day in the summer, the spa may host as many as a dozen Newcomers, more if Jesslyn pulls off the Regatta as planned."

"That's what concerns James," Eva said. "He had to leave for London this morning to see about his family. All we can do is be vigilant. Question the reason for every fellow to be here."

That was a tall order. Even with Jesslyn's help, would Doctor Bennett be able to handle such a task? He might end up treating the very people they wanted captured!

But of course, he didn't ask for help in such matters. "I'll do what I can," he said. "Now, if I may finish my work, I'll leave you two to talk."

Eva stepped back toward the door. Panic pricked Abigail, and she jerked up her free hand to halt her friend. "Stay, please, Eva. My mother is busy, and I would prefer company."

She didn't dare say the word chaperone, but her friend seemed to understand, for she returned to her spot at the foot of the bed with a commiserating smile. Doctor Bennett, however, frowned just the slightest, and she couldn't tell if it was her request or her wound that troubled him.

"Any pain?" he asked, taking her arm in his warm hands and studying the stitches.

So easy to study him in return. Those lashes were more gold than brown and long enough to make the ladies sigh in envy. A depression marked his cheek, less ruddy than the rest of his skin. A scar perhaps? And those lips…

She made herself focus on her wound instead, though she had to crick her neck to see all of it. Was the mark less red than yesterday?

He raised his gaze to hers, and she realized he was waiting for her answer.

"Only a little pain, when I move it," she allowed.

When his brows went up, she sighed. "Well, I must move it once in a while. Some things require getting out of bed, sir."

"I can think of nothing more important than your health, madam," he countered, gaze returning to her wound.

"And how do you suggest I use the chamber pot?" she demanded.

His mouth twitched, as if he was fighting a smile. "I will allow that sort of exception." He glanced up again. "Have you needed the laudanum?"

She'd almost given in last night when the ache had consumed her. "No."

He released her to turn and pull a fresh bandage from his bag. "There is no silver cup for enduring pain, Miss Archer. If you need the medicine, use it."

"I told you, it makes me nauseous. And there's no silver cup for vomiting either, sir."

A laugh popped out of him, and Eva giggled. Abigail's shoulders came down. But, when next he spoke, it was directed at her friend as he began bandaging Abigail's wound anew.

"You have always struck me as a reasonable person, Mrs. Howland. Perhaps you can convince your friend to have a care for herself."

"I don't know how I gave you the impression that I'm reasonable, Doctor," Eva said, the twinkle returning to her blue eyes. "The previous Earl of Howland called me headstrong. I believe Abigail and I share that trait."

Abigail grinned at her.

He finished quickly and picked up his bag. "I'll check on you this evening, Miss Archer."

"Twice in one day," Abigail teased. "How did I earn such an honor?"

"By being headstrong," he replied. He nodded to both of them. "Good day, ladies."

Eva watched him out. "You've certainly set his back up."

"Well, he sets mine up, so we are even." She patted the bed beside her. "Come. Talk to me. Tell me of something beyond these walls."

Eva came to sit, settling her lavender skirts about her. "I wish I had thrilling tales to share, but things have been quiet the last few days since we captured Harris. As far as we know, no one has broken into the castle."

Castle How had seen a number of mysterious events the last few weeks—lights appearing in the window, strangers flitting through the Great Hall. All had now been laid at the foot of Mr. Harris, the French agents for whom he worked, and others who had since departed the village.

"Then you think the French will still land," Abigail said.

"If they do, we'll be ready," Eva promised. "Mr. Greer will be exercising the militia three days a week starting tomorrow. James will take over when he returns. In the meantime, I'd feel more assured if we could find the remaining French agents."

"So would I," Abigail told her. "And I fear Doctor Bennett will not be up to the task. He simply doesn't know a Regular from a stranger. And he's more likely to argue logically than to take action."

"Unlike you," Eva said with a nod to her bandage.

"Unlike me," Abigail said primly. "But I can promise you—I'll be keeping an eye on Grace-by-the-Sea, and our new physician."

Abigail Archer was certainly a redoubtable woman. Linus caught himself smiling as he walked to the spa that morning. His father had treated more gunshot wounds than any physician would prefer, and Linus had seen more than his share of soldiers begging for something to kill the pain. She bravely fought through. A shame that meant she sometimes fought him as well.

He didn't like being a few minutes late, but at least no one was waiting for him, and his first appointment wasn't until half past ten. He unlocked the door and ventured inside.

The quiet, the peace, settled over him like a warm blanket. Whoever had designed the spa at Grace-by-the-Sea had known exactly what he was about. One wall held windows looking down toward the cove and the sea beyond. The other walls, all the color of that sea on a clear day, surrounded the space with calm. Potted palms here and there whispered of warmer climes. The pale stone fountain in the corner promised a refreshing drink. Now, if he could just get that fountain to work.

The fluted basin still showed a faint circle of orange, marking where the mineral waters had once pooled, so he knew the pumping mechanism had worked at some point. No matter which way he twisted the little rod below the basin, nor how many times, the fountain would do no more than dribble water down the carved central stand of stone. A gurgling below suggested more waited. He had no idea how to free it.

Well, they'd hired a physician, not an engineer.

He was still tinkering with it when his guests began arriving.

The first two were gentlemen, Mr. Donner and Mr. George. They had started attending the spa when he had begun his post. Both had dark hair and ready smiles and dressed like London dandies. Neither required medical treatment, or at least not that he could see. They certainly had not approached him about any concerns. They seemed content to sit in the wicker chairs by the windows and wait for others to join them.

The next visitor to arrive made his way straight to Linus's side. "Quiet this morning," he mused, glancing around.

Linus smiled at his colleague. Doctor Robert Owens had appeared at the spa only the other day. Round face wreathed in wrinkles, short-cropped hair now white and thinning, he nevertheless exhibited an energy that Linus envied. Now he rubbed his hands before his tailored blue coat as if he couldn't wait to begin work.

"I hope that it will be worth your time shortly," Linus told him. "If not, I fear you'll have nothing to tell the spa owner in Scarborough."

Owens returned his smile. "Oh, no need to worry, dear boy. I'm learning all sorts of things at Grace-by-the-Sea. I'm sure my superiors will agree it was worth my time to visit to see how you all do things here."

Perhaps as an example of what not to do at a spa.

Over the course of the next hour, Linus did his best to welcome each visitor and attempted to determine their reasons for coming to the spa. Most seemed more interested in meeting others than in being treated, and he could only hope that Miss Chance would take pity on him and return soon. It was challenging enough seeing each one settled. Now he found himself studying every countenance for more than signs of illness.

Were there truly French agents among them?

He could not discount the possibility. The worrisome proximity of the southern coast of England to France had been a key consideration in his decision to move Ethan to Grace-by-the-Sea. Napoleon was said to have amassed thousands of ships and soldiers across that narrow body of water, ready to embark at a moment's notice to cross the Channel and invade England. Defenses had gone up from Dover to Cornwall. Every county had had to develop plans on how to safeguard its people, livestock, and wheeled conveyances.

Still, Grace-by-the-Sea seemed an unlikely landing spot. The cove might be sheltered, but it was small. On the other hand, it was the only area of low bank leading up to the Downs for miles, and the other bigger harbors were guarded by trained soldiers and marines.

But to see treachery, villainy, in every new face? Unthinkable!

He had settled all the guests and was back at the fountain again when he became aware of an increase in the noise level. Turning, he found that Miss Chance had entered the spa along with half a dozen people who had apparently been regular attendees before he had taken his position. He'd met one—Mr. Crabapple. His rheumy eyes and jerky movements begged for Linus's medical attention. Unfortunately, like the others, he studiously avoided Linus, coming instead to sit opposite a silver-haired fellow at the chessboard near the fountain.

Miss Chance went to the tall desk by the door. When Linus joined her, she was consulting the large book open there.

"No others appear to have signed in since you arrived," she said, voice soft as she flipped back a page. "Yet I see at least one Newcomer in the room."

"I don't tend to ask whether they're visiting for the first time, so I never suggested they sign in," Linus told her. "Is that of particular importance?"

"Very," she assured him, raising her blue gaze off the paper. "We have three classes of visitors, sir: Newcomers, Irregulars, and Regulars, and they must be treated accordingly."

She made the categories sound as important as animal, vegetable, and mineral.

"As I would treat any regardless, I fail to see the distinction," he said.

"Whereas my treatment of them must vary considerably," she said. "See Mrs. Harding, there by the windows?"

An older woman with auburn hair and a physique in robust health stood surrounded by gentlemen, Mr. Donner and Mr. George among them. "She would not appear to require my services," he noted.

"Indeed, sir. She comes for the company. She has stayed here from spring to autumn for years. I have no need to instruct her about the village shops, the location of the assembly on Wednesday, the timing of church services."

He would not have thought to instruct anyone on those matters. "Ah, I see. But you would have to share such insights with those new to the spa."

"And those who come only occasionally," she agreed. "And everyone must sign the welcome book. It is helpful for you and me to match faces to names and names to needs. And it allows acquaintances to find each other."

She made it sound logical. "I begin to see why your Regulars value you as they do. Thank you for agreeing to return to the spa."

She nodded. "It is my pleasure. How have you been getting on otherwise? I trust you found the examining rooms to be sufficient."

"More than sufficient. Though I cannot convince the fountain to do more than bubble."

"There's a trick to it. Let me show you."

He spent the rest of the day learning.

"I had no idea of the responsibilities," he told Abigail Archer when he went to check on her and pick up Ethan that evening. "It seems I should have informed the

Inchleys to retrieve the dirty glasses and bring fresh ones. I'd been attempting to sanitize the few we used myself. I didn't know to alert Mr. Ellison to bring things for tea. We haven't hosted tea since Miss Chance left. And I would have been lost attempting to manage my first assembly. I cannot thank you enough for insisting that I approach her."

Sitting up in her bed, she smiled. She appeared to be in excellent health: color in her cheeks, a sparkle to her green eyes. She'd draped a short jacket of a similar shade of green about her shoulders. The color made the ginger of her hair and lips more noticeable.

"Did your mother put up your hair?" he asked. All too easy to focus on the warm color, estimate the thickness, imagine the feel of it. Ahem.

She raised her uninjured arm to touch a hand to the braid about her head. "Yes. Why do you ask?"

Linus collected himself. "Just making sure you're following doctor's orders."

That brought the familiar light flaring into her eyes. "I don't follow anyone's orders, sir."

"A slip of the tongue," Linus assured her.

She leaned forward. "Then we are agreed I may rise from this bed?"

"We can consider it tomorrow," he hedged. "Until then, continue the regime I prescribed."

She made a face as she leaned back. "May I at least have something better than gruel? Mother tells me the Mermaid has a lovely beef stew tonight."

"I cannot advise red meat," he started, but he could see her stiffening, as if building up the energy to fight him. "However, if you concentrate on the vegetables instead, I will allow it."

"How very generous of you."

He had not been aware those words could be said so venomously.

"Until the morning, then," he replied and went to collect his son.

Once more Ethan walked with him down High Street, head bowed as if he counted each stone they passed. The stillness at the spa had been restful. The silence now made Linus's shoulders feel tight, as if his muscles had suddenly pulled themselves into a ball. Not so long ago, when Linus had come home from his practice at the end of the day, Ethan would have told him stories—castles he'd built with his blocks, mathematical problems he'd solved. Now he spoke only when necessary.

"How are you and Mrs. Archer getting along?" Linus asked as they turned onto the path toward the cottage.

"She's very kind," Ethan allowed, head still bowed. The sea breeze ruffled his hair.

"Oh?" Linus encouraged. "How so?"

"She lets me draw as much as I like, and she brings me treats from the bakery."

Why was he suddenly jealous of a baker? "We could purchase treats as well. Nothing too sweet and not often enough to disrupt your diet, of course."

"Yes, sir," Ethan said dutifully. He climbed the steps to the cottage as cautiously as an old man.

Linus almost slammed the cottage door shut behind them. But no. He would not allow such a display. Ethan deserved better.

And Linus knew why the display was so tempting. He was frustrated, with himself and their situation. Catriona was to have been his partner, the mother to their son. Her charm, her beauty, had won his heart, but marrying her had been a mistake. She'd craved a life he could not give her, a life he still didn't fully understand. In the end, she'd chosen that life over him and their son and left them behind. He still struggled to forgive her for her choices.

But he refused to let Ethan see any of that. His son

deserved to live without the fears, the burdens.

If only Linus could find a prescription that would help the two of them find happiness again.

# CHAPTER FOUR

ABIGAIL TOOK PARTICULAR PLEASURE FROM the look on Doctor Bennett's face when he came to bring Ethan and check on her the next morning. As his son went to the dining room where her mother had hot chocolate waiting, the physician stopped in the middle of the sitting room and narrowed his eyes at her.

"I distinctly recall saying we might consider you getting out of bed," he said.

Abigail rose from the sofa, her burgundy-colored skirts falling about her feet. It had taken an hour of practice that had left her sweating, but she could stand without putting either hand on the seat to help her. "I did consider it, and then I attempted it, and you can see for yourself that I am fine."

His gaze swept over her, as if he was examining every inch, and her cheeks heated.

"Your color is too high," he said, bringing his gaze to meet hers. "You obviously overexerted yourself."

Abigail shook her head. "Have you ever considered that my color has less to do with my health and more to do with your infuriating suggestions?"

He frowned. "I suppose that's possible. And how am I to examine your arm now that you're clothed?"

"Ha!" She twisted to show him the white satin lacing on the long full sleeves. "Eva Howland let me borrow the gown. You have only to untie the ribbons, and the fabric will fall aside."

He looked skeptical, but he dropped his bag on the sofa and began loosening the ribbon to run it back through the embroidery-edged holes.

Abigail glanced toward the dining room. Her mother was sitting calmly, sipping at her cup and nodding at something Ethan was saying. She had explained the function of the gown to her mother, but surely the woman had some opinion about the fact that her daughter was being partially undressed less than twenty feet away.

Doctor Bennett, thankfully, seemed more fascinated by the gown than what was inside. "Ingenious," he allowed as the bandage came into view. "I'll have to suggest this to the next lady I treat who has had the misfortune to be shot in the arm."

Was he teasing her? Abigail turned her head to watch him. He was busy unwrapping the bandage, large hands quick but gentle. The scent of mint caught her nose. His cologne, perhaps? Or the soap he used?

"Any pain?" he asked.

Abigail gathered her wits. "None. I haven't used the laudanum either. And I ate an entire bowl of stew with no nausea. I'm ready to go about my day."

"Not until the sutures have been removed," he said, gaze on her wound.

"So, remove them."

He turned to retrieve the new bandage. "In another ten days."

"Ten days!" Abigail stared at him. "Jesslyn Chance walks down the aisle in four. Nothing will keep me from her side."

"Fever?" he suggested calmly, lifting the new bandage from the bag. "Gangrene?"

"Surely they are no longer considerations," she protested. "I can stand, move. I am dressing and undressing myself with assistance. It is only a one-hour ceremony, sir."

"One hour of standing," he reminded her, beginning to wrap the bandage around her arm. "The attendants remain on their feet along with the bride, groom, and minister, at least in the weddings I've attended. That doesn't count the preparations beforehand or the wedding breakfast afterward. Such an event will tax your strength."

"You, sir, know nothing of my strength."

He finished rewrapping the wound. "Tie up the ribbons yourself, then."

She scowled at the dangling ribbon, then at him. "That's not fair. It's impossible to do one-handed."

"As will be many tasks if you lose that arm." He snapped shut his bag. "I hope you will think about what I said. We can speak further tonight."

Abigail gritted her teeth as he headed for the door. He might know more about medicine, but she knew her own capabilities. She would not wait for him to return tonight. She would go up to the spa and prove to them all she was sufficient. She needed no one's help to live her life.

Least of all his.

Stubborn, prideful, willful! Linus found himself walking faster than his usual pace around the corner of Miss Archer's shop and forcibly slowed his steps. Why couldn't he make her see reason? He knew what gunshot wounds could do to flesh; he'd heard the screams of soldiers as their limbs were amputated. Worse were those who had to wait, eyes sunken, faces sweating, as they begged for mercy.

He stopped, swallowing. Was that sweat on his own brow? The sea breeze seemed inordinately cool otherwise. And here he'd thought himself beyond such memories now.

As he drew in a breath, he became aware of another gaze. Through the window of Mr. Carroll's Curiosities across the street from him, the dapper shopkeeper looked at him in concern. Then he held up one finger. Linus had only reached the shop door when he hurried out.

"For your son," he said, offering a book from the many Linus knew crowded the shop. "I thought the drawing of the octopus particularly intriguing."

Linus gazed down at the book. "Denizens of the Deep," he read. "Very interesting. I'm sure Ethan would enjoy it."

Mr. Carroll leaned closer, his gaze magnified by his spectacles. "He was in the other day. Couldn't stop looking at the pages."

"Then I should pay you for this," Linus said.

The shopkeeper stepped back, raising both hands before his paisley waistcoat. "Not at all. It is my pleasure to be of service. Tell young Master Bennett he is welcome to visit any time." He bustled back inside before Linus could thank him.

Funny how a little kindness went a long way. He was certain the sun hadn't been shining so brightly a moment ago. Tucking the book under his arm, he continued to the spa.

Only to find it open and full.

Ladies lounged in the wicker chairs; couples promenaded. The silver-haired fellow, who he now knew as Lord Featherstone, and another Regular called the Admiral were playing chess while Mr. Donner attempted to catch the naval man's attention over some matter that seemed of great importance. Mr. Crabapple was absorbed in what Mrs. Harding was saying, Mr. George hanging on her every word as well. Doctor Owens was sampling the spa water cascading from the fountain, crystal glass in his hand, journal tucked under one arm.

"You, madam," Linus told Miss Chance, who was standing guard over the welcome book, "are a wonder."

She smiled at him. "Good morning to you as well. You should know the latest gossip is that a press gang has been plying its trade along the coast, and no man is safe. And there was an altercation at Upper Grace last night, the next village on the Downs. The constable there claims it was thieves, but some reported to have heard gun shots. I would downplay the former rumor, as no one in the spa is likely to be impressed into the Royal Navy, and I would reassure them concerning the latter rumor. We have few weapons at Grace-by-the-Sea, Abigail's wound notwithstanding."

"You continue to amaze me," Linus said, setting down the book from Mr. Carroll.

"I've been working at the spa long enough it's not much effort, sir."

"You give yourself too little credit," Linus insisted.

"I fear you have the same fault." She lifted a small leather-bound journal from behind the desk and held it out to him. "I've had any number of requests for your attentions, so I started you an appointment book. Your first patient today arrives in a quarter hour—Mrs. Rand. She's an Irregular. My father treated her two years ago when she complained of pleurisy. I've left his case notes on the table in the first examining room should you care to familiarize yourself. One warning—she is sensitive to loud noises."

Linus stared at her. "I shall speak to Mr. Greer. He must know this spa will only function properly when its leader is at her desk." He seized her hand and kissed the back, then strode to the examining room, feeling lighter than he had in weeks. Now, if only he could find a way to get through to Abigail Archer.

Abigail marched into the spa in time to see Linus Bennett press a kiss against Jesslyn's knuckles. She stopped, blinking, but the vision did not go away. Her heart was pounding in the most alarming way as he turned from her friend and strode to the closest examining room, but she doubted the tempo had anything to do with her wound. She made herself continue toward the welcome book.

Jesslyn must have seen her coming, for she picked up her pink muslin skirts and hurried to meet her. "Abigail! I'm so glad to see you up and about."

Abigail accepted her hug, careful to keep her bandaged arm to one side. "Thank you. But I must ask. Did Doctor Bennett just kiss your hand?"

Jess blushed. "Yes. I gather he's had difficulty settling into the spa. He was grateful for the help."

"Well, I'm glad he recognized your incomparable talents," Abigail said, shoving aside any lingering emotion. She would not be jealous of the woman she loved like a sister, especially over a man she barely tolerated. "So, everything back to normal?"

"Nearly," Jess said. "Eva tells me we must be on the lookout for strangers." She spread her hands. "Every Newcomer is a stranger. Five arrived this morning alone."

"And some never progress beyond Newcomer," Abigail said with a look to the open examining room, where Doctor Bennett stood, head bowed, as he studied the parchment in his hands.

"He's trying," Jess said.

"He certainly is," Abigail agreed. "And what of Maudie? Did he decline to allow her to work?"

Jess leaned closer and lowered her voice. "She's been helping Eva Howland, what with the magistrate and his mother out of town. And I wasn't sure how Doctor Bennett would take to her. Not everyone appreciates Maudie's view of the world."

Jesslyn's aunt, Maudlyn Tully, was an older woman given to fancies. Most in the village understood. Even the Regulars conversed with her easily. How would Linus Bennett react to the tales of pirates, fairies, trolls, and mermaids Maudie liked to spin?

Two elderly ladies entered the spa just then. One was tiny and wizened, but her companion was far taller and sturdier. Abigail couldn't help admiring the fine embroidery on the smaller woman's indigo wool gown. If the plainer Carmelite-patterned cotton of the larger woman's dress was any indication, one was the mistress and the other paid companion. The little lady scampered as quickly as a mouse to the Welcome Desk and clutched the polished wood with both lace-gloved hands as if afraid she might blow away.

"Miss Chance, how good to see you," she said in a voice that trembled as much as the rest of her. "Am I late?"

"Not at all, Mrs. Rand," Jess assured her as her companion came up behind her with an apologetic smile. "Our new physician, Doctor Bennett, is expecting you. And good morning to you as well, Miss Turnpeth."

The companion beamed as if pleased to be remembered, but Mrs. Rand looked toward the examining rooms, pale blue eyes wide. "Is he particularly fearsome?"

Oh, but Abigail could tell her tales. She kept her mouth shut and smiling.

"No," Jess promised. "He's quite reasonable. Miss Archer, here, was a recent patient. She recovered faster than expected under his care."

That was overstating matters, but the little woman

turned her gaze on Abigail, face hopeful. "Did you find him a caring soul, dear?"

She didn't want to frighten the woman, but she couldn't lie. "Doctor Bennett is very focused on ensuring his patients receive the best care he can manage," Abigail allowed.

The statement seemed to disappoint Mrs. Rand, for she slumped. "Oh. Well, I suppose there's nothing for it. Come, Tildie."

With another apologetic look around, her companion followed her to the examining room door.

"Now that's one interaction I'd like to see," Abigail said, tilting her head to try to keep the lady in sight.

"Examinations are private," Jesslyn reminded her.

"You assisted your father," Abigail countered. Linus appeared to be bowing over the lady, or maybe he was just bending closer to catch her words. And when had she started thinking of him as Linus?

"I only assisted when necessary, and he was my father," Jess replied. "I doubt Doctor Bennett would be comfortable with anyone assisting him."

So did she.

Still, Mrs. Rand must have requested that Linus leave the door open, for Abigail could see a great deal of their interaction. With Miss Turnpeth a patient shadow in the corner, he listened to Mrs. Rand's chest, then peered into her eyes, nose, ears, and mouth. But what surprised Abigail was the way he stood, nodding and listening, for a full quarter hour according to the bronze wall clock across from her, to what Mrs. Rand was so earnestly saying.

"Is she very ill, then?" she murmured to Jesslyn, who was making lists on paper. By the titles of the lists, they had to do with the Regatta.

"Not unless she's contracted a dozen diseases since last she visited," Jess said, noting something on one of her lists. "Father thought her maladies stemmed from loneliness, but he made sure to give her a thorough examination, just to be certain she wasn't actually ill."

Linus appeared just as thorough. When he ushered the lady out a short time later, she was smiling.

He escorted her and Miss Turnpeth to Jess and Abigail. "Miss Chance, Mrs. Rand would like to be reacquainted with our village. I told her you would be glad to accommodate."

"Indeed I would," Jess assured her.

"Then I'll leave you in her good hands. Miss Archer, if I might have a word?"

His smile was all congeniality, but his words came out clipped. Still, Abigail stepped aside with him, drawing him closer to the harpsichord in the corner.

Immediately, his smile faded. "What are you doing? Are you intent on cutting up my peace?"

Abigail raised her brows. "Your peace? Since when is a physician more concerned with his feelings than his patient's?"

Those grey eyes looked surprisingly heated. "It is precisely your health that concerns me, madam. Has nothing I've said made the slightest impact?"

"I have heard your concerns, sir. You fear fever, infection, the inability to use my arm, the plague, for all I know. I am persuaded you are being too cautious. Look." She started to raise her wounded arm.

"Don't!" he barked. He grabbed her arm and held it still. "If you will believe nothing else, believe that I am trying to save your life, Abigail."

"Oh!"

At the sound of the cry, Abigail managed to tear her gaze away from Linus's face. Mrs. Rand clutched her chest as she crumpled toward the floor.

# CHAPTER FIVE

LINUS PRESSED ABIGAIL'S ARM AGAINST her
chest. "Don't move." He then dove across the floor to
catch Mrs. Rand before she collapsed.

"My heart," she whispered, gazing up into his face.

"Is a much stronger organ than you know," Linus
assured her.

Several of the other guests had hurried over and now
surrounded them. He glanced up to meet the blue-eyed
gaze of Lord Featherstone.

"My lord, would you help Mrs. Rand back to the
examining room?" Linus asked.

"It would be my honor," the silver-haired lord said. He
crouched beside Linus and smiled to the widow. "If I may
be so bold, my lady?"

Mrs. Rand fluttered her lashes. "Certainly, my lord."

He lifted her easily and carried her back to the room.

"Nicely done," Miss Chance murmured to Linus as he
straightened. "He'll be able to dine tonight on the story,
and she keeps her dignity."

"I'm learning," Linus murmured back. Then he turned
to resolve his bigger concern.

Abigail stood, head high, feet planted, and uninjured
arm cradling the injured one. But her face was bunched,
as if she was struggling not to cry.

Linus was at her side in two steps. "You're hurting.

Where? How badly?"

"I'm fine," she said, gaze on the examining room door. "If my actions caused her harm, I will never forgive myself."

Linus lay a hand on her good shoulder. "Neither of us knew that even raised voices would overset her. Now, if you're certain you don't require my help, I should see to her."

"Go," she said.

He went.

And the entire time he listened to Mrs. Rand's strong pulse, checked her lungs and throat again, he felt Abigail watching. She could not be so fascinated by his work. He'd used the same approach on her. True, many physicians refused to actually touch their patients, preferring to diagnose through questions and observation. He found tallying the basic functions—heart, respiratory system, eyes—to provide invaluable information. Was Abigail watching because she was still so worried about the lady? He sent her a quick look, and their gazes met.

Why was it so hard to look away?

He forced his attentions back to his patient. "You are hale and hearty," he assured Mrs. Rand, straightening from his examination.

"But I feel so weak," she protested. "I think I should rest. Perhaps Lord Featherstone would be so good as to escort me back to my rooms at the Swan?"

Linus kept his face neutral. "I will inquire."

He stepped out into the spa only to discover that the number of guests had grown. He couldn't spot Lord Featherstone or Miss Chance. Doctor Owens had disappeared as well. His colleague must have slipped out of the spa earlier, otherwise he would surely have offered his assistance when Mrs. Rand had collapsed.

Abigail was standing by the fountain, catching water in a glass with her free hand. Was it that ginger hair or the lady herself that drew his attention, every time?

He made his way to her side. "I did not prescribe that."

She raised the glass in toast, water sparkling inside. "Yet I drink to your health nonetheless." She swallowed a mouthful and made a face.

Linus did his best not to laugh. "Mrs. Rand requested Lord Featherstone's help returning to the inn. Have you seen him?"

She nodded toward the windows. "Try Mrs. Harding's set. Though he has given way to Mr. Crabapple, our good baron still enters the lady's orbit on occasion."

"You should go home and rest," he said.

"You should see to real patients, sir, not those of us who have recovered."

She was recovering. He knew that and was thankful. Yet he felt a certain disappointment. All too soon these conversations would no longer be necessary. A good physician worked himself out of a job, his father had always said. With a shake of his head, he went to make arrangements with the baron.

He'd just seen his lordship and Mrs. Rand out, the lady leaning heavily on the baron's arm and her companion right behind them, when Mr. Greer entered. The tall, lanky apothecary moved with his head thrust forward, hands clasped behind the back of his brown coat. Linus suspected a weakness of the spine, but the Spa Corporation president had never asked his advice on the matter. He went to meet him nonetheless.

"I see we are quite busy," Greer said, peering around Linus into the Grand Pump Room. "Excellent. I knew all that was needed was a good physician."

"Not all," Linus told him, leading him further into the room. "It was remarkably still until Miss Chance returned."

"Miss Chance?" He squinted toward the welcome desk, where Abigail was now standing beside the spa hostess.

Then he drew himself up. "She is not supposed to be here. Forgive me for not coming sooner to deal with the matter." He pushed past Linus and strode for the desk.

Linus hurried after him.

Both Abigail and Miss Chance watched the Spa Corporation president approach, Miss Chance with a pleasant smile, Abigail with narrowed eyes, a look with which Linus was all too familiar.

"Miss Chance, I must protest," Greer blustered. "I made it quite clear we had no further need for your services."

"You had no further need," Abigail put in. "Doctor Bennett wisely disagreed."

His benefactor aimed a frown his way.

"Miss Chance is better organized and has a greater understanding of our guests than I will ever have," Linus told him. "I have learned that people come to the spa for the society as well as the medical advice."

"But the expense," Greer protested. "We cannot be expected to pay two salaries."

"Then take hers out of mine," Linus said.

They all three gaped at him.

Abigail recovered first. "Nonsense. A good physician is worth his wages, as is a good hostess. Look around, Mr. Greer. I suspect when you speak to Mr. Lawrence, you will find we've had more subscriptions than usual."

Miss Chance nodded, ringlets bobbing. "I've had three inquire today alone. And once word begins circulating that the Earl of Howland visited recently, I expect more will follow."

His lordship had indeed visited last week, but she could not know the famed and feared Lord Howland was on his deathbed. He had confided in Linus that his London physicians gave him no more than a month to live. But then, perhaps his heir would come to the spa as well. The Howlands owned the castle on the headland, after all.

"I will speak to Lawrence," Greer promised. "In the

meantime, Doctor, I had another purpose for visiting the spa. I came to tell you about our local militia, organized by our magistrate to protect the village from invasion by the French. We meet three times a week. Every gentleman takes part. You'll want to join, of course."

He made it sound as if training for war was nothing more than joining a gentleman's club. Linus knew the true cost some soldiers paid for their efforts.

"I will tend any wounds incurred in defense of the village," Linus said.

"Of course," Greer replied. "And you'll be expected to drill as well. We muster on Mondays, Wednesdays, and Fridays every week for an hour or more on the fields above the spa. Treacle, our tailor, can make you a red coat. He has quite a number to work on, but I'm sure he'll move our physician to the head of the list." He smiled benignly.

Linus refused to argue with his employer. "My position at the spa and the health of my patients prevent me from drilling." He turned purposely to Abigail. "Do you require escort home, Miss Archer? I'm sure Mr. Greer would be delighted to assist."

Greer blinked.

"I hadn't finished my business at the spa," Abigail said, voice not nearly as sweet as Miss Chance's.

"Neither had I," Greer said with a frown at her, as if she'd been the one to presume on his time. "And we have not settled on your rank or position in the militia, sir."

Linus ignored him. "I'm afraid I must insist, as your physician," he said to Abigail. Then he glanced at the apothecary. "I'm not sure if you are aware, Mr. Greer, but one of your militiamen had the poor aim to shoot Miss Archer."

Greer washed white. The change was so abrupt Linus would have been alarmed under other circumstances.

"A tragedy," he murmured. "I didn't realize you were

suffering, Miss Archer."

Linus expected her to correct him. Instead, she put a shaky hand to her brow. "Terribly, Mr. Greer. I only wish the fellow who shot me knew of the trials I must endure because of his thoughtlessness. Why, if it weren't for Doctor Bennett's unrelenting care, I shudder to think what might have become of me."

Linus stared at her.

"Then, please, allow me to see you home," Greer begged.

She came around the desk to lean on his offered arm. "You are too kind. And perhaps we might discuss the finances of the spa on the way. I'm certain we could find the funds to support Mrs. Tully as well."

"Now, see here," Greer started, but Abigail moaned, and her knees buckled.

Linus caught her before she fell. "Abigail! What's wrong?"

She bravely pulled herself upright and out of his arms, then drew a deep breath as if marshalling every ounce of energy. "I will survive, Doctor Bennett." She leaned closer, and her green gaze brushed his. "You owe me," she whispered, before she obliged Greer to lead her out.

Abigail managed to extract herself from Mr. Greer's company at the door of her shop, but not before he'd promised to fund Jesslyn's salary without pilfering from Linus's and consider paying Jesslyn's aunt to work part time. Thoroughly pleased, she let herself into the shop.

Silence greeted her.

The spa might be crowded with guests, the other shops with visitors. But here no customers marveled over the pottery Mrs. Catchpole created from clay banks down the shore. No gentleman debated which of Mr. Josephs' wrought-iron work to purchase. And no lady fingered Mrs. Mance's tatted collars and asked about the price.

Which also meant no one was getting paid.

Unacceptable. She had started this shop to make a difference, for her and her mother and for the other families in the village for whom income wasn't always reliable. She would not fail them now. She propped open the door with one of Mr. Josephs' shoe stands and set about dusting and sweeping.

The first customers wandered inside within a quarter hour. She recognized the dark-haired fellow from the spa. He'd arrived just before the fracas at the castle. Like the others, he moved from display table to display table, picking up this, considering that. But he stood before the paintings the longest. Abigail finally went over to check on him.

"Do you prefer landscapes or sailing ships?" she asked him with her best shopkeeper's smile.

He spared her a quick glance before returning his gaze to one of her more recent pieces, showing the castle on the headland with the waves pounding the cliffs below. "In truth, I'm not certain," he admitted. "I was thinking about what I'd heard recently. Is it true there are caves under Castle How?"

"Quite true," Abigail told him. "I hinted of the entrance there, where those two boulders part the waves. The area is called the Dragon's Maw for those teeth-like boulders as well as the roar the waves make when they strike the cliff."

"Fascinating." He continued studying the piece a moment. "And you can access the castle from those caves, then?"

A chill ran up her spine. Why would he care? Eva had asked her to be alert to any strangers in the village. Mr. Donner—or was it Mr. George? The two were usually

joined at the hip—had arrived a little sooner than she
might have thought the French agents to appear, but perhaps Eva and the magistrate had mistaken their dates.

"I believe the access from the caves to the castle is well
guarded these days," she said, keeping her smile in place.
"Are you interested in sailing, Mr. Donner?"

He didn't correct the use of his name, so she must have
guessed correctly. "I suppose I'll need to be," he said,
turning at last from the painting. "I understand there will
be a fine regatta here in the next month. I wouldn't want
to miss that."

"Then you intend to stay in Grace-by-the-Sea so
long?" she pressed.

His smile looked equally contrived. "For the foreseeable
future. I find it a most welcoming place and well-suited
to my purposes. Now, forgive me for monopolizing your
time, Miss Archer. I know you have other customers
eager to speak to you." He inclined his head and saun-
tered out the door.

And she vowed to keep an eye on him.

But he was right, and she had others she must attend to
at the moment. She kept busy answering questions and
taking payments until she saw Mr. Carroll across the street
locking his door. Then she ushered out the last shoppers
and started for the back of the space, where a curtained
doorway led to her studio and the flat beyond. Her paintings whispered to her, but she didn't dare answer. Like it
or not, she wasn't ready to lift a paintbrush. And if she
thought about losing the ability to paint, she would go
mad.

She came into the flat to find her mother in a chair
by the window, embroidery hoop in her lap and silken
thread sliding off one edge.

"Where's Ethan?" she asked.

"I sent him to the Mermaid to ask about dinner," her
mother answered. "He should be back shortly. How was

your visit with Doctor Bennett?"

"I didn't go to the spa to visit Doctor Bennett," Abigail told her, coming to join her. "I went to prove I'm recovered. And I returned quite a while ago. I was working in the shop. Nearly one hundred pounds worth of product went out the door this afternoon. I'll send word to pick up the disbursements by the end of the week."

Her mother took another stitch. "That's good news. I know the other families will be very pleased." She glanced up, then frowned. "Though Mrs. Howland may have something to say when she learns you managed to dirty her pretty gown."

Abigail looked down. The front of the dress was spotless, the skirts as full and rich as they had been when she'd first donned them. The left sleeve was fine. The right sleeve...

Was speckled a rusty brown.

"Oh," she said, plopping down on the chair beside her mother's. "I seem to have opened the wound."

Her mother set aside her sewing. "I'll fetch Doctor Bennett."

"No," Abigail said. "Don't. I'm sure it's nothing serious. Help me. We must clean this up before Ethan returns."

# CHAPTER SIX

SHE WAS BACK IN BED, smiling brightly, when Linus arrived that evening.

"Your excursions took their toll, I see," he observed, coming around the bed to set his case on the table.

"I merely thought it wise to rest while I could," Abigail replied. "I feel fine."

"No pain?" he asked, regarding her.

She refused to blush. "None. And I wish you'd stop asking. I begin to feel abnormal because I don't have pain."

"I can safely say there is little normal about you, madam."

"I beg your pardon," Abigail sputtered.

He held up both hands. "I meant no offense. You are in every way an exemplary model of health, intelligence, and talent."

Hard to be annoyed with him after such a statement. "Then you are satisfied I'm sufficiently healed to attend Jesslyn's wedding?"

He pulled back her sleeve, then frowned. "This isn't the bandage I put on this morning."

"Oh?" she said, finding the bed suddenly harder than she remembered.

"No. The Misses Pierce have ordered the material I prefer, but I've been using my own supply until it arrives. This isn't as absorbent, and the weave is loose enough that pieces could stick to the wound."

Abigail sighed. "You're right. I bled a little. Mother changed the bandage for me."

Immediately he was all action, unwrapping the wound as he spoke. "Does it itch, sting?"

"No," Abigail admitted. "And I don't feel the least feverish."

"We'll check that in a moment."

He was so concerned her own worries multiplied. The last layer stuck to the stitches, and she winced as he eased it free.

"I'll leave your mother another length of proper bandage, in case it's needed when I'm unavailable," he said. He peered at her arm, and Abigail craned her neck to see as well. Two of the stitches stuck out like the thread on a girl's first embroidery sampler, and the edges of the trough were definitely redder than they had been that morning. She bit her lip waiting for his diagnosis.

"You've put a strain on it, no doubt," he said. That grey gaze rose to meet hers, and something shot through her, nearly as sharp as the bullet. She couldn't look away.

He lay a hand on her forehead as if claiming her for his own. Even as the thought made her shiver, he yanked back his hand as if the touch had scalded him.

His tone, however, was its usual calm. "You don't appear feverish, though I don't like the chill that went through you."

Neither did she.

"Have your mother stay with you tonight and send word if there's any change," he ordered, dropping his hand. "I'll check on you in the morning."

That seemed a long time away. Abigail made herself nod. She kept her mouth closed and counted to three hundred in her mind as he rebandaged the wound. That didn't stop her from noticing how the candlelight brushed his hair with gold.

Her mother came in after he'd left with Ethan.

"I take it you need watching," she said, eyeing Abigail as if she might suddenly fly up out of the bed and through the roof.

"I'm fine," Abigail assured her. "I'll call if I need help."

Her mother shook her head. "No, you won't. I've been waiting for that call for nearly ten years, and it's never come."

Abigail leaned back against the headboard. "You sound as if you would have preferred it if I was weak."

"No, dear, not weak," she said, dropping her gaze and shifting on her feet so that her saffron-colored skirts brushed the hardwood floor. "Just…willing to accept that others need to be needed sometimes."

Abigail sighed. "If I've ever run roughshod over your feelings, I apologize. But someone had to take charge when Father died. Did you like being the village charity case?"

"The previous vicar was kind," she allowed.

"From pity," Abigail argued. "We had one room, one bed, and all our food and clothing were donated. Now we have a flat, a business, respect. We don't have to wait in hope that others will support us."

"Yes," her mother acknowledged. "And I rarely see you."

Frustration nipped at her. Abigail rubbed her forehead and prayed for patience. "I have also apologized for that. But I must paint, I must see to the shop. I was not born to be a lady who sits about all day doing embroidery."

Her mother slumped, and too late Abigail remembered how she filled her days.

"And embroidery, alas, is all I appear to be good at," her mother muttered.

"Never." Abigail threw back the covers, climbed from the bed, and went to enfold her mother in a one-armed hug. "You gave me life, kept me safe from Father, instilled in me a purpose. You know Gideon adored you."

She sniffed. "I miss your brother so. I wish he would write and let us know how he fares."

They had not heard from Gideon for nearly six months now. He was serving with Wellesley in India, and Abigail couldn't help fearing for his safety even as she deplored the cruel war there that decimated its people.

"I know, Mother," she murmured. "But I'm here. Now, what did Mr. Hornswag have to say about dinner?"

Her mother brightened as she pulled back. "A nice ham and pea soup. I have a loaf from Mr. Ellison. Shall I bring you some?"

"I'll join you in the dining room," Abigail said.

"But Doctor Bennett…" her mother started.

"Will have to accustom himself to disappointment," Abigail said, going to fetch her bed jacket and determined to put the handsome physician from her thoughts, at least for the moment.

Linus walked his son home down High Street. Ethan's silence continued to concern him, though, at the moment, it was a blessing. His mind offered noise enough.

He knew his role as physician. He'd taken an oath to abstain from every voluntary act of mischief and corruption, to refuse to dole out poison when asked. Indeed, he worked to give his patients only the best—his attention, his knowledge, his experience, his time. It didn't matter their gender, age, prestige, or wealth. Disease and infirmity knew no prejudice. He focused on healing, improving conditions, easing suffering.

But this evening, when he'd looked into Abigail's eyes, he hadn't seen a patient needing his care. He'd seen a woman—beautiful, vibrant, vital.

And that scared him.

He did not have a wealth of experience with women. He'd been studying for his profession since he'd been a youth, first under his father and then at the college in Edinburgh. He'd known what he wanted, where he was going. And then, he'd met Catriona, and all his carefully made plans had fluttered away like parchment caught in the wind. That experience had proven he knew little about love and marriage, and he had no plans to try again.

Surely he was wiser now. Surely his youthful passions had cooled. Abigail might intrigue him with her fiery hair and attitude to match, but he could admire without embroiling himself further.

Couldn't he?

After a difficult night, Linus was certain he had mastered whatever maggot had entered his brain the previous evening. He dropped Ethan off and checked Abigail's wound. He was congratulating himself on his professional approach when he caught himself inhaling the scent of peaches that clung to her. He made himself lean back.

"I am satisfied yesterday did not give you a setback," he said, depositing the used bandage in his bag.

"Excellent," she said. "Then I can attend Jesslyn at her wedding."

"Let's see how the next day or so goes," he suggested.

He glanced up in time to see her face puckering. "You must make a decision, sir, and I pray it is the right one. You cannot deny me the opportunity to celebrate my dearest friend's wedding."

He would if he thought it would endanger her health, but he decided not to argue the point now. "Perhaps a few more sedentary pursuits in the meantime."

That didn't seem to make her any happier. She wiggled on the bed. "What about going to watch the militia practice with Mother and Ethan?"

"I thought they only met Monday, Wednesday, and Friday," he said. "Today is Saturday, if I recall."

"It is," she allowed. "But Mr. Carroll came by last evening to let us know they were conducting a special drill today. Everyone else is going."

"And you think this will be a particularly edifying sight," he said, turning for his bag again.

"Oh, the last few drills have been highly entertaining," she assured him. "And I understand they hope to start with muskets today."

The snap of his case closing sounded as if a musket had gone off in the room instead. Every muscle in his body tensed. "That may not be wise."

She frowned. "Why not? Surely they must fire away from onlookers."

"And one of them shot you," he reminded her. "I cannot advise repeating that event."

Her chin came up. "You cannot advise anything entertaining, it seems."

All at once he heard Catriona's voice again. *I rode hard, drove fast, and danced late before I was married and had a child. You even joined me, sir. Why should any of that change now?*

He'd argued and lost, and she'd lost her life in the process.

"If you are determined to go," he told Abigail, "I'll accompany you. I'm sure Miss Chance will want our guests to attend such a stirring spectacle."

Abigail inclined her head. "Then we will see you there."

Her friend was just as eager, Linus discovered when he reached the spa a short time later. All their guests were discussing the upcoming drill as if they were about to view the king's victory parade. Even Mrs. Rand cancelled her appointment with him to join them.

"Such a thrilling event, all those gentlemen," she enthused. Her companion, Miss Turnpeth, nodded agreement.

"Are you certain you wish to attend?" Linus felt compelled to ask. "I understand there will be some gunfire."

Her gaze slid to the left, where some of the gentlemen were reminiscing about their time in the military. "Then I will be sure to stand very close to Lord Featherstone."

Linus hid a smile.

"Surely you don't find this fascinating," he said to Doctor Owens, who was walking beside him as they all set off up the hill. The day was warm and cloudless, and a breeze that smelled of brine set the grass to rippling.

"I have seen far better," his older colleague agreed, tugging his top hat down on his head. "But I came to experience all Grace-by-the-Sea has to offer, and this appears to be quite the event."

Linus still doubted.

At the top of the hill, approximately thirty men, less than a third of whom had any sort of uniform, were milling about in the center of the field. All along the edges, others sat on blankets or stood in groups. A few had carried up chairs and now reclined on them. He spotted Abigail, her mother, and Ethan with Mrs. Howland and an older woman dressed in deepest purple and excused himself from Doctor Owens to join them.

"Will they have cannons?" Ethan was asking Mrs. Archer.

"I'm afraid not," Abigail answered for her. "As it is, this is the first time they've tried firing muskets on command as a group."

"Guns, bah," the older woman declared. "They'd do better to enlist the aid of the trolls. Now, there's a troop that knows how to brawl."

Linus shook his head, sure he must have misheard her.

Or perhaps the village called the soldiers from a neighboring militia unit trolls.

"But they aren't as good at sailing as the mermaids," Mrs. Howland allowed with a nod to him.

Even as he returned her nod of greeting, the older woman drew herself up, only bringing the top of her head to his breastbone. "Mermaids don't sail. What would they do with their tails?"

Abigail wrinkled her nose. "Not to mention the smell under such close quarters."

Had he somehow wandered into another realm? He glanced at Ethan, who was watching the women avidly, then to Abigail, who grinned at him. She'd donned the gown with the slashed sleeves again and put a green patterned wool shawl about her shoulders. One side was slipping, and he had to fist his hands to keep from reaching out to drape it more securely about her slender frame.

Mrs. Howland took pity on him. "We're delighted you could join us, Doctor. We just made the acquaintance of your charming son. I understand he hopes to be an architect."

He did? He looked again to Ethan, who squirmed and dropped his gaze as if he were guilty of some misdeed.

The older woman was eyeing Linus up and down. "I see nothing wrong. Have you warts on your toes? Pocks on your chest?"

Linus kept a neutral face with difficulty. "No, thank you for asking."

She shook her head. "Then I cannot see why Abby would take you in such dislike."

Abigail pressed her lips together a moment as if trying to hold back laughter. "Perhaps if you were to spend a little time in his company, Mrs. Tully," she managed, voice choked.

Minx. But he could only conclude that this little lady was Jesslyn Chance's aunt. They looked nothing alike.

This lady had grey curls clustered tightly about her round face and a sharp, assessing light in her eyes. Nor did they act alike. At least, he hadn't noticed Miss Chance discussing the probable habits of trolls and mermaids.

"Troop, assemble!"

Greer's command echoed across the field, and all the spectators turned to watch the men of the Grace-by-the-Sea militia sort themselves out in a long, uneven line. Ethan moved closer to Linus, body stiff.

Greer, in a red coat with white facings edged in silver braid any captain might envy, strode down the line, nudging this one forward, that one back. Then he positioned himself in front of them.

"Thank you all for coming," he said, voice carrying. "Your village appreciates all you do to keep us safe."

"Better than being conscripted or picked off by the press gang," someone called, and others nodded.

"Be that as it may," Greer continued with a stern look up and down the line, "there have been rumors of strangers in the area—clothing and blankets being taken off the line, produce being plucked from gardens." He thrust a finger into the air. "We must be vigilant, valiant, in doing our duty."

"Are we going to shoot?" another of the men called, as if he had better ways to spend his time.

Greer dropped his hand. "As we discussed yesterday, we will be adding the rudiments of firearms to our drills while our magistrate is in London."

"Takes that far to be safe from them, does it?" Abigail murmured to Mrs. Howland, who giggled.

Ethan shifted on his feet.

"Who's teaching us, then?" someone asked.

Greer stood taller. "I will be your instructor for now."

"Why?" someone else asked. "You've already proven you can go off half-cocked."

Greer flamed as snickers sounded.

"Well, if he can hit Miss Archer in twilight, maybe he could hit a French soldier in broad daylight," another teased.

So, Greer had been the one to shoot Abigail. Small wonder he'd quailed yesterday at the spa when reminded of her injury. Linus glanced at her and saw merriment in those green eyes. They shared a smile that made the day feel oddly warmer.

"Attention!" Greer barked, and even Linus's gaze snapped forward. The laughter snuffed out as would-be soldiers straightened their shoulders.

"Right face," Greer commanded.

Beside him, Abigail sucked in a breath, and Mrs. Tully clasped her hands as if praying.

To a man, they pivoted on their heels.

"Forward, march!" Greer ordered.

The youngest of them, drum slung about his narrow chest, set the beat, and they tramped across the field.

"Left face!" Greer called.

Again, they turned.

"Ooo," Mrs. Howland enthused. "Right and left. James will be pleased."

Some of the others went so far as to applaud. Ethan mimicked them. Again, Linus felt as if he had missed something.

Greer had them march a while longer, then lined them up again. But his audience was growing restless. Ethan had crouched on the grass and appeared to be studying it as if he suspected it of hiding pirate treasure. Abigail, her mother, and Mrs. Howland were chatting, while Mrs. Tully continued to regard Linus as if trying to find hidden flaws. He could have told her he had any number. He looked toward the spa group, where Mrs. Harding was fluttering her lashes at Doctor Owens while Mr. Crabapple's face bunched as if he were about to burst into tears. Mrs. Rand was leaning so heavily on Lord

Featherstone's arm that the baron stood lopsidedly, and
the Admiral had closed his eyes and begun snoring, while
Mr. George attempted to keep him upright. Only Mr.
Donner showed any interest in the activities.

"The Hound of the Headland came this way once,"
Mrs. Tully said to no one in particular.

Linus focused his attention on the troop.

"The commands for firing are simple," Greer was
saying. "You already know shoulder arms. The next is
present arms."

Two of the company moved forward and offered him
their guns.

"No, no," Greer told them, waving them back into line.
"Present arms means to hold the weapons out in front of
you vertically."

"Like we was going to shoot you?" someone asked,
and Linus couldn't tell if the fellow was eager to try or
concerned about the prospect.

"Like this," Greer said, drawing his side pistol and holding it out.

Eight muskets, two dueling pistols, and an assortment
of knives, swords, and a pitchfork stuck out at him in
return.

Greer lowered his pistol. "Where are your guns?"

"Most of us don't own one," Mr. Lawrence, the Spa
Corporation treasurer, told him. "And it isn't as if Grace-
by-the-Sea has an armory."

"Well," Abigail said, "that is going to be a problem.
What will they do if the French arrive?"

"Spit in their eye," Mrs. Tully said darkly.

Ethan stood. "I think they're very brave. Perhaps I'll be
a soldier when I am old enough."

"Absolutely not."

The words left Linus' mouth before he could stop
them, and he found himself the focus of all gazes. At least
Abigail appeared to understand why he feared for his son,

as her eyes dipped down with her mouth. Mrs. Howland and Mrs. Tully looked disappointed in him. Mrs. Archer seemed to be more shocked at his unpatriotic declaration.

And Ethan curled in on himself as if Linus had struck him.

# CHAPTER SEVEN

ABIGAIL KNEW THE HURT SPREADING across Ethan's face, the tightness pressing his shoulders in. Likely it hurt to draw breath. How many times had she slunk away from her father's temper?

But Linus Bennett wasn't a man like her father. Her father had never listened to anyone's concerns the way Linus did. When she or Gideon had been hurt or sick, he'd left all care to his wife. Still, the important thing right now was Ethan.

She slipped her good arm about the boy's shoulders. "Soldiers are fine fellows. My brother is one. But architects are fine fellows too. There are even soldier architects. Plenty of time to decide which way you want to go. And whatever you decide, I'm sure your father will be proud of you."

She glanced up and met Linus' gaze, determined to make him agree with her. But his face mirrored a similar pain.

"I am always proud of my son," he said.

Ethan's head came up, eyes wide in hope.

A dozen questions crowded her mind, but now was no time to ask, not with her mother watching her that way and Mrs. Tully narrowing her eyes. Keeping Ethan close, she turned to watch the militia.

Unfortunately, Mr. Greer must have realized the drill

was going against him, for he dismissed the troop a short time later. Their audience began packing up to leave as well.

"Never could abide beatings," Mrs. Tully said with a scowl to Linus. "By rod or by word. Men have been haunted for less."

Mrs. Howland linked her arm with the lady's. "I feel the need to refresh myself with our marvelous mineral waters. Let's visit the spa. We might even ask Doctor Owens to join us." She nodded to where his colleague stood watching the Grace-by-the-Sea militia shamble past.

"He may be a troll," Mrs. Tully confided in Linus before suffering herself to be led away.

As her mother beckoned Ethan to her side, Linus stepped closer to Abigail. "Has Mrs. Tully always been this way?" he asked, clearly bewildered.

"From before I was born," Abigail told him. "She married a sailor, who was lost at sea, and she retreated to a fantastical world for comfort."

She waited for him to begin diagnosing illness and prescribing cure, but he merely nodded. "If that brings her solace and no one else harm, then I can only applaud her. Others have found far more deleterious methods of dealing with such pain." His gaze moved to his son.

"May we go now?" Ethan asked her mother.

She took his hand and gave him a smile. "Of course. But I think we should stop by Mr. Ellison's before we go home."

Ethan's eyes brightened, then he glanced at his father and some of the joy leaked away. "I'm not supposed to have treats."

Her mother deflated, but Linus flinched.

"Mrs. Archer's offer is very generous," he told his son. "Make sure you thank her when you accept it."

"Yes, sir! Yes, ma'am. Thank you." He hurried along

beside her mother toward the village.

"Please thank your mother for me as well," Linus said, watching them. "It's been a while since anyone took such an interest in him."

He'd opened a door, and she didn't hesitate to walk through. "Has his mother been gone long, then?"

He started moving, and she fell into step beside him. Jess and the spa guests were just ahead, but Abigail felt as if it were only her and Linus on the wind-swept Downs.

"She died eight months ago," he said, gaze on the dusty track before them. "It was a carriage accident. Ethan was ill at the same time. He was insensible for three weeks. I couldn't even tell him. We weren't sure he would survive."

"How horrible." She had to touch him. Her fingers wrapped around his arm and held tight. "I'm so glad he's all right now."

"For which I will be forever grateful."

He didn't pull away, but his gaze had gone to the distance, as if he saw Ethan even now, on a bed from which he might never rise.

"Small wonder you do not want him to become a soldier," she said, "traveling far from you."

His gaze speared back to her. "It isn't the distance that concerns me. My father was an Army surgeon. He took me and my mother with him as he served in India and the American colonies. When he deemed me old enough, he had me assist in his work. I know the dangers soldiers face—disease and injury and battery. I still see their faces in my dreams. You will forgive me if I hope my son doesn't have to endure any of that."

Was pain contagious? She felt as if his pierced her heart. "Certainly, sir," she agreed. "I pray my brother, who is serving in India now, doesn't have to endure any of that either. But I am thankful for his courage and valor as well as the courage and valor of those who serve with him.

I can only hope the Grace-by-the-Sea militia can attain such heights."

He cocked his head as if studying the men, who were heading down into the village. "They have much to learn."

"As do we all," Abigail assured him.

They were nearly at the spa. Jess and most of the others had already entered, as had Eva, Mrs. Tully, and Doctor Owens. Mrs. Rand was clinging to Lord Featherstone's arm as if she would never let go. Abigail knew the feeling.

She tugged Linus to a halt. "Before you go in, I must repeat my request to attend Jesslyn's wedding. You can see I'm fine."

He gazed down at her, and Abigail gave him her best smile, hoping she looked the picture of health. "I'll think on the matter and let you know this evening."

He could not know how hard it was to maintain her smile as he took his leave of her.

She caught up with her mother and Ethan as they were coming out of Mr. Ellison's bakery with a plump cinnamon bun to share and accompanied them back to the house. Ethan chatted with her mother, face open and eager, and she could only be glad he'd recovered from his father's outburst.

Still, he had no sooner finished his treat before he was back at his drawings.

"He needs more to occupy his time," Abigail told her mother, who was gathering her embroidery things. "At his age, he should be out playing pirates or chasing butterflies on the Downs."

"He is nine, dear," her mother said with a fond look his way. "Many boys his age are off at school. And you heard his father: he has no desire to have Ethan anywhere near any sort of weapon, very likely even the wooden swords Gideon used."

"It wasn't just Gideon," Abigail reminded her. "Jess and

I used them whenever we could steal them away from him."

Her mother sniffed. "I remember. I still have them."

Abigail grinned. "Go find them. Ethan and I can have a go."

It took more than she'd expected to convince her mother to allow her the use of the old toy swords and then even more time to convince Ethan it was perfectly fine to try them. They had no yard at the shop, but the tide was out, so she took him down to the shore. A few of the fishermen were darning their nets. They smiled as Abigail passed, sword up and at the ready.

"Been a few years now, Miss Abby," one called.

"Far too long," Abigail assured him.

Her mother followed, a blanket and bandages up in her arms, as if she fully expected casualties.

"We're not going to strike each other," Abigail told her and Ethan as they made their way out onto the pebbled shore. "We're merely going to practice the forms. Now, then, young sir, stand like so." Mindful of her injured arm, she clasped the hilt with her left hand and turned her body sideways.

Across from her, Ethan took up a similar stance, sword in his right hand.

"You see how you present a smaller target this way?" Abigail asked. "Now, bring up the blade like so."

"It's actually wood," he reminded her, but he brought up the sword at the angle she'd used.

"True," Abigail allowed. "And very good stance, by the way. Now, attempt to strike me, between the shoulders and the hips, if you please."

Ethan's blade dipped with his frown. "But you said we wouldn't strike each other."

"And so we won't. I merely ask you to attempt it. I'll parry. Watch."

Face still tight with obvious doubt, Ethan gave a half-hearted swing, and she knocked the blow aside.

"See? Now, my turn."

She jabbed toward him, and he scrambled back.

"Escape is always wise," she said, pursuing him, "but you may have to fight at some point. Try striking me again."

He lunged, as fast as a wasp, and she barely managed to parry in time. "Oh, well done!"

Even as Ethan grinned, a voice from the shore shouted, "What do you think you're doing!"

Linus stormed down the beach, unable to believe what he'd just seen. Was she intent on maiming herself or his son?

Ethan lowered his sword and backed away, even as Mrs. Archer hurried up to put her arms protectively around him. Abigail brandished the weapon at Linus.

"It's only a game," she informed him, tone turning icy again. "No harm done."

"No harm done?" He skidded to a stop on the pebbles to stare at her. "Have you lost your senses entirely? What about your arm?"

She rolled her eyes heavenward. "Why do you think I'm fighting with my left hand?"

"I did suggest this might not be wise," her mother put in.

"So you don't listen to her either," Linus said.

Abigail glared at him, chest heaving. "I listen. I simply choose to take a different path."

He could almost hear Catriona's voice instead of hers. Why couldn't he get through to her? She'd come far from her injury, but she must understand she wasn't out of danger yet.

But if she wouldn't listen to words, perhaps she would heed action.

Linus held out his hand. "Ethan, give me that sword."

His son edged warily forward and handed him the weapon. Wood. Painted silver and nicked any number of times over the years. As he'd been coming down the hill, he'd been certain they were metal, and his fears had propelled him to their sides. Still, wood could bruise, and the right strike could break open her wound.

"I wouldn't have hurt her, Father," Ethan said, brows tight together.

Linus nodded. "I believe you, Ethan. But accidents happen."

His son washed white, and Linus only wanted to call back the words. Ethan knew more than most what harm an accident could do. Before Linus could respond, his son scurried to the safety of Mrs. Archer's arms. Her generous mouth was a tight line as she too glared at him.

Well, he was used to playing the villain. It was a small price to pay to keep his patients safe and healthy.

He turned to Abigail. "Here's my proposal: you defeat me in a sword fight, and I will allow you to attend Miss Chance's wedding. I defeat you, and you stay at home and put away these things for the foreseeable future."

"You are not my father, sir," she retorted. "You have no authority over me."

He inclined his head. "Only that of a physician caring for his patient." He brought up the sword. "Of course, if you think me too likely to win…"

"Never." She brought up her own sword and saluted him with it. "Lay on, sir."

He had barely assumed the stance before she drove at him.

He shoved the sword away, circled out of reach, but still she came, like a storm sweeping across the Channel. How she managed not to tangle her feet in her skirts was beyond him. Right, left, lunge, swing. If these had been real, he might have feared for his life with such ferocity.

"Give him what for, Miss Abby!" someone called, and he realized they had an audience. Besides the fishermen, Mr. Ellison and his son had come out of the bakery, and the Misses Pierce and three of the lady spa guests were hurrying out of the linens and trimmings shop to watch the spectacle.

Abigail shot them a grin, and he lunged. She parried in time.

"Oh, no, you don't!" She returned to the attack.

"How are you fighting left-handed?" he demanded, giving way before her.

"Jesslyn and I learned both ways," she said, feinting to his right and lunging to his left. "Her father said you never know when you might lose an arm."

So, she'd listened to the previous doctor, just not to him.

He redoubled his efforts, but she was quicker than a cat, and now they were all cheering for her. He even heard Ethan's voice among the calls.

It was lowering.

It was exhilarating.

Back and forth they went, up and down the shingle. He'd learned the blade from soldiers serving with his father, done rather well in bouts at Edinburgh. No gambit he tried, no feint he attempted, got under her guard. He was most likely going to lose.

But her blows were becoming softer, less frequent, and he could see the perspiration dotting her forehead. She'd been mostly abed since her injury. If he kept the fight going, he could probably outlast her. But she had won the match and her point.

Along with his admiration.

He put up the sword and held up his other hand. "I concede. Seldom have I had a more skilled opponent.

Forgive me for interrupting a master at her work."

She lowered her weapon as well as she dipped him a curtsey. "I will accept a rematch at any time, Doctor Bennett."

Applause echoed from the shoreline. She bobbed a curtsey at her devoted audience as well. Then she turned to Linus.

"I assume you had some purpose for coming down the hill besides being drubbed at swordplay."

He chuckled. "I thought to check on Ethan after this morning. Clearly, he was fine. While I'm here, I will ask Miss Pierce the elder to make you a sling to support your arm during the wedding festivities."

"A sling!" Abigail raised her sword as if ready to take him on anew. "And how will I look accompanying Jess down the aisle with an ugly great band over my gown?"

"Ask her to make it of material that matches your gown, then," he countered. "So long as it is lined with lamb's wool and keeps your arm relatively immobile, I don't care what it looks like."

"Oh. Well." She relaxed. "I suppose that would work. Thank you. Will I see you tonight?"

He inclined his head. "And every day until I am certain you are fully healed."

She nodded and called to her mother and Ethan. Then she sailed past him, her mother hurrying in her wake.

"That was well done, Father," Ethan said as he accepted the sword back from Linus. "You almost beat her." He followed the women up to Hill Street.

Leaving Linus to return to the spa, which he suspected could never hold such enjoyment as time spent with Abigail.

# CHAPTER EIGHT

H E WASN'T SO BAD AFTER all. Abigail smiled as she walked her mother and Ethan back to the flat. He'd stood his ground on what he believed to be the best course of action, but he'd been willing to concede defeat. A lady could admire a gentleman like that.

"I would be very grateful to learn more about swordplay from you, Miss Archer," Ethan said as they came back into the flat. He still held one of the two swords and showed no signs of wishing to give it up.

"And I shall be very glad to tutor you," Abigail assured him. "Perhaps we might find some other lads your age interested in joining us."

He glanced up at her. "There are boys my age in my class with Mr. Wingate. But they all have brothers or fathers to teach them."

Once more loneliness seemed to wrap around him like a cloak.

"My father wasn't much of a teacher," she said, earning her a frown from her mother. "But you saw your father. He was rather good."

A grin popped into view, warming her. "He was, wasn't he?" As quickly as it had come, the smile faded. "But he's too busy."

"He has a very demanding occupation," her mother said, reaching out a hand to pull the sword from Abigail's grip. "And a great responsibility."

Ethan sighed. "I know."

"But the days are long right now," Abigail reminded him. "Perhaps we can convince your father to spend a little more time having fun."

"Maybe." The word held very little hope. He surrendered his sword to her mother.

She should open the shop, but she could not like the set to his shoulders, as if the entire world had suddenly crashed down upon them. "Suppose you show me what you've been drawing," she said.

Light flared in his eyes, and he hurried to bring her his sketchbook.

The drawings were rough, but certainly better than hers at that age. She recognized a number of the buildings in Grace-by-the-Sea—the bakery, Shell Cottage, St. Andrew's, the spa. And a few fanciful pieces with sea serpents and dragons.

"Very nice," she said. "I can see you have a keen eye for detail. That bodes well for an architect."

"And an artist?" he asked hopefully.

Her heart melted. She put an arm around his shoulders and gave him a squeeze. "Certainly an artist. When you're ready, I'd be happy to let you try your hand at something bigger in my studio."

His eyes widened, and his cheeks turned pink as he beamed at her.

Something uncurled inside her, reached for the light of his smile. She had never thought to be a wife, much less a mother. She had a hard enough time getting along with her own mother. But perhaps the key ingredients were commonsense, encouragement, and love.

Those, she could manage.

Linus had thought he'd undergone the worst the day could throw at him—the apology to his son, his defeat to Abigail—but Miss Chance had other ideas. He'd just escorted Mrs. Rand to the door when the spa hostess approached.

"Another appointment?" he asked with a smile.

Her smile was much sweeter than anything he'd ever managed. "No, sir. An invitation. I hope I may count on you and your son joining us for our wedding and the festivities afterward."

He'd already determined that none of the guests were able to refuse her, but he'd thought himself immune. Now the need to agree tugged at him. She had been an enormous help to him at the spa, but a wedding? He wasn't sure he was ready to attend one. It would only remind him of what he'd lost when all he wanted was to be happy for what she'd found.

"Someone should watch the spa," he demurred.

She raised her finely shaped brows. "I expect most of the guests will come to the wedding, as will the members of the Spa Corporation board. I'm sure no one would mind if we closed. And you will have to do without me for a few days afterward while Lark and I take our honeymoon trip."

He had yet to meet her betrothed, but he knew the fellow fortunate indeed. "The Lakes District, perhaps?" he suggested.

"No," she said without a hint of disappointment to miss the scenic wonders there. "Lyme Regis. I want to compare their shops and assemblies to ours."

He laughed. "No one could ever claim you aren't devoted, Miss Chance."

"To my village and to my groom, sir," she promised. "Please say you'll come."

He could not make himself refuse.

Nor could he keep Abigail abed. He continued to check on her every morning and every evening, and she continued to press against any bounds he might suggest. Before the wedding even arrived, she had convinced him she could reopen her shop on a permanent basis and undergo fittings for her gown. But, though he appreciated the truce they'd found, he held his ground on painting.

"I need to finish a canvas as a wedding present for Jess and Lark," she protested two days before the wedding as they stood in her sitting room, her mother helping settle Ethan at the dining room table. "It will only take a few hours."

"Before your injury, I saw you with paint spattered on your cheek and in your hair," he argued. "Do you know the sorts of chemicals involved? I will not chance them reaching your wound."

"Very well," she agreed, dropping her gaze.

That had been too easy. He knew how readily she disobeyed orders the moment he left her. There had to be some way he could protect her.

"Perhaps it would help if I saw where you create your works," he said.

She blinked. "I don't usually allow anyone to see the paintings before they're done, but very well. This way."

She led him through a door and down a short corridor to a room off the shop. Wide, multipaned windows looked south and let in light muted only by the shade of the building next door. Every wall was eclipsed by massive canvases, leaning here, on easels there. Some were blank, the creamy white waiting for inspiration. Others had charcoal sketches outlining ocean, cliff, trees, and clouds. A few bore the mark of her brush, showing the power of waves, the peace of moonlight.

He'd seen her work for sale in the shop and knew the hold the landscape paintings could take on him and anyone else who viewed them. The one closest to the door drew him even now. The focus was on a choppy sea, with the moon huge on the horizon, the light gilding a path toward the viewer.

"That's the one I intend to give Jess and Lark," she said. "I call it A View Forward. It seemed fitting for their marriage."

"They will be delighted with it," he assured her. He turned to meet her gaze. "And they will understand when you deliver it late."

She sucked in a breath, and he held up one finger. "I have seen the pieces in your shop and those in this room. If I find any changed, I will ask the magistrate to confiscate your paints."

"The magistrate," she snapped, "is out of town."

"Miss Chance's betrothed, the Riding Surveyor, then. He sounds like the sensible sort. And he would not want to see his bride's dearest friend harmed."

"You are the most opinionated, hard-hearted fellow I know," she fumed.

"Guilty, madam," he said with a bow. "Now, if you'll excuse me, I should get to the spa." He straightened and left.

She was considerably less friendly when he had her mother show him the shop and studio the next day, but at least she'd heeded him at last, for he saw no progress on her work.

And then it was the big day. So many people would be attending, in fact, that the usual Wednesday night assembly had been cancelled in favor of the party to follow. Ethan dressed in his Sunday clothes—navy breeches, navy coat, tan waistcoat, and a short-collared shirt—and ran a wet comb through his hair.

"Very distinguished," Linus assured his son when he turned for his inspection.

"You too, Father," he said with equal solemnity. Linus

could only hope his black coat and breeches would look elegant and not funereal.

As they started up High Street for Church Street, others joined them: Mr. Carroll in a blue velvet coat that made his eyes brighter behind his spectacles; Mrs. Rinehart, the milliner, with a hat covered in peacock feathers; the Misses Pierce in frilly muslin gowns they'd no doubt sewn for the occasion. He and Ethan took a pew near the back of the church. There wasn't room anywhere else.

Ahead of them, he recognized the members of the Spa Corporation board; shopkeepers like Mr. Treacle, the tailor; and innkeepers like Mr. and Mrs. Truant of the Swan. They and all the spa guests crowded into the little walnut box pews, light coming through the stained-glass windows making jeweled patterns on their fine coats and gowns. The tall fellow at the altar near the vicar must be Larkin Denby. His attendant looked enough like Miss Chance to be her brother.

Everyone stilled as she entered from the nave to stop at the foot of the aisle, and Mr. Denby's face lit. Linus shook his head. Had he looked so besotted when Catriona had come to take his arm? How blind he'd been to the future, so certain that his love would help her change, grow, even as her love made him a better man.

Or a bitter one.

"She's very pretty," Ethan whispered.

He followed his son's gaze only to find himself staring. Abigail stood next to Miss Chance, wearing a high-waisted, long-sleeved gown of soft rose, a ginger sash tied under her bosom. Her hair was piled up and fixed in place with pearl-headed pins. Draped across one arm and tied at her waist was a shawl with a paisley pattern, rose and teal and purple mixing. Miss Chance might be all the sweetness and light of springtime, but Abigail was the blaze of a summer sun, offering warmth, energy.

Hope.

He'd worried this wedding might endanger her recovery, but he'd overlooked a far greater danger.

To his heart.

# CHAPTER NINE

JESS AND LARK'S WEDDING WAS everything Abigail could have hoped. The love on Lark's face as he took his sweetheart's hand to say their vows brought tears to her eyes. What woman wouldn't want such a look aimed her way?

As she turned to follow them back down the aisle at the end of the service, more than a hundred gazes watched. One caught hers.

Linus Bennett, eyes soft and face wistful, as if he too hoped for such a love.

Blushing, Abigail hurried from the church.

More people waited outside. Voices rang with wishes for good health, good fortune, large families. The progress of the wedding party through the churchyard was interrupted a dozen times as women pressed flowers into Jesslyn's arms and men shook Lark's hand while offering words of wisdom. Abigail joined the others waving as the flower-decked carriage, on loan from Mrs. Harding, whisked the happy couple, Mrs. Tully, and Lark's mother to the assembly rooms for the feast and festivities to follow. Then Abigail moved into the grand procession walking down Church Street and up to the assembly rooms.

"When you get married," her mother said, strolling beside her in her best church dress of cerulean blue silk, "I hope for such a turnout."

"I doubt anyone in Grace-by-the-Sea could match this," Abigail told her, adjusting her sling to keep her arm from bumping the people around them. "Even James and Eva Howland's wedding wasn't quite so well attended."

Her mother lifted her chin, setting the silk orchid on her bonnet to bobbing. "They came for the magistrate, and they came for their spa hostess. They'll come for their physician too."

"Then perhaps you should be planning Doctor Bennett's wedding instead of mine," Abigail joked.

Her mother blinked. "But dear, they are one and the same."

"Now, Mother," she started.

"May we join you?" Linus asked as he and Ethan came alongside them in the procession. Ethan looked up her hopefully. She offered him a smile. How mature he looked in his Sunday best. How sad his mother was not here to see it.

"Of course," her mother said before she could answer. "Don't you look handsome, Ethan, and you as well, Doctor Bennett. I'm sure Abigail agrees."

Abigail brightened her smile. "Everyone looks very festive."

Linus nodded toward her arm. "I see you managed to contrive a sling."

Abigail touched the shawl draped strategically to protect her injured arm. "Miss Pierce the younger found the perfect complement, and we are negotiating to sell similar items in the shop."

"And should I then expect to see more arm injuries in the area?" he asked.

He was teasing her. A light shimmered in the grey of his eyes, like sunlight skipping across the waves. Warmth spread through her.

"No arm injuries," she assured him, "but I hope the fashion will catch hold."

Her mother offered her hand to Ethan. "Walk with me, sir, and I will tell you all about your village."

Ethan took her hand, and she went ahead of them, leaving Abigail to walk with Linus.

"Perhaps I should listen," he said. "I still feel like a stranger here."

"Then you have not seen the admiring looks cast your way," Abigail told him. "You are much respected, sir. Grace-by-the-Sea has needed a physician for some time."

He grimaced. "Yet there I am, stuck in the spa. Your case is the only one I've been asked to consult on in the village."

Abigail glanced at him. "You want to treat everyone?"

"Certainly. When I became a physician, I vowed to treat all. I assumed there would be more need at the spa, but, most days, my appointments fill up less than half of my time."

Abigail snapped a nod. "Then we must see you put to better use. Give me a day or two, and I'll work it out."

His brows went up. "Very kind of you, but I wouldn't want you to exert yourself on my behalf."

"Why not? Jesslyn isn't the only one good at organizing things. By the way, Eva and I talked. We will come help at the spa while Jess is away."

"Do you expect me to break the place?" he asked.

Abigail laughed. "Well, it's been known to happen when one puts a gentleman in charge."

"And your shop?" he asked.

That had been more difficult to arrange. Who could she trust?

"I decided to enlist the aid of Mrs. Truant at the Swan," she told him. "She knows something about handling money and keeping things organized from her work at the inn, and she doesn't supply me with any goods, so she should be an impartial clerk when it comes to selling items to customers."

They reached the assembly rooms then. He stood in the doorway and blocked anyone else from entering so she had pride of place going through the door. Protecting her arm, of course.

"I must sit with Jess and the wedding party," she explained as they followed her mother and Ethan into the long, high-ceilinged room, which had been decorated with flowers and crape streamers.

"Then perhaps I'll see you later," he said, giving her a bow.

Why was it so hard to walk away? Abigail had to make herself go take her seat. As Jess's attendant, she warranted a place high on the table. So did Lark's family, including his mother, sisters Rosemary and Hester, and Hester's six-year-old daughter, Rebecca. The adults all nodded their greetings as she approached. Rebecca was too busy squirming in her pink satin dress.

As Abigail took the chair Mr. Inchley's younger son held out for her, she spotted her mother, Ethan, and Linus taking places farther down. Doctor Owens and some of the other spa guests settled around them. Jess had decided against precedence and allowed her other guests to sit where they preferred.

"Miss Archer." She turned to find Quillan St. Claire bowing beside her. Raven-haired, broad-shouldered, and well-favored, he looked particularly dashing today in his naval uniform. She'd only met him a few times but always with great delight. Mrs. Tully might praise a fellow in a red coat, but there was something commanding about a naval officer. Rosemary Denby must have agreed, for she raised her lorgnette off the front of her azure gown and studied him through it.

"Captain St. Claire," Abigail acknowledged. "A pleasure to see you."

"And you," he assured her, gaze traveling down her frame and lighting with appreciation that brought a blush to her cheek. "I wonder, would you save me a dance later?"

Rosemary's lorgnette tumbled from her fingers.

Abigail was nearly as stunned. Once she would have leaped to accept his offer. Now she could only smile her regrets. "I fear I must decline. My arm isn't up to such challenges yet. It took the utmost persuasion to convince Doctor Bennett to allow me to attend the wedding."

"Ah, yes," he said, eyeing the shawl. "Your gift from the Grace-by-the-Sea militia. I'd forgotten. Another time, then."

"Assuredly," Abigail promised.

"I'm certain other ladies will be glad to take her place," Rosemary went so far as to suggest.

He bowed. "You honor me, Miss Denby. But I dance rarely. Bum knee, you know."

She frowned as he made his way down the table.

Odd. It was as if he'd singled her out. Abigail had been hoping he'd ask her to dance the last few times he'd attended the weekly assembly. Now, she didn't feel the least disappointed to refuse him. Instead, her gaze sought out Linus, and lingered.

"I had no idea the village held so many people," Doctor Owens was saying beside Linus as the first course was served, a white soup smelling of savory onions and herbs.

"Miss Chance is highly respected," Mrs. Archer, on his other side, put in before nodding to Ethan to try the soup.

At least she was encouraging something more than sweets at the moment. Linus had a feeling his son would be stuffed with sugar by the end of the meal. He would have to have a discussion with the lady about a healthful diet for growing children.

"I recognize a few acquaintances," Owens said, glancing around. "Lord Featherstone there with Mrs. Rand. Crabapple with Mrs. Harding. Donner. George. But what of that fellow speaking with Miss Archer?"

Linus glanced up the table. He hadn't met the man either, but he couldn't like the way his arm rested on the back of Abigail's chair as if he intended to embrace her. He leaned too close, his smile too smug, as if he was assured she would be swayed by anything he requested. He obviously didn't know the lady well.

"Mrs. Archer?" Linus asked, keeping an eye on the fellow. "Who is that?"

She must have glanced up the table too, for she answered readily enough. "Captain St. Claire. Abigail finds him rather dashing, but I have other hopes for her."

So did Linus.

Immediately he schooled his face and his thoughts. He had no claim on Abigail. She had every right to speak to whomever she chose. But he couldn't help a smile as she sent the fellow packing, his face hinting of disappointment.

"Surely that's a naval uniform," Doctor Owens said, spooning up his soup. "If there is a marine unit nearby, I'm surprised they aren't training the militia."

"He is here alone, on half-pay, I believe," Mrs. Archer supplied. "He was injured at the Battle of the Nile and has been recuperating at Dove Cottage ever since. It's at the top of the hill beyond the assembly rooms. Everyone accords him a fine gentleman."

"If he is injured, perhaps we should call on him," Doctor Owens mused. "Or has he other medical care?"

"Doctor Chance, our previous physician, attended him," Mrs. Archer said. "Here, now, Ethan, let me help you with that roll. They can be tricky things to butter."

"I would feel remiss if I did not attempt to make his

acquaintance," Doctor Owens told Linus. "I introduced myself to Mr. Denby earlier this week, offering my congratulations. I would have spoken to your magistrate as well, but he appears to be out of town."

"In London," Linus clarified. "I expect him back shortly."

Owens tsked. "Both your magistrate and your Riding Surveyor away at the same time. I certainly hope your militia is up to the task of protecting the area should the French strike. That drill last week did not reassure me of their ability to handle weapons."

The way Abigail had been wounded came too easily to mind. He glanced up the table again.

She was watching them. Meeting his gaze, she smiled, and his heart rate accelerated. Ridiculous organ. He gave her a nod before turning purposefully toward Owens again.

But he could not seem to manage his thoughts or his gaze. Always they drifted to Abigail. When she rose to toast the happy couple and the candlelight set her hair to flaming. When her laughter over something Mrs. Tully had said drifted down the table to tickle his ear. When the dancing started, and she bravely sat alone to watch the couples on the floor, her gaze longing.

How fine it would be to take her hands, twirl her down the line.

What was he thinking? Her arm would not bear the strain. He should commend her for remembering that, when she clearly wished to dance.

Leaving Ethan with Mrs. Archer, he ventured to Abigail's side in time to hear her refuse an invitation from Lord Featherstone, who bowed himself off.

"Your abstinence now will reap dividends in the future," Linus promised her, taking the baron's place at her side.

She stuck out her tongue at him.

Linus started laughing, and she gave in and joined him.

"It is more difficult to refuse than I expected," she admitted. "I love to dance."

Another thing she had in common with his late wife. But dancing hadn't been exciting enough for Cat. Every chance she'd taken had been riskier than the last. Could he trust that Abigail had a different disposition?

"You must persevere," he told her.

She cast him a glance. "I am well aware of that, Doctor. But thank you for making sure my memory was more sound than my arm."

He inclined his head and went to collect Ethan before Mrs. Archer could ply his son with another sweet roll.

It was worse the next day at the spa. No matter what he did, which way he turned, Abigail was there.

She and Mrs. Howland came in shortly after he unlocked the door, Abigail in her slashed-sleeve gown and Mrs. Howland in lavender. He hadn't expected many visitors that day. Most had attended the wedding, and the festivities had continued until after the sun had set at ten. He'd heard some industrious souls singing their way through the village at about that time. Surely their guests would sleep late.

Abigail and Mrs. Howland apparently had higher expectations, for they set about counting glasses and setting out pamphlets.

He had just ventured toward the fountain to start the impeller when Abigail approached him with the appointment book Miss Chance—no, Mrs. Denby—had started, balancing the open book on one gloved hand.

"You have no one scheduled for this morning and two in the afternoon," she explained, "Mrs. Rand at one and Mr. Crabapple at half past three." She glanced up to meet his gaze with a smile that made the room brighter. "If others request an appointment, do you have a preference for timing?"

"Fill up the afternoon first," he said, trying to ignore

the scent of her. Why did he smell peaches? Was he simply reminded of them by her coloring?

"Very good," she said. "Do you need help starting the fountain?"

It was lowering to think Mrs. Denby might have let her in on all his deficiencies. "No, thank you. I can manage."

She nodded. "You'll do well. Eva and I are merely here to help." She turned for the welcome desk.

And the light seemed to dim. He shook his head. Nothing had changed because Abigail moved away from him—about the room, about his life, about his future. He must remember that.

But as the day wore on, he was very glad for her company. Mrs. Harding had elected to remain abed to recover from her exertions, and Mr. Crabapple moped so much it required the combined attentions of Lord Featherstone and the Admiral to wring a smile from him. Mrs. Rand felt the lack of attention from the baron and had no less than three attacks before her appointment that afternoon. Doctor Owens had not made an appearance, so Linus could not even appeal to him to speak to the lady. And Mrs. Rand did not want to listen to him.

"My physician in Berkshire tells me I am delicate," she said after the third attack. "I would not expect a lesser fellow to understand."

He had never been one to brag of his accomplishments, but Abigail had no such trouble.

"I would feel the same way," she told the lady as she helped her to sit up from where she'd collapsed, strategically near Lord Featherstone and the chessboard. "That's why I'm so grateful for a physician of Doctor Bennett's skills. Few spas can claim their medical staff are both Edinburgh-trained and have attended some of the finest families in London."

Mrs. Rand peered at him more closely, as if his pedigree must be written on his forehead. "Indeed. Impressive."

He wasn't sure if it was Abigail's praise or the lady's change of heart, but every appointment for the remainder of the afternoon was filled, and he had six more scheduled for the next day.

"How does Jesslyn manage it?" Mrs. Howland, who had insisted he call her Eva, asked as Abigail saw the last guest out that afternoon. "I could sleep for a week!"

"I had a splendid time," Abigail told her, returning to their sides by the welcome desk. "Perhaps tomorrow, you could ask Mrs. Tully to come play. The music should be soothing."

"She plays the harpsichord?" Linus asked, glancing at the lacquered instrument in the corner, which had remained silent since he'd arrived.

"Very well," Eva assured him. "And I will request that she not play a dirge."

Linus raised his brows.

Abigail glanced around. "Is there anything else we should do before closing?"

"No," Linus said. "I'll collect a few case notes to review tonight, then lock up. You two go. And know that you take my thanks with you. You have my everlasting gratitude for your help."

Eva smiled, but Abigail's look would stay with him a while.

"I'll let Ethan know you're on your way," she said. "See you shortly."

He could hardly wait.

Why did he keep fighting the notion? Something about her invigorated him. She was a talented artist, inspiring others with her work. By the way she cared for and encouraged Ethan and had come to rescue the spa while Mrs. Denby was gone, she had a kind heart. She knew how to champion what she believed in, regardless of the arguments arrayed against her. None of that meant he had to enter a courtship. He could enjoy her company,

her engaging conversations, yes, even their spirited dis-
agreements, without falling in love.

Still, he moved swiftly through his remaining tasks. He
shut off the fountain, made sure the water drained from
the basin. It wouldn't do for guests to arrive in the morning to a cloudy pool or specks of sediment. He hadn't
had to light any lamps, but he made sure they were all
out nonetheless. Finally, he gathered the case files for the
morning patients, added fresh supplies to his medical bag,
and went to shut and lock the door, juggling both bag
and files in the process.

His solitary walk home with Ethan beckoned. Perhaps he could pay for dinner for Abigail and her mother
instead. He could imagine him and Abigail sitting around
the dining table, laughing over the day's events, talking
to Ethan and Mrs. Archer about their activities. His son
always seemed more relaxed around Abigail and her
mother. He could see why. They both exuded a warmth
and energy that beckoned people closer.

He was turning from the door when someone grabbed
him from behind and shoved a sack over his head.

# CHAPTER TEN

"HOW DID IT GO?" HER mother asked when Abigail walked in the door that evening. Book open on his lap as he sat beside her mother on the sofa, Ethan looked up with a smile.

"Very well," Abigail told them both. "I am in even more awe of Jesslyn's skills, though. It took Eva and me both to replace her, and I'm certain we still missed a few things."

"I'm sure Doctor Bennett is grateful for your help," her mother said.

"He was very nice about it." Abigail turned to Ethan. "And he'll be right behind me, so you should probably gather your things."

"Yes, Miss Archer." He slid off the sofa and began to collect his books and drawings.

Abigail watched him a moment, then beckoned to her mother, who rose and joined her closer to the door. "I don't suppose you used those swords recently?"

"No," her mother admitted. "We've kept mainly indoors before the wedding and today. But I'm so enjoying having someone around the house again."

"I'm sure you are," Abigail allowed. "But Ethan deserves to have something more to do than study with the vicar and draw."

She was glad to see her mother nod. "The youngest Lawrence boy is taking lessons with him. I imagine they might be friends. I'll speak to Sadie about the two spending time together outside of lessons."

"The Greers' youngest daughter should be about their age," Abigail murmured. "Perhaps we could include her too."

Her mother wrinkled her nose. "Girls and boys have little in common at this age."

"You forget," Abigail said. "Jess and I joined with several of the young lads our age to romp about the village. At nine, we were learning to sail and whacking each other with Gideon's swords whenever we could sneak them out of his keeping."

She shuddered. "I remember the bruises. Your father wasn't pleased."

"Father was never pleased," Abigail told her. "With any of us."

Her mother put a hand on her arm. "Hush, now. Ethan might hear you."

Abigail pulled away, feeling as if the touch had stung as much as her mother's words. "We don't have to be silent anymore, Mother. There's no need to protect Father's reputation. He's been dead for ten years."

Her mother's eyes widened. "I never asked you to be quiet for his sake. I did it for you and your brother and me. It was bad enough we lost the church pew. I didn't want to lose the lease on the house as well."

Ethan had stopped working to watch them, face puckered in obvious concern.

"It's all right," Abigail assured him. "The lease on the shop and flat is paid for the next ten years. No one will force us out." She looked to her mother, who pressed her lips together.

Why did her mother persist in protecting her husband's legacy? Habit? Pride? Fear? Abigail's father had certainly made an impact on their lives. He'd been a stern man on the best of days; his word had ruled his house. Gideon had kept his head down, like Ethan, and Abigail had hidden behind her older brother. But when their father had been drinking, he became something else entirely.

"I think he's one of your aunt's trolls," Abigail had confided in Jess once as they had scoured the shore for shells to add to their collections. "All he wants to do is smash things."

Dishes, furnishings, her mother's embroidery—all had fallen foul of her father's rages. She'd never known what might set him off, an unkind word from the mill in Upper Grace that employed him to cart their wares around the area, an overcooked meal, a disagreement with the vicar. What had started at home had gradually trickled out into the village. He'd been destroying the public room at the Mermaid on a memorable night when its owner, Mr. Hornswag, had called the constable for help. The constable had enlisted the aid of the previous vicar. They'd both gone down under her father's fists. That's when the vicar had removed the family name from the church pew.

Her mother had never wanted to talk about any of it— to Abigail and Gideon, to acquaintances in the village, to the vicar who had made it clear she and her children were still welcome to attend services. She'd insisted Abigail and Gideon tell no one about the anger inside their home either.

"It's our shame to bear," she'd said.

Only Jesslyn and her parents had known the full of it, Jesslyn and her mother because Abigail had to have someone to whom she could pour out her heart, and Jesslyn's father because he'd had to deal with the injuries of the men her father had harmed that night. Abigail had tried apologizing to him once, and his answer had been an offer to teach her to fend for herself. She was still practicing the lessons he'd taught her. One had been to be kind to her mother. It was the hardest lesson of all.

She made herself smile for Ethan's sake. "So, what's for

dinner tonight?" she asked.

Her mother brightened too. "Mr. Hornswag said he would wait for my order. I was hoping Doctor Bennett and Ethan could join us."

Ethan looked at her eagerly. "More salmon?"

"It is a rather nice fish, isn't it?" Abigail agreed. "An excellent suggestion, Mother. Let's see what Doctor Bennett says."

But Linus didn't arrive. A quarter hour passed, then a half. He should have left moments after she and Eva had gone through the door. Could someone have come seeking his aid? Or had he merely lost track of time?

After three quarters of an hour, Abigail rose from where Ethan had been showing her his book on sea life. "I'll pop up to the spa and fetch your father. It's probably just an overzealous visitor detaining him."

"I'm not worried," Ethan said. "There are very few carriages in Grace-by-the-Sea."

Her mother cocked her head. "Why would you worry about carriages, Ethan?"

"Mother died in one," he said, calmly turning the page.

Abigail felt chilled. "Well, it's very clever of you to notice the lack of the things here. I'm sure your father will have a good explanation for his tardiness."

"He must work," Ethan said, turning another page. "He saves people from terrible illnesses. He saved me. I almost died too."

Her mother sprang up from her chair and went to enfold him in a hug. "There, now, my dear. You're safe here. Your father is very wise and very good. And Abigail is one to fight for those she loves."

Abigail was so taken aback she couldn't speak for a moment. Did her mother truly see her that way? She certainly tried to stand up for her principles. She never wanted to feel like a victim again.

"We'll all be fine," she told them both. "Ethan, I'll be

right back with your father."

Her mother released Ethan with a watery smile and followed Abigail to the door. "Are you certain you should go alone? We could ask Mr. Carroll to check."

"It will only take a moment, Mother," Abigail promised. "This is still Grace-by-the-Sea. Nothing happens in broad daylight. And the sun won't be down for hours yet." With a smile she hoped betrayed none of her thoughts, she hurried out.

All the shops were closed and most of their guests had returned to their lodgings as she climbed the hill to the spa. The memories of her father faded away to be replaced by concern for Linus, but no distinguished doctor strolled toward her. Indeed, the only movement was a piece of parchment blown on the wind. Abigail bent to retrieve it.

No sign of infection or inflammation. Expect the swelling to go down within the fortnight.

Were these case notes?

She looked around again. There, against Mrs. Mance's rosebush, another piece. And another in the hedge in front of Shell Cottage, the new Denby home. Something was very wrong.

She slipped the pages into her sleeve, snatched up her skirts with her good hand, and ran to the spa.

The door refused to open. Locked. She knocked anyway, then waited, but no one answered.

"Doctor Bennett," she called through the portal. "Linus, are you there?"

In the distance, other doors closed, voices sounded. None were his.

Her pulse pounded hard and fast. Where could he be? Had he had an urgent request to help another villager who was ill or injured? Why would he have dropped his case notes? And wouldn't he have found a way to send word to his son? He was so careful of Ethan, so concerned for his wellbeing.

And hers.

She moved back to the road, looked left, right. No sort of accident in view, no huddle of people around a door, no one hurrying for the apothecary or the vicar.

Where was he?

Perhaps he'd gone to his cottage to collect something first. Of course, that was about a ten-minute walk from the spa. Plenty of time to go there and return to her shop and Ethan. And the pages in her sleeve cried out their doubts.

What could have happened?

Her worrying spun her in a circle, and, for the first time in a long time, panic reached for her. No, she would not allow it to gain a hold. She was no longer a child, squeezing herself as small as possible in the corner of the bedchamber, praying her father wouldn't come in, that his storm of anger wouldn't break over her head this time. Gideon had protected her while he was there, but she couldn't blame him for escaping when he could. She had learned to rely only on herself. If there was something to be done, she must do it. She'd fought for a place for herself and her mother, fought to regain the respect of the village.

Yet how did she fight something she couldn't see, couldn't name?

"Abigail!"

She whirled. Linus was stumbling down the hill from the crossroads. She ran to him, threw her good arm around him, and held him tight. "Oh, Linus! I was so worried."

"It's all right," he murmured against her hair, hand pressed to her back. "Now, let go before you reinjure your arm."

Abigail jerked away to stare at him. She'd been too pale when she'd first run to him. Now color blazed back into her face.

"My arm?" she fumed. "You disappear for more than an hour and worry us all sick, and your concern is for my arm?"

"My concern is always for my patients," he said, gathering his dignity close. She had buried her face in his cravat when she'd come to him or she might have seen the wonder and joy that had no doubt crossed his face when he'd found himself wrapped in her embrace. "I'm sorry I worried you."

Her face bunched. "Of course you worried us. Where were you? Mother, Ethan, and I have been waiting."

"Again, my apologies, but I had little say in the matter. When I came out the door, I found men waiting for me."

"Who?" she asked with a frown. "The only house above the village belongs to Captain St. Claire. Is he ill?"

"It wasn't the captain, at least, I don't think he was involved." He angled his head to look at her arm. No sign of blood, but that didn't mean she hadn't broken a stitch.

"Come inside," he said. "I'll explain."

Her mouth worked, and, for a moment, he thought she would refuse. Then she nodded. As he dug out the key, she tugged some parchment from her sleeve.

"Your case notes," she announced. She thrust them at him before sailing past, nose in the air.

He offered her a bow that did little to thaw her annoyance. The light from the south-facing windows brightened the space sufficiently that he could cross to one of the examining rooms, leave the battered case notes, and return with a fresh bandage.

She sighed at the sight of it. "I'm fine, Linus. This isn't

necessary."

"I will examine you at your flat, with your mother present," he assured her, tucking it into his depleted bag, "but I'd rather have this conversation here, where I don't have to frighten Ethan."

Immediately she was all attention. "What happened?"

"I was kidnapped," he said, and her eyes widened. "Two men, by the number of hands on my person, though neither spoke. They covered my head with a sack, bound my hands behind me, and marched me to a waiting wagon. What time is it?"

She blinked at the non sequitur, then glanced at the bronze wall clock. "Nearly half past six."

"Then I've been gone more than an hour," he realized. "I estimate they drove me for about a quarter hour each way, and it took me another half hour to tend to the patient."

She seized on the word. "A patient? Someone was ill?"

"Injured," he corrected her, thinking back. "Gunshot wound to the thigh. My captors pulled me out of the wagon and led me into the inner room of a house, then took off the sack. The place smelled of dust and decay. There was a man sitting on a crudely constructed wooden chair. The walls were plaster, no paper. The floors hadn't been swept for some time."

Once more she stared at him. "What has that to do with anything? You were kidnapped!"

"And I'd very much like to know by whom," he assured her. "The more I remember about the circumstances, the better our chances of locating the place again."

She drew in a breath and nodded. "You're right. Sorry. Go on. What else do you remember?"

"There was nothing else in the room except a washbasin with water. Plain white. Porcelain."

"Common, then," she agreed. "In fact, it very much sounds like a tenant farmer's house."

"Possibly, but they weren't farmers. The two who had captured me backed from the room before I could catch a glimpse of them. The injured fellow had a cap that covered most of his hair. Dark brown eyes, the beginnings of a mustache and beard, brown or black. He refused to speak to me."

"None of this makes sense," she protested. "You heard the militia the other day. Most of the people in the area don't even own a gun. How could this fellow have been shot?"

"Perhaps because he attempted to steal food and clothing from a real farmer."

She gasped. "The French agents!"

"Exactly," Linus agreed. "By refusing to speak, they hid even their voices from me. But they wanted me to know who they represented. It was almost as if they were taunting me. You see, they'd draped a French flag over the back of the chair."

She shook her head. "The villains! But why did they let you see one of them and live?"

He'd been afraid they wouldn't. But he wasn't about to tell her that, or the fact that his first emotion on considering the matter had been regret that he wouldn't see her again.

"Because they may still need me," he said. "I fear the wound is grievous, much more serious than yours. He was feverish when I arrived. They'd already attempted to dig out the ball. I finished the job and bound him up, but I won't be surprised if he needs more treatment."

Like a teakettle, she'd built up enough steam to sound off again. "They cannot go around kidnapping people at will. We will protect you. We'll go to the magistrate."

"Who is out of town," he reminded her. "As is Mr. Denby. And your constable cannot be expected to dance attendance on me."

"We don't have a constable at present," she explained.

"He retired, and no one saw the need to replace him. We have few crimes in Grace-by-the-Sea." She stiffened. "I know, the militia! Mr. Greer will take a dim view of someone troubling our physician."

He sighed. "Mr. Greer was instrumental in giving me this position, for which I will always be grateful, but I'm not sure the village militia is ready to confront French soldiers, even with one of them injured. Someone else could get hurt."

"Right." She raised her chin. "There's nothing for it, then. We will take the road of last resort. We'll call an emergency meeting of the Spa Corporation board."

# CHAPTER ELEVEN

H E HAD NEVER MET A more determined woman. It was surprisingly invigorating.

"You collect Ethan," she said, starting for the spa door. "I'll alert Mr. Lawrence. He can send his children to fetch the others." She glanced at the clock as she passed it. "Meet at the Swan's private parlor at half past seven?"

Linus hurried to intercept her before she could leave. "I would rather keep you out of this. If anything should happen to you…"

She waited, and he could not make himself say what his heart demanded.

"You could reopen your wound," he finished lamely.

She cocked her head. "By walking to the jeweler's and then to the Swan? Doubtful. Besides, I am a member of the Spa Corporation board. You'll need me there to ensure a quorum. Now, hurry. I'll walk you as far as the shop to make sure no one else takes off with you."

It was rather humbling that he needed protection, but he could think of few better. He wouldn't want to tangle with Abigail Archer on a mission.

"Mr. Ellison and Mr. Bent, the former employment agency owner, generally sided with Mr. Greer," she explained as they started down the hill. "I don't know how Mrs. Catchpole, Mr. Bent's replacement, will vote. This will be her first meeting. Mr. Lawrence and Mrs.

THE ARTIST'S HEALER 105

Kirby generally make up their own minds. It's Mr. Greer you'll have to convince."

She was right, Linus saw when they all regrouped a short time later. Unsure how long the meeting would go, he'd left Ethan with Abigail's mother.

The Swan's private parlor was a paneled room that boasted a large fireplace of pale, rough stones; a brass chandelier; and a long plank table that could seat twenty on its flanking benches. A high-backed chair stood at either end. Mr. Greer went to take up his place at one. He nodded Linus toward the other. Mr. Lawrence; Mr. Ellison, the baker; and a buxom blonde who had introduced herself as Mrs. Catchpole slid onto one of the benches. Abigail and the leasing agent, Mrs. Kirby, took up positions on the other, Abigail as close to him as possible. He tried not to be gratified by the fact.

"Come to order," Mr. Greer called, though no one had been saying a great deal. As the last voices quieted, he nodded down the table. "First, allow me to welcome you, Doctor Bennett, to your inaugural board meeting, and Mrs. Catchpole as well. I can assure you, we generally give a few days' notice before calling one." He regarded Abigail pointedly.

She must have taken that as her cue, for she promptly launched into her reasoning, voice crisp. "An incident occurred this evening that must be brought to your attention. Normally, I'd speak to the magistrate, but he's out of town. So, I appeal to this august group instead. There are French agents in our midst."

They all regarded her.

"And?" Mr. Greer prompted.

"And? And!" Abigail sputtered. "And we must capture them."

A bold statement, but Greer shook his head with a sigh. "Miss Archer, the militia here in Grace-by-the-Sea and the officers of West Creech are aware of the issue. This body can do nothing useful to assist."

"Even if they threaten our physician?" Abigail demanded

Every one of them stiffened, and all gazes latched onto her.

"Who'd bother our physician?" Mr. Ellison demanded, massive frame quivering. "We didn't hire him to offer him out to strangers."

"Highly irregular," Mr. Lawrence agreed, tugging down on his waistcoat.

Greer alone seemed less incensed about the matter. "How exactly does this threaten Doctor Bennett?" he asked.

Abigail looked to Linus.

Right. It was his turn to present them with the facts. "When I was locking up this evening," he said, glancing around the table, "I was seized, bound, and carried off by two men to tend a third with a gunshot wound to the thigh."

Greer washed white. "What?"

Mrs. Kirby, whose hair was a vivid shade of red, leaned forward to meet his gaze around Abigail. "Did you get a good look at them?"

"A sense of their location?" Lawrence added.

"Neither," Linus assured them. "My head was covered by a sack during travel. I only saw the patient I was to tend. But I can tell you this: the wagon in which they placed me traveled uphill as we left the spa—I felt the inclination. Then the bed flattened out for a while. From the amount of time I was away from the spa, I'd say I traveled approximately a quarter hour along the Downs to a vacant house. I can provide details."

Greer leaned back against his chair. "It must have been near Upper Grace. This has nothing to do with us."

"Nothing!" Abigail cried. "They kidnapped our physician."

"And returned him unharmed," Greer pointed out patiently. "I see no reason to get involved."

Abigail stared at him. "These are French agents, sir. It is our duty to call out the militia."

All gazes now swung to his. Greer stuck out his chin. "I refuse to trouble our valiant men for something so vague. Besides, we have musters coming up that cannot be delayed."

It was as Linus had suspected. Greer saw the militia as a gentlemen's club—all good show and good cheer.

Abigail must have realized it as well, for she shook her head. "So, our militia is nothing more than a spectacle to entertain visitors, give us all a false sense of security."

Greer's color returned and deepened. "Certainly not, but neither are they to be sent out for every little inconvenience."

"I can't say I agree," Mrs. Catchpole put in. "Going out to search for these Frenchies would give the militia something more useful to do than trampling the grass. Besides, what if these fellows decide they need a vicar next? Or an apothecary."

Greer blinked as if he had not considered that.

Lawrence looked to Linus. "Are you under the impression, Doctor Bennett, that these fellows might return for you again? Or anyone else?"

Linus shrugged. "It's quite possible. I did what I could for the injured man, but he needs more attention than I could provide. If they don't come for me, they might accost the other physician who is visiting at present, Doctor Owens."

Lawrence's look veered to Greer. "We cannot have them troubling a guest."

Greer nodded thoughtfully. "Very well. I'll send word to the encampment at West Creech. They can search any vacant houses between here and Upper Grace."

"I'll give you a list of vacant leases," Mrs. Kirby offered.

Something brushed his boot. Abigail's smile was smug. He returned the pressure against her slipper.

"We should also ensure Doctor Bennett's protection," Mrs. Kirby continued. "Assign the militiamen to take turns guarding him and the spa."

Well, that might be overdoing it. Linus opened his mouth to refuse, but Abigail spoke first. "An excellent suggestion. There are thirty men in the troop. If each one took an evening and night, they'd only have to stand guard for a day a month."

"A month!" Greer frowned at her. "How long do you intend for this to go on, Miss Archer?"

She raised her chin. "Until someone has the foresight and courage to capture these renegades, Mr. Greer."

"I can defend myself," Linus said in the silence that followed. "Now that I know of the danger, I can be on alert."

"There, you see?" Greer spread his hands. "There was no need for concern."

"And what of your son, Doctor Bennett?" Ellison pressed with a frown his way. "Are you confident you can protect him as well?"

The baker could not know the doubts that leaped up at the suggestion. He had nearly lost Ethan once. He would not lose him now. The French had proven they knew more about the village than anyone had expected. If they needed a physician again, and they could not reach him, would they go after Ethan instead, to use his son as leverage against him?

Some of his concerns must have leaked out, for Abigail put a hand on his arm. "He's right, sir. Let us help you."

Linus met her gaze, allowed himself to slip into the kindness shining there. Then he nodded. "Very well. I will do as this body advises."

As she gave his arm a squeeze, Mr. Lawrence glanced between him and Greer. "And what does this body advise?"

Abigail straightened in her seat. "I move that we assign Doctor Bennett and his son a bodyguard from the moment the spa closes until it opens in the morning. This bodyguard will be chosen from among the men of the Grace-by-the-Sea militia with experience in using firearms accurately."

"Well, that narrows the field," Lawrence muttered.

Greer drew in a breath. "Very well. All in favor?"

"Aye," answered Abigail, Mrs. Catchpole, Mrs. Kirby, Ellison, and Lawrence in unison.

"Let the record show that I disagreed," Greer said. "But the motion passes. I'll speak to Mr. Hornswag tonight about who to assign."

"I'll send my oldest to you tonight," Lawrence promised. "He's our drummer, and he knows how to shoot."

The lad couldn't be more than a few months over the age of fifteen, the youngest a male might enroll in the military. Had Linus merely added another for whom he was responsible?

Insufficient. That was all Abigail could think. Davy Lawrence was a fine young man, but she could not imagine him fighting off three determined French soldiers. A shame she couldn't be there to protect Linus and Ethan. Thanks to Doctor Chance, she knew how to fence at least. But she and Linus could not spend the night together in his little cottage unless they were married.

For a moment, she imagined it. Her paintings on the walls, Ethan out on the shore playing catch-me-who-can with friends, Linus coming home from the spa after she'd closed the shop. He'd cross to her side, take her in his arms, and...

"He is the stuff of dreams, isn't he?"

Abigail blinked. The meeting had ended. Everyone was getting up to leave, and Mrs. Catchpole was smiling at her.

Abigail regarded her. "I beg your pardon?"

Mrs. Catchpole held up her hands. "No offense meant." She nodded to where Linus was speaking to Mr. Lawrence and Mr. Greer, offering them the details of his kidnapping so they could advise the officers at West Creech. "I asked you the same question twice, but it was clear where your thoughts were."

Hopefully not that clear, but her cheeks heated nonetheless.

"I'm just concerned about him," Abigail told her.

"Course you are. We all are. At least we should be." She narrowed her brown eyes at Mr. Greer. "Stay on our exalted president, and make sure he follows through."

"I will," Abigail promised. "Was there something else you needed?"

"Nothing as important as that," Mrs. Catchpole assured her. "And if there's anything I and my staff can do to help, just let us know."

Abigail did one better. When Linus arrived to drop off Ethan and check on her the next morning, she left at his side.

"I take it nothing further happened last night," she said as they came around the building. "Davy Lawrence acquitted himself well?"

"He was asleep at the table when we woke this morning," Linus said with a shake of his head. "I sent him home."

"We'll do better tonight," Abigail promised.

He shot her a glance. "You will not be taking a turn, Abigail. While I appreciate you and Eva's help, I cannot like involving you in this."

"I did not intend to take a turn," she informed him.

"And Eva and I are only helping at the spa until Jesslyn returns." She nodded to Mr. Carroll, who was just opening his shop. He hurried out to intercept them.

"So it's true," he said, sunlight gleaming on his spectacles. "We have French spies in the area."

Abigail could not wonder how the news had spread so quickly. There had been five people at the board meeting last night besides her and Linus, more than enough to ignite a fire of gossip in the village.

"Three of them, to be exact," Abigail said. "Somewhere between here and Upper Grace. Tell everyone to look sharp."

"I will," he promised. He nodded to Linus. "I'm on rotation to serve you three days from now. I will pray we capture them before then."

"I'm sure that wasn't a comment on his abilities," Abigail assured Linus after he'd thanked the shopkeeper and they'd continued up the hill.

"Very likely not," Linus said. "But do we need to tell everyone what happened?"

"Absolutely," Abigail said. "The more who know, the more who can watch over you."

He did not look comforted. She still made sure to tell Eva everything the moment her friend arrived at the spa that morning with Mrs. Tully. Jesslyn's aunt did not look pleased to be back in the spa, her narrowed gaze darting about as if she expected trolls to pop out of hiding.

"We'll keep Doctor Bennett safe," Eva promised, hands on her lavender skirts. "I'm sure Lord Featherstone and the Admiral could assist. We might even get our two dandies, Mr. Donner and Mr. George, to do more than ogle the ladies." She nodded to where the two younger men were lounging in chairs near the windows, watching a set of Newcomer sisters who were promenading with their mother.

Abigail turned her gaze to the welcome book instead.

"I know Jesslyn was being cautious of Newcomers. Anyone who arrived in the last fortnight could be suspect."

"Mr. Donner and Mr. George included," Mrs. Tully declared.

Eva wrinkled her nose as if she could not imagine the two dandies involved, then dropped her gaze to the book as well. "That's at least two dozen people."

"We should interrogate them," Mrs. Tully said. "Ferret out their secrets. I'm sure the fairies will help."

Eva put a hand on her arm. "I have a more important task for you. Will you play for us? It will distract the French from our intentions."

"They won't suspect a thing," she vowed before marching herself to the harpsichord. She spread her purple skirts to sit, and a sonata sprang from her fingers.

"Well done," Abigail told Eva. "Now, about these interrogations…"

"Polite inquiries," Eva amended.

"You may be polite if you like," Abigail said. "Just rule out the females. Linus seemed certain he was kidnapped by men. That leaves us with eleven. If you take five and I take six, we can question each and determine whether more drastic action is needed."

Eva agreed, and they put their plan into place that very morning.

Abigail made sure to start with Mr. Donner. The handsome brunette had moved closer to the chessboard, where Mrs. Harding was watching Mr. Crabapple take on the Admiral.

"Plotting strategy?" she asked the Newcomer.

Donner smiled at her. "Always. A gentleman could learn a great deal from watching more seasoned campaigners."

Indeed he could. "Forgive me, sir, but I don't recall which part of England you call home."

"London," he said readily. "Is that not where all the best

people reside?"

Convenient answer. Arrogant too. She rather thought some of the best people resided in Grace-by-the-Sea. "And your family? Have they some fine estate in the country?"

His face tightened. "No, Miss Archer. They do not."

"Ahem." The Admiral affixed them both with a steely-eyed look. "We are attempting to wage war here. A little quiet would be preferable."

Abigail curtsied and returned to the welcome desk. Donner had proven more slippery than she had expected. All she could say she knew about him was that he had decided to prolong his stay. He might be a French agent, or merely an impoverished member of the gentry determined to pretend to more. These interrogations were decidedly tricky.

She had a little more success with Mr. George. Once approached, he was happy to converse with her. In a few minutes, she learned that was from nearby Wiltshire and had loving parents and six charming sisters. She had thought his friendship with Mr. Donner of long duration, but he admitted they had struck up an acquaintance on the stage on the way to the spa. As for Mr. George, he had come with hopes of acquiring a better connection to Society at lesser expense than traveling to London.

Doctor Owens regaled her with stories of the patients he'd treated, some with rather stomach-turning ailments, before she found a way to escape. The other three gentlemen she attempted to question were more interested in flirting than direct conversation. Eva fared no better.

"As innocent as the day is long," she lamented as she and Abigail regrouped at the welcome desk.

The best they could do was be watchful. Linus had appointments with patients for the first two hours, all female, so it was simple enough to ensure no Newcomer approached him. As the morning wore on, however, he came out of the examining rooms and mingled more with the guests. He spoke at some length with Mr. Crabapple, Lord Featherstone, and the Admiral. Mrs. Tully put herself in his path and shook her finger at him. Abigail was about to effect a rescue when Doctor Owens pulled him aside for a private word. Linus's gaze veered to Abigail. She stood straighter under it. He excused himself from his colleague with a nod and came to join her.

"I have been told you are badgering the guests," he said, though his smile was amused. "I find that unlikely given how hard you and Eva work to keep the spa running well while Mrs. Denby is away. What are you up to, Abigail?"

"Only doing my duty," Abigail said. "If there is a French agent watching you, it stands to reason he must be a Newcomer. Eva and I are merely making sure of their innocence."

"And possibly endangering yourselves in the process," he said, brows coming down. "Besides, Mrs. Denby and I already reviewed all the recent guests. None seemed suspicious."

"Perhaps you aren't as suspicious as I am," Abigail countered.

Just then, a gentleman strode into the spa. She'd seen him in St. Andrew's in recent months. One of the fishermen? He apparently recognized her as well, for he hurried to her side. "Miss Archer. Can you point me to the new physician?"

"I'm the physician," Linus said. "Doctor Bennett, at your service, sir."

He grabbed Linus's arm, and Abigail bristled.

"Come with me," he told Linus. "Please. My wife's having our baby, and her sister says all she can see is the buttocks. It's stuck. You have to help us."

"I'll get my bag," Linus said.

"And I'll come with you," Abigail added.

# CHAPTER TWELVE

L INUS DIDN'T HAVE TIME TO argue with her. Eva must have overheard their conversation, for she came running with his medical bag. He was just thankful he'd already restocked it that morning. He followed the man from the spa, Abigail by his side.

"This is our third," the fellow was saying as they hurried down High Street for the cove, his worn brown coat flapping. "The first two were so easy we thought we could do it with only her sister to help. But something went wrong."

"The fact that your wife brought two children into the world stands in her favor," Linus told him. "But a baby in the wrong position is never easy."

"You're Mr. Evans, aren't you?" Abigail asked the father as they passed Mr. Carroll's.

He nodded, brown hair beginning to stick out around his narrow face. "That's right, miss. Came here two months ago to stay with my wife's sister, Ruthie Jannesy. She kept writing us and writing us about how good it is to live in this village." His hopeful smile faded as quickly as it had come.

"It is a good village," Abigail promised him. "You'll see. Are you along the cove, then?"

"Yes, miss. This way."

They came out along the shore and turned for the east,

Mr. Evans's legs eating up the rocky path. Abigail scurried along beside Linus. While he appreciated her trying to help, he could not like her pallor. The ginger of her hair stood out around a white face, and she kept her injured arm close, as if it pained her. He could only hope she would stay outside when they reached the little stone cottage on the opposite side of the cove from his.

She came in right behind him.

Unlike his cabin, this one had a single room, though a wooden ladder near the hearth led up to what was no doubt a loft. Normally, the family would likely have slept there, but Mrs. Evans was lying on a pallet against the white-washed back wall, blankets piled around her. Her dark hair hung limply around a face drenched in sweat. The younger woman holding her hand must have been her sister. Their eyes were nearly as wide as those of the two young children, perhaps six and four, huddled against the adjacent wall, one with her fist shoved in her mouth as if holding back her fears.

"Right," Abigail said to the children, moving around him as he headed for the mother. "I'm Miss Archer, and I know a secret. It involves cinnamon buns. Follow me, and I'll whisper it in your ear."

The two little girls edged closer to her, and she shepherded them out the door.

Clever woman.

Linus knelt beside the mother. Her sister had draped the covers around her as if protecting her modesty, but he could see the mound of her belly, the hand that pressed against the pain.

"I'm Doctor Bennett," he told her with a smile. "Let's see what we can do for your newest little one, shall we?"

He wasn't sure how long it had been, but the sun didn't seem to have moved much when he stepped out of the cottage again. The sea breeze cooled the perspiration on his forehead and his bare arms where he'd rolled up his sleeves. Abigail was at the shore below the cottage, tossing rocks into the water with the children. He wouldn't have thought that would hold such fascination, until she cocked her good arm and threw. The stone skipped across the waves three, four, five times before it sank. The youngest clapped her hands with delight.

Mr. Evans came out of the cottage, bundle in his arms. "Sally, Mary, come meet your little brother."

The girls turned and ran to their father. Linus stepped aside to let them pass.

"Success, I take it," Abigail said, moving to join him.

"Mother and son are doing fine," he said, taking in a deep breath of the briny air. "Thank you for your help with the girls. Their mother was as worried about them as she was the birth. I have a question for you, though."

"Oh?" she asked, brows rising.

"What's the secret with cinnamon buns?"

She smiled as she leaned closer, breath brushing his ear and her peachy scent teasing his nose. "They're sweeter when they're shared."

Linus had to stop himself from reaching for her as she leaned back. "Perhaps we should test that theory," he said.

"Only if we bring one back for the girls," she said. "I promised."

"Give me a moment." He went inside to fetch his coat and bag, then returned to the cove and washed in the brisk, salty water.

"And they'll be all right?" she asked, eyeing the cottage.

"I'll check on them tonight on the way home." He rose and shook the water from his fingers.

"I'll speak to Mrs. Mance and the vicar," she said as they started around the cove. "I'm sure baby clothes and blankets can be donated. And Mr. Hornswag will want to send down dinner tonight."

Linus smiled. "I'm sure that would be appreciated."

They walked up to the bakery together, where Abigail procured three buns—two for the family and one for her and Linus. After delivering their gift, she led him to a rough driftwood bench along the cove and sat to divide their spoils. The fishing boats rode at anchor, their crews already home with the day's catch. The cove might have been abandoned, except for him and Abigail, and the shoppers up on High Street were heading for the spa.

The sun warm on his face, a gull calling overhead, Linus's muscles relaxed. He took a bite of the roll and savored the spicy cinnamon.

"I don't imagine you get much call to birth babies," Abigail ventured. She'd left her bonnet at the spa, and sunlight set her hair to gleaming.

"Doubtful," he allowed. "But I'd assumed I would be treating the villagers as well. I was surprised there were no examining rooms set aside for them, no separate entrance to the spa."

"Doctor Chance had such rooms in his home," she explained, "but that was Shell Cottage, where Jess and Lark will be living now. The cottage you were given isn't large enough."

"And poorly located on the harbor," he agreed.

She licked icing from her fingers. "We must find you a bigger house."

He could not look away from the shine of sugar on her lips. She must have noticed, for she cocked her head and returned his look.

Once more his heart started pounding. He could not ignore its demands this time.

"You're right," he murmured. "Cinnamon buns are better shared." And he leaned forward and kissed her.

She tasted of sugar and cinnamon, sunlight and sea

breeze, and every other good thing he could imagine. Her touch, her sigh, carried him like a wave. He made himself lean back before he could sink.

Her eyes were closed, lashes as dusky as cinnamon fanning her cheeks. Her lips were parted, as if she would breathe him in. Slowly, she opened her eyes and gazed at him in wonder. "You kissed me."

"I did," he agreed, willing his heartbeat to slow. "It seemed...necessary."

"Perhaps it was." She seemed more bemused than annoyed. "Do you intend to make a habit of it, sir?"

The very idea sent his pulse rocketing again. "I hadn't thought that far."

She pursed her lips, which only made him want to kiss her again. "Most unusual for a physician. I thought you always considered consequences, looked to outcomes."

Generally he did, but his heart had other ideas when it came to her. Still, a gentleman didn't kiss a lady without expectations being raised. She had every right to an explanation, even if he could not bring himself to apologize for such a kiss.

"I find you attractive," he said. "I admire your talent with a canvas, your determination. And you had sugar on your lips."

She raised a ginger brow. "I can think of a dozen ways to remove it without you kissing it off."

"A dozen, eh?" Linus couldn't help his smile.

"Do you doubt me?" She raised her chin in a gesture of defiance he had come to know well. "I could have eaten more of the bun. I could have sipped water or tea. I could have requested a napkin from Mr. Ellison. I might have brushed it off with my fingers." She slid her fingertips across the soft flesh. "I could have licked it off." Her tongue flicked out.

"That is sufficient demonstration," Linus said, feeling the need to stand and look out toward the cool waters of the cove. "I apologize for doubting you."

She rose as well. "Apology accepted, for the doubt and for the kiss. We should report to the spa, but I have one stop to make first."

"Another cinnamon bun?" he asked, trying not to look eager at the thought.

"No, Mrs. Kirby's leasing agency. I want to see about another house for you."

It was likely the least important thing in that moment. He would have patients waiting at the spa. Eva might need her help. There were French agents plaguing the village! But Abigail had to do something immediately, or she'd likely kiss him again.

And why? What was wrong with her? After seeing the tragedy of her parents' marriage, she'd never thought to wed. Of the men with whom she'd associated closely over the years, the only two who weren't despots were Doctor Chance and Mr. Carroll, and neither had been disposed to look at her as a possible partner. Neither had particularly stirred her spirit either. She certainly hadn't hoped for a kiss! Even Quillan St. Claire seemed all brash bravado, and she'd never dared to look deeper.

Linus Bennett was different. Those grey eyes could brim with compassion, and he truly listened to what others said. He was willing to admit when he didn't know something and equally willing to learn from his mistakes. And he admired her painting and determination. But as a physician, he was used to ordering people about. Could she live with such a man?

Not that he'd asked her for a commitment. Indeed, as they walked through the village, he seemed determined to ignore the matter, head up and look on the distance.

Perhaps it had been an aberration, brought on by the emotions of the birth.

"I believe Mr. Lawrence is signaling us," he said.

She glanced around him. The jeweler was standing in the bow window of his shop, pointing down at a display of rings.

Wedding rings.

"You mistake him," Abigail said, scooting around to put herself between Linus and the shop. "He seems to be dusting his wares."

He frowned. "And Miss Pierce the elder?"

Abigail looked toward the linens and trimmings shop, where the older sister had come out, lace draped along her arm like a wedding veil.

"Is airing her goods," Abigail said with a furious shake of her head at the lady, who pouted. "I imagine some get quite musty on the voyage from Ireland."

He did not look convinced as she hurried him up the street to Mrs. Kirby's home.

The lady was in residence and happy to discuss the matter with them on her wide front porch overlooking the cove. She seated them on the wicker chairs there and had her housekeeper bring out lemonade. Abigail explained the situation, then drank deeply. She certainly didn't want any more sugar on her lips.

Just another kiss.

"I know the perfect house," Mrs. Kirby said, as if she hadn't noticed the color climbing in Abigail's cheeks or perhaps attributed it to the exertions of their walk. "I showed it to Mrs. Howland the other week. A fine four bedroom with a study off the entrance, perfect for an examining room."

Abigail swallowed the tart liquid. "Why didn't the Howlands take it?"

"Mrs. Howland preferred to be away from High Street," Mrs. Kirby said, leaning back in the wicker chair. "But I would think that location a benefit for a doctor. Easy access for his patients. And it's just up the street from Shell Cottage, where they used to see their physician."

So Abigail would be close to Jess. No, no! This house wasn't for her. It was for Linus and Ethan. She would not be living in it.

"I can show it to you now, if you'd like," Mrs. Kirby offered, glancing between them.

Linus started to shake his head, but all at once, Abigail wasn't willing to share him with the spa again so soon.

"That would be delightful," she told the leasing agent.

Mrs. Kirby went to fetch the key.

"I have appointments this afternoon," he reminded her, large hands cradling the glass.

"None that cannot wait," Abigail said. "At least look at the house to see if it's something you might want to pursue."

He regarded her a moment, and Abigail dropped her gaze. Silly, really. It wasn't as if he could see what she was dreaming.

Could he?

"Very well," he said, and a tingle shot through her.

The leasing agent returned and led them up the street to a tall stone house with green shutters on the multipaned windows. The front garden overflowed with flowers, and an old, curly limbed tree in the back shaded it from the summer sun.

"The four bedchambers are all upstairs," Mrs. Kirby explained as she let them into a wide entry hall with a warm wood floor. "One could be used as a study. And there are quarters above the carriage house in the back for staff."

They wandered through the rooms. Easy to imagine sitting on that settee there by the window in the wide withdrawing room, her mother's dishes in the mahogany hutch built into the dining room wall. Ethan would love

the bedroom nearest the tree. They'd have to watch that
he didn't climb out the window into it as he grew older.

And there she went daydreaming again!

Linus spent the most time studying the room to the
right of the entry, which Mrs. Kirby had suggested could
be his examining room.

"The house would be ideal," he finally told the leasing
agent. "How much for a year's lease?"

She named a price that raised Abigail's brows. Linus
thanked her and told her he would consider the matter.

"Too dear," he said to Abigail as they started for the spa
at last. "It would take more than half my salary at the spa."

"Let's not rule it out just yet," she said as he paused to
look up and down the street. "Having you able to treat all
comers would be a great benefit to the village. It would
help Upper Grace and the outlying farms as well. Perhaps Mr. Greer could negotiate an agreement with the
owner."

He took her good arm and started across the street.
"Who owns the land in the area?"

"Approximately half belongs to the Earl of Howland;
the rest is divided among Lord Peverell and a few yeo-
man farmers. I'm not sure where this house falls."

He stopped at the corner of Church and High Street,
hand lingering on her arm. She didn't pull away.

"Why don't you go up to the spa?" he suggested. "I'll
ask Mrs. Kirby about the matter."

"No need," she assured him. "We'll see her Sunday at
St. Andrew's. I'm sure the house won't be let before then."

"Nevertheless," he said, "I would prefer that you continue on to the spa."

Abigail frowned at him. His gaze had narrowed, his
body tensed. This couldn't be about the house.

"Why?" she asked. "What's wrong?"

He leaned closer. "A gentleman has been following us

since we left the bakery. I would prefer to know you're safe before confronting him."

# CHAPTER THIRTEEN

SHE DIDN'T BUDGE. HE HADN'T really expected that she would. This was a woman who looked danger in the face and went after it tooth and nail. So, he shifted his position to put his back to the fellow and stepped to the left to allow her a view down the street.

"Big man," he murmured. "Keeps his distance. Do you see him?"

She nodded, gaze focused beyond him. "Tough visage too. I wouldn't want to tussle with him."

Linus nearly sagged with relief. "Then please do as I ask, and go up to the spa."

"And miss all the fun?" Her gaze met his, and her green eyes sparkled. She stepped around him and raised her voice. "Jack! Jack Hornswag! Come make yourself known to our physician."

Linus turned as the burly fellow approached. Dressed in a rough coat and trousers, a red, bushy beard hanging down to the middle of his chest, he loped up to them and came to a stop to pull off his cap. "Miss Abby, Doctor Bennett. I'm your escort this evening, sir. I just thought I'd practice a bit first."

"Mr. Hornswag is the proprietor at the Mermaid," Abigail explained, smile this side of smug again. "Mother and I have been relying on his staff's cooking for years."

He grinned, betraying teeth stained yellow. "My best

customers. I've known her since she was a girl."

For some reason, that sobered her. "I'm glad to see you're on duty, but who's minding the inn?"

"Thought I'd give Arnie Williams a try. He's my latest cook," he confided in Linus. "It's only one night, and he could use the experience. Plus, he's big enough to bust a few heads if needed." He barked a laugh.

Hornswag looked as if he could bust a few heads himself. His protection would certainly intimidate the French more than that of young Mr. Lawrence.

"Thank you for the assistance," Linus told him. "We were just returning to the spa. Will you join us?"

Hornswag shuddered, an earthquake on a mountain. "Not me. Too many fancy sorts there. I generally cater to the men who work with their hands. No offense meant, sir. I'll just keep an eye on the place until you're ready to leave."

Linus thanked him again, then turned with Abigail for the spa.

"Don't feel foolish for mistaking him," she said as if she could read Linus's face so well. "You're still learning everyone in the village. And he is rather large."

Could she read his mind as well? "I'm not used to requiring protection."

"It's as much for Ethan as it is for you," she reminded him. "And I admit to sleeping easier knowing you're safe." As if she heard the same tender concern he did, she hurried on. "We have needed a physician for some time. I don't intend to hand him over to the French."

And he had needed someone who cared.

Impossible to doubt it, though he hadn't been willing to admit it even to himself until now. But once he had admitted it, the thought refused to leave him. It hovered over him as he saw to his patients then updated their case files that afternoon.

Growing up, he'd been one of the few lads among the

families following the drum. He had relied on the company of his mother and father until they'd both passed. Small wonder he'd found it hard to make friends at Edinburgh. Not that he'd had much time for such things with his studies. He would never have met Catriona if not for an invitation from a professor to join him at a friend's house for dinner.

Her father had been a wealthy banker who donated to the school. The house, the food, had impressed Linus. It had been soup and bread most nights for him. One look at Cat near the head of the table, and he hadn't been able to look away. He'd never understood why she'd sought him out for further acquaintance among her dozens of admirers. He had not fit into her set of horse-mad, sporting enthusiasts. But he'd convinced himself he loved her and that she returned his love. He was no longer sure of either.

Yet was what he began to feel for Abigail any different? She too was a beautiful woman with a propensity for finding trouble. Cat had generally made her own trouble by taking risks in the name of fun. Abigail risked all for what she believed in—a position for her friend, the safety of her village. It was hard to find fault with such zeal.

But that didn't mean he had to kiss her, even if he had to argue himself out of kissing her again.

One kiss—a moment's aberration brought on by the heat of the moment. Two—or three or four—kisses, a statement he was not prepared to make.

But his new neighbors thought otherwise.

"I am very thankful for the care you've shown Abigail," Eva said as she brought the teacart to the empty examining room that afternoon so he could have a cup. "She is an amazing woman. Don't you agree?"

He glanced out the open door to where Abigail was speaking with Mrs. Rand before noting something in his appointment book. "Indeed I do."

"Excellent," she said with a smile. "I hope to hear good news soon."

Jack Hornswag voiced his opinion as he escorted Linus down to the Archers. Abigail had gone ahead while Linus finished locking up the spa.

"Fine woman, Miss Abby," he said, falling into step beside Linus and dwarfing him in the process. "A lady to be respected and admired."

Linus could only nod agreement. If he spoke, he might betray too much.

"I was very glad to see neither her nor her brother took after their father," Hornswag continued. "Tragic case, that."

Linus frowned. "Was he ill long?"

Hornswag snorted. "I wouldn't call illness what a man brings on himself. Mean as the distance is long, that one. Made a mess of my public room more than once. Rumor was he made a mess of his home as well. Never did know what his sweet wife saw in him. No one missed him."

Linus could not imagine Abigail growing up with a tyrant of a father, nor her gentle mother marrying such a fellow. Had she learned her determination by standing up to the man?

Her mother seemed to have borrowed some of that determination, for she took his arm and drew Linus aside as soon as he entered the flat that evening while Jack waited at the door.

"Abigail is fetching dinner from the Mermaid," Mrs. Archer told Linus, eyes bright in a face that was beginning to wrinkle with cares. "And Ethan is gathering his things. I just want you to know you have my blessing."

She was so fervent, but she could not mean what he thought. "Blessing?" Linus asked.

She smiled. "To propose to Abigail, of course. I already think of Ethan as my grandson, so it will be easy."

Easy, she said, as if adding another person, another

family, to his life was anything less than complicated. If his own conflicted feelings weren't enough to give him pause, he had to consider Ethan. His son had been through so much in the last year. Was he any more ready for Linus to marry again?

"You seem to be getting on well with Mrs. Archer," Linus ventured as they walked home, Jack lumbering a respectful distance behind. Linus hadn't wanted to frighten his son by mentioning the kidnapping; he'd only told the boy that the village wanted to ensure their safety at the odd hours he worked. So the boy didn't question their hulking shadow now.

"She's very nice," Ethan agreed, gaze on the pebbles at his feet.

"And what of Miss Archer?" Linus asked, shoulders tensing.

"She's nice too," Ethan allowed, shifting the books he carried. "She's a little like Mother."

Now his throat and back felt tight as well. He forced his voice to come out neutrally. "Oh? In what way?"

"She'll talk to me, play games with me, but she doesn't get tired of me like Mother did."

An ache spread through him. If only he could assure Ethan his mother had never tired of him, but he couldn't. Cat had hated motherhood, seeing it as one more chain to bind her. He couldn't even assure Ethan she had loved him. If she had truly loved her son, or Linus, she would never have taken such risks.

"Miss Archer is a singular lady," he said instead. "I'm glad you've had the chance to become better acquainted."

"Me too," Ethan said. "I heard Mrs. Archer tell Mr. Carroll she hopes you'll get married. That might be nice."

Linus stumbled on the path and righted himself in time to climb the steps to the cottage door. "You wouldn't mind if I brought home a wife, a new mother for you?"

Ethan looked up into his eyes at last, face drawn. Was

Linus mad to see hope as well? "So long as she doesn't leave us like Mother did."

Linus lay a hand on his shoulder, so small, so fragile. "None of us knows when we'll be called to Heaven, Ethan, but most people don't actively seek to leave now."

"I know," Ethan said. "I was worried at first you'd go after her, because that's what you always did. Mother would dash off, and you would go find her and bring her home. But you stayed with me this time."

Tears were burning his eyes. Linus went down on one knee and wrapped his arms about his son. "I will always stay with you, Ethan. You are my son. I love you. So long as there is breath in my body, I will be here with you."

Ethan lay his head on Linus's shoulder, and he felt the sigh go out of him. "When they hear Mother is dead, everyone says I must miss her. Is it bad that I don't miss her so much?"

"No." Linus pulled away to look his son in the face. The downturned eyes, the tight cheeks, tugged at his heart. "You didn't know your mother well. She wasn't as much a part of your life as some mothers. Missing her or not is entirely up to you and quite natural."

He nodded as if drawing comfort from the words. "Good. I'd miss you more, though. You mustn't let those Frenchies capture you again."

Linus's brows shot up. "Where did you get the idea I was about to be captured by the French?"

He glanced back at Hornswag, who grimaced, and Linus could only wonder how much he'd overheard.

"Mrs. Archer was talking with Mr. Hornswag the other day," Ethan admitted. "And Charlie Lawrence in my class with the vicar mentioned it as well. Mr. Wingate, the vicar, said we should pray for your safety."

Linus rose. "With such men as Mr. Hornswag at my back, I am perfectly safe. And so are you."

Now, if he just knew what to do about Abigail.

Linus Bennett did not attempt to kiss her again the next couple of days. It was rather disappointing. Of course, she hadn't encouraged his kiss and had not planned on a courtship, which usually went with such a kiss. She'd met very few men who could be trusted, in the long run. Yet, Linus seemed like he should be added to that number.

She watched him at the spa on Saturday and at services and the spa on Sunday. Militiamen came and went, and the French agents made no more attempt on his person. She and Eva had worked out the details of running the spa, and all went well. Everyone seemed happy, healthy. Four more gentlemen Newcomers arrived, and she or Eva interviewed them closely.

"Distressingly normal," Eva said with a sigh.

Abigail couldn't argue. Then again, she couldn't complain either. She wasn't afraid to jump into the heat of battle, but peace was nothing to cry over.

She still wondered about Mr. Donner, but he too behaved with distressing normality. While Mr. George slept late Sunday, Mr. Donner attended services and appeared to be a model congregant. The only oddity about him was the length of his stay. Some spent the entire summer or even the year at Grace-by-the-Sea, but most visited between a fortnight and a month. Mr. Donner and his friend were approaching a month now and showed no sign of leaving.

She went so far as to ask Mrs. Kirby about their leases.

"Neither has a lease," the lady reported as they walked out of the services that Sunday to a trickle of rain. "I believe they are staying at the Swan. Mrs. Truant mentioned she was glad for such accommodating gentlemen. It's not often she and her husband have such long-term guests. Not many can afford it, and those that can usually lease instead. Of course, Doctor Owens and Mrs. Rand have also extended their stays, I understand."

Which raised the question of Mr. Donner's income. He dressed well, but not extravagantly, and wore neither gold fob nor diamond stickpin. Could he have stolen those clothes? From whom? Surely any gentleman in the area missing clothing would have reported it to the magistrate's house, even if James Howland was out of town at the moment.

"Any news on whether Doctor Bennett will be taking that house?" Mrs. Kirby asked hopefully, glancing to where Linus and Ethan were visiting with the vicar. "I had another inquiry."

"Perhaps you could hold off on giving an answer," Abigail said. "I want to bring up compensation at our next board meeting. That may sway the decision one way or the other."

"Well, I'd certainly prefer to see it go to the doctor," Mrs. Kirby assured her. "If the income from the spa warrants it, I'm all for increasing his salary so he can take the house."

With everything so prosaic at the spa, they certainly had the income, at least at the moment. Somehow, she knew Mr. Greer would argue nonetheless.

On Monday morning, Linus removed her stitches.

"The scar will remain, I'm afraid," he told her as he examined the wound. At least she didn't have to wear her nightgown in front of him anymore. Eva's slashed-sleeve gown could also soon be returned to its owner, after a thorough brushing, of course.

"Only to be expected," Abigail allowed. She caught herself admiring the wave of his hair over his forehead and made herself look at the white pucker of flesh instead.

He leaned back. "I'd give it a few more days before you start painting again. I'll continue to check it when I stop by for Ethan."

Once she would have railed at the delay. Now she could only smile and thank him, grateful that their quiet conversations would continue a while longer. She was even a little disappointed when Jess and Lark returned from their honeymoon later that morning, and her friend took up her place at the spa.

"The two of you were wonderful to step in while I was gone," she told Abigail and Eva as they stood around the welcome book. "Everything looks just as it ought, and everyone seems content. I cannot thank you enough."

"It was our pleasure," Eva assured her. "I'll just take my leave of Doctor Bennett. I want to prepare Butterfly Manor for James. He should return from London by this evening."

Abigail shifted on her feet as Eva hurried away. She should leave too. Mrs. Truant would want to return to her duties at the Swan instead of staffing All the Colors of the Sea, Abigail's shop. Yet she felt as if she'd been wrapped in another bandage, one that tied her to the spa.

She glanced across the room to where Eva was speaking to Linus. As always, he leaned slightly toward her, eyes on her face, and nodded as if in understanding and appreciation of what she was saying. She had never met a man so attentive to his patients, his colleagues. Her.

"I wonder, Abby," Jess said. "I know you must have a great deal to do at the shop, but perhaps you might spare a few hours every day to help me."

Her gaze snapped back to her friend. "Anything. What do you need?"

"There are a hundred details that must be settled regarding the Regatta. I'm not sure I can manage them and the spa too."

Her smile was as sweet and engaging as ever, but Abigail had known her friend too many years to miss the light in those big blue eyes.

"You know I'm always delighted to help," Abigail told her, "but you have managed the spa and events like the Regatta for years. Why is this time any different?"

"Because," she said, "this time, I have a very important project to manage in addition to those."

Project? Her friend was entirely able to take on the French army, let alone the three agents hiding among them, but she surely wouldn't have heard about Linus's kidnapping so soon.

"Oh?" Abigail asked with a frown. "What would that be?"

Jess's smile widened. "I must make sure my dearest friend and our good physician live happily ever after. And you're going to help me with that as well."

# CHAPTER FOURTEEN

GUILT PULLED ON LINUS AS he walked Ethan to the Archers the next day. He had always prided himself on clear, directive conversations with his patients. Bad news must be given with compassion, an opportunity for healing or comfort. Good news must be tempered with admonitions on how to maintain health. Never had he knowingly lied to a patient.

Until now.

He'd told himself it was from an abundance of caution. He was only considering Abigail's profession, her willingness to take risks. The truth was that she was healed, and he had only delayed telling her because he didn't want to stop seeing her.

No more. It wasn't fair to her, and he was only darkening his character by such behavior. He must think of her first.

Even if he thought of her all the time.

So, he made a show of examining the wound one last time as she perched on the sofa and Ethan and her mother conversed in the dining room. Tiny dots showed where the stitches had been. A white line, like an arrow pointing toward her elbow, marked where the bullet had traveled. Her skin was pink and warm. Healthy. Soft.

He drew in a breath and released her. "Lift your arm for me."

She did so, palm down.

"Any pain?" he asked.

"No," she admitted, holding it steady in mid-air. "But it feels heavier than normal."

"A little weakness is only to be expected," Linus allowed. "Go easy on it, and the strength will return with time."

She lowered her arm. "Then it's done? I can resume my work, my painting?"

Linus leaned back. "I see no reason why not."

She launched herself at him.

Linus caught her, held her close, breathed in the scent of ripe peaches. The silk of her hair brushed his cheek. Her arms hugged him tight. He didn't want to move.

"Oh, thank you, Linus," she said. "I'm so relieved. It's felt like forever."

And only a day. He made himself smile as she disengaged. "I'm glad the outcome was what we hoped for."

Yet, now he found himself hoping for more.

Abigail couldn't wait to return to her painting. Besides, Jess was playing matchmaker, and her friend was rather famous for her skills in that area. What was it, more than a dozen marriages in the last four years alone? Well, she was fair and far off this time. She was fully capable of managing the spa this morning, and the Regatta too. After giving her mother the good news, Abigail hurried down the corridor for her studio.

The light, the quiet, wrapped around her as she stepped through the door. She could almost feel her darlings crying for her attention. Was that dust gathering on her canvasses? It was not to be borne! She set to cleaning with a will. If her arm protested a little, it was only to be expected.

Her mother found her there later that morning.

"Ethan and I are going to the shore to watch the fishermen come in with their catches," she announced. "Would you like to join us?"

"Perhaps another time," Abigail said, studying the painting she'd wanted to give Jess and Lark. "But thank you for asking."

Her mother left.

Before she'd been shot, she had laid on the expanse of blue for the ocean, but she needed teal and navy and white to bring out the depths and heights of the waves. She set about mixing her paints—Mr. Carroll obligingly ordered them from London for her—to make up the right colors, covering her oblong wooden pallet with blobs of rich shades. She'd lived along the shore her entire life, seen the cove and the Channel beyond on every sort of day, from wind-driven to calm, from balmy to bleak. She knew how many colors there were in the sea.

When her pallet was ready, she approached the canvas, brush in hand. A dab here, a stroke there, and the Channel waters began to come to life in all their glory. But the sky was missing, and she had just the shade. She reached up, started to sweep her brush across.

Her arm balked. Worse, it positively trembled. Fear poked at her. Enough of that. She raised her chin and pushed harder.

Pain shot through her, and the brush clattered to the floor, splattering paint against her leather shoes.

Abigail clamped her arm to her side, bit her lip to keep from crying out. Linus had warned her, again and again. Had she damaged her arm beyond repair?

Fingers shaking, she set down the pallet and removed her smock to drape it over the only chair in the room, then let herself out. Voices murmured from the flat, but she could not face her mother now, confess her fears.

Mother would only worry. She was worried enough as it was. She slipped down the corridor and into her bedchamber to fetch the sling she'd worn to Jess's wedding. The shawl warmed her skin, but not her thoughts.

"Ethan is telling me about the creatures in the ocean," her mother hailed as she came back through from her bedchamber. "Fascinating. Come listen."

"I should open the shop," Abigail said. "Perhaps later."

Better to think of someone other than herself. Mrs. Truant had done a fine job of managing things, but dust had accumulated in the shop too, so she wielded a cloth with her good arm between helping customers who wandered in.

A few were local. Mrs. Catchpole stopped by for a payment. She was brimming with news of the area.

"They say Doctor Bennett will be taking a house to treat us all," she told Abigail, eyes wide as if watching for a reaction.

"That's the hope," Abigail said, counting out the coin the lady was due.

"And did you hear?" The employment agency owner leaned closer, curls bobbing. "There was a press gang at Ringstead a few days ago. Caused quite a panic. If they came through Scratchy Bottom, they could be here soon."

"Alert Mr. Greer," Abigail told her. "We'll keep our men close if we must and call out the militia if we can't."

Most of her customers, though, were from the spa. Having met her there, they seemed more disposed to buy from her now. And share a little gossip. Mr. George, it seemed, had quarreled over some matter with Mr. Donner and the two were sitting at opposite sides of the spa.

"Though I expect they will make up shortly, like gentlemen should," Miss Turnpeth, Mrs. Rand's companion, told Abigail as she paid for the tatted collar she'd admired.

"Doctor Bennett tells me your injury is healed," Doctor Owens said as he brought her a leather wallet he had decided to purchase. "I wanted to add my best wishes for the future."

That's right—he cared for patients at a spa too. Perhaps she could speak to him instead of Linus, keep her fears to herself for the time being.

"I understand I will be stiff for a while," she said, wrapping the wallet in tissue. "I suppose some pain is to be expected."

She thought he might disabuse her of the notion, but he merely smiled as he handed her the coins to pay for the piece. "Pain is part of life, I find."

She might have thought that when she was younger. She, her mother, and her brother had borne the pain of her father's misdeeds. She'd hoped for better news when it came to her arm. "But it should return to full function?" she pressed.

"Very likely," he said with a benign smile. "And I believe I heard you are helping Miss Chance with the Regatta now. An interesting event for a spa."

"But a practical one for Grace-by-the-Sea," Abigail said, returning the parcel to him and trying to fight off resignation. "We've had fishermen and boats in the cove since before the Romans arrived. Showing them off comes naturally."

"And visitors arrive from up and down the coast as well, I believe," he said. "How do you keep track of them all?"

Abigail leaned against the counter, suddenly as heavy as her arm. "The captains send registrations to Mr. Hornswag at the Mermaid, naming the time they will arrive. Jess records the information and compares it to previous years. She has a ledger going back decades, to when her mother and grandmother were in charge of the event."

"Another of her books," he said fondly. "I'd love to see it. It might give me an idea of how to stage such an event in Scarborough."

Abigail made herself straighten as other customers came through the door, laughing and talking. "But I thought Scarborough had its own Regatta. One of the captains mentioned doing well there last year."

"Yes, but we can always improve," he insisted. Tucking the parcel under his arm, he bid her good day and made way for the others.

Abigail worked until she saw Mr. Carroll closing up across the street. Everything had gone so well she might almost think her arm was back to normal. Her studio whispered from behind the curtain separating it from the shop, but she passed it for the flat. Perhaps tomorrow, after she talked with Linus. Whether she liked it or not, he was the only one she truly trusted to address her concerns.

She was watching Ethan sketch when Linus returned that evening. Her mouth feeling dry, she rose to meet him.

"I had a few questions about my injury," she told him. "Would you mind?"

"Not at all." He raised his voice. "I'll be a few minutes, Ethan." He looked to Abigail. "How might I be of assistance?"

Abigail caught herself rubbing her arm and dropped her hand. "I tried painting earlier. It didn't go well."

"I explained some stiffness is to be expected," he reminded her.

"Stiffness, certainly. But pain?"

He frowned. "What were you trying to do?"

"Just paint," she assured him.

"I understand, but what exactly? Perhaps you could show me."

Abigail stiffened. He'd asked her once before to show him her studio. It had been difficult then; it seemed impossible now. She didn't share her workspace with anyone. Painting was personal; she put a piece of herself into every picture. It was hard enough to watch her work walk out the door, but at least she knew it was going with someone who admired it. To share its creation? No. It was as if he'd asked her to attend church naked.

"Perhaps I can just mimic the motion," she said.

"You could," he allowed, "but the pain might have been caused by the weight or the friction of materials against each other. I could diagnose the problem better if I could see how the action played out."

So, to make sure she healed, she had to share every part of herself. She'd faced impossibilities before. She could do it again. "Follow me," she said.

She felt him behind her as she walked down the corridor to the studio. The swish of her muslin skirts over the wood floor sounded overly loud. Once through the door, she tied on her smock again. She had to scrape the hardened paint off her pallet first, then prepare a fresh batch, only a little, only to demonstrate. It wasn't as if she was really painting in front of him. Still, she found breath difficult as she rubbed the brush against her pallet, then faced the canvas.

"I was fine so long as I confined myself to a narrow field," she said, dabbing the cerulean over the base. "But I need to use bolder strokes if I'm to cover the sky." She forced in a breath and swept across the canvas.

Pain lanced her, and she cried out, jerking to a stop.

Immediately he was at her side. "Easy. Give me the brush."

It fell from her fingers, and he set it aside. His strong hands cradled her arm. "Relax. Let me move it."

She tried, but her muscles tensed at his touch. He rotated her arm this way and that, gaze on her face as if looking for the least twitch. She remained still until he stretched out her arm, then she gasped.

He lowered her arm carefully. "I believe it's merely

your muscles protesting being put back into action." He turned for the brush and offered it to her. "If I may?"

She wasn't sure what he meant to do, but she accepted the brush. He positioned himself behind her, right arm aligned with hers, then cupped her wrist.

"Any exaggerated movement up or down or right or left will be tricky for a while. Make your movements small for now, like this." He swept her brush back and forth. Her muscles tightened, but no pain pierced her.

"Better?" he asked against her ear.

Suddenly quite good. "Yes," she managed.

"Excellent." He lowered her arm, but he did not release her, and for a moment, she stood in his embrace, his chest against her back, his hand holding hers.

"I've never painted in front of anyone," she murmured. "It's not something easily shared."

"Then I am all the more honored," he said.

His hand trailed up her arm, rested softly on her wound. "Give it time, Abigail. It will heal."

She didn't want him to leave. "And you, Linus? Will you heal as well?"

"I wasn't aware I had been injured."

She turned in his arms, made herself face him. Those grey eyes were curious, his brow lined as he gazed down at her.

"You lost your wife," she said, "the mother of your child. That must leave a mark."

His throat constricted as he swallowed. "Even more than I would have imagined."

She wanted to know this other woman who had held his heart. "Tell me about her, Ethan's mother."

He sighed, then nodded as if making up his mind.

"Catriona was bright and beautiful and possessed of boundless enthusiasm. But she also had moments of deepest despair. I think that's what drove her to be forever mobile. She was trying to outrun the darkness."

Sadness slipped over her, like twilight had come to the village. "That must have been a difficult way to live."

"It was. I was naïve enough to think love and marriage and then motherhood would change her. They didn't. She grew ever more frantic. Her father suggested some-place more stimulating than my quiet practice outside Edinburgh. He arranged for me to take over from a physician in London. But moving there only made things worse. I tried modifying our diet, removing all liquors from the house. She did not appreciate my intentions. On one occasion, she threw her perfume bottles at me."

Abigail might have reacted as poorly if someone claiming to love her had reordered her life. She reached up and traced the mark on his cheek. "Your scar. Is that how you gained it?"

He shuddered, as if her touch had gone deeper, to the hurt inside. "A minor injury. My greater mistake was in pressuring her to show more of an interest in our son. She rebelled against the confines of motherhood, so much so that she took up racing her curricle, as if the scandal meant nothing. She overturned it one day taking a turn too fast. She was thrown out and died on impact."

Pain and loss echoed in his voice. She'd been right. He hadn't healed. "I'm so sorry," she murmured. "How difficult it must have been for you—to be father to a grieving son while you hurt as well."

His shoulders sagged, as if he felt the hurt even now. "I did what I could, but I still doubt it was enough. Surely he should be more lively, more confident, yet what if liveliness is merely the beginnings of his mother's erratic behavior?"

"You fear it inherited?" One look at his face confirmed as much. "You forget, sir. Ethan is as much his father as his mother. His quiet nature may be a reflection of you."

"And yet I would not wish that for him either. I feel as if I've been wrapped in a bandage for months, unable to move, to breathe."

She couldn't stop herself. She gathered him close, held him gently. "You are safe here. Grace-by-the-Sea welcomes everyone."

"Even flawed Newcomers?"

She heard the hope in his voice. "Especially flawed Newcomers. And we do all we can to help them become beloved Regulars."

"Beloved," he murmured. "I like the sound of that."

"So do I," Abigail whispered. She raised her chin, and he lowered his head to meet her. His lips brushed hers, trailed across her cheek to return to her mouth. She trembled with his touch, but she did not step away. This was too perfect, too true.

At length, he drew back, face so sad she almost reached for him again. "Be patient with me, Abigail. I'm trying."

"I am your patient, sir," she said with a smile. "And I would like to be your physician."

He returned her smile. Oh, that was so much better. "What do you prescribe, Doctor Archer?"

All at once, she knew. "Enjoyment, fresh air, and good food. Preferably all together. In short, sir, I advise you to take a day off tomorrow and go on a picnic with me, my mother, and Ethan."

# CHAPTER FIFTEEN

S HE WAS SURPRISED AND DELIGHTED when he agreed to the idea of a picnic.

"You'll see," she told him as she walked him back to the flat from her studio. "It will be just the thing."

His smile offered hope.

Ethan and her mother were more enthusiastic.

"Excellent idea," her mother proclaimed. "I'll ask Jack Hornswag to arrange for a hamper. I think I still have your brother's kite."

"Is it difficult to fly a kite?" Ethan asked, eyes shining. "I'd like to try it."

"With your perspective on angles, you'll be brilliant at it," Abigail assured him. "We'll see you both tomorrow, say half past noon. That way we miss the muster."

"And I have a few moments at the spa," Linus agreed.

"Very clever," her mother said after they'd left. "I'm so glad you're taking his courting seriously."

"Doctor Bennett isn't courting me, Mother," Abigail told her, gathering up the last of Ethan's drawings for the day. One showed a man, woman, and boy, all holding hands. The woman had reddish hair.

Her mother put her nose in the air. "When a gentleman stops by twice a day to see a lady, I call that courting."

"He stopped by twice a day to tend my wound and arrange for Ethan's care," Abigail reminded her. "That's not courting. That's business."

Her mother eyed her. "I see no difference."

Abigail shook her head. "I should not encourage you. Jesslyn is bad enough. She is certain Linus and I should make a match."

Her mother gave a little bob, skirts rising and falling with her heels. "Excellent. Dear Jesslyn has never failed when she set her hand to matchmaking."

Abigail wasn't so sure of that. Despite Jess's exemplary record, she had done all to help Mr. Crabapple pursue the Widow Harding, and the lady remained unattached.

"She will have her hands full this time," Abigail said. "Linus Bennett isn't sure of me. Of any lady, I begin to think. His heart has not healed from his wife's death."

Her mother sobered. "Neither has poor Ethan's. But you can help there."

"I'll do what I can," Abigail told her.

"And agree to his courting?" her mother nudged, brows up in hope.

Abigail smiled. "You are incorrigible. But I am becoming accustomed to the idea that he and I might suit."

Her mother clasped her hands before her chest. "Oh, wonderful! I can't wait to hear the banns read in St. Andrew's."

Abigail caught her hands. "Not just yet. Linus and I have a long way to go before agreeing to marry."

The picnic proved as much.

The Bennett men arrived the next day precisely on time. She would not have expected otherwise. Her mother wasn't quite ready. Also not unexpected.

"I have the perfect blanket," she called, head buried in a cupboard beside her bedchamber, spring green skirts swinging as she dug. "I know it's here somewhere."

"We can take the one off my bed," Abigail offered.

Her answer was a thud of something falling from a shelf.

"She did find the kite," Abigail told Ethan and Linus with a smile. Ethan smiled back. Linus looked a bit nervous, if his darting gaze and hands clasped behind the back of his navy coat were any indication.

"And we added a fine tail," Abigail tried. "I'll show you how to fly it, Ethan, when we reach the castle."

She thought Linus might suggest she go easy on her arm, but he merely nodded.

Ethan's eyes, however, widened. "We're going to the castle?"

He must have seen the Earl of Howland's hunting lodge. The building had been designed to resemble a medieval castle, complete with rounded towers at each corner. The thing was visible from many spots in Grace-by-the-Sea.

"We are indeed, or at least the lawns leading up to it." She nodded to the wicker hamper Mr. Hornswag had sent over. "Think you can carry that that far, Doctor Bennett?"

Linus shook himself, then went to take each leather handle. As he lifted them, his brows went up. "What did you pack?"

Her mother bustled back into the room, plaid blanket bundled in her arms. "Ham, cheese, rolls, a bottle of lemonade, tin cups, a slicing knife, a cutting board, napkins, Abigail's sketchbook, Ethan's sketchbook, sketching supplies, and a book of poetry. Oh, and someone will need to carry Abigail's parasol."

As Linus looked impressed, Abigail wrinkled her nose. "Do I even own a parasol?"

"You must," her mother said, folding the blanket. "I found it last night when I was looking for the kite. It might provide shade if we need it."

It might at that, Abigail saw when they embarked shortly afterward. The sky was cloudless, the air warming, as they climbed the path leading up to the headland. Linus went first, carrying the hamper and making it look surprisingly easy. Ethan followed, holding the kite protectively close. Her mother came next with the blanket, and Abigail brought up the rear, holding a fringed lime-green parasol she couldn't remember seeing before.

The wildflowers had faded since she'd last visited the headland a fortnight ago, but heads of red, pink, blue, and white still poked up among the grass. Ringed by trees and a wide lawn, Castle How stood tall and stately, the pale stones gleaming gold in the sunlight. Beyond it, the Channel stretched endless.

Abigail stopped to regard it. "That color. That's what I need to capture for Jess and Lark's painting. Every shade of blue."

"Green, too," Ethan said beside her. "And brown."

She squinted against the light bouncing off the waves. "You're right. Very observant. And spoken like an artist."

Ethan's cheeks pinked as he smiled at her.

"There," her mother said, nodding to a patch of lawn partly shaded by trees. "The perfect spot for our picnic."

Linus carried the hamper over, waiting only until she had spread the blanket to her liking before setting it down at one end. Abigail and Ethan came to join them.

She tilted her head to the sun, and the breeze fanned her cheeks. "West-southwest wind today. That means we'll need to run in that direction if you want the kite to fly."

"Yes, ma'am, please," Ethan said, clutching the kite closer still. She and her brother had decorated the diamond-shaped piece of parchment with charcoals so that it resembled a mighty falcon. Patches here and there told of collisions with a tree, and, once, her father's fists. The new rag tail held bright gingham, sprigged muslin, and printed cotton, remnants of gowns others had donated to them during the time they had lived on the village's charity.

Linus frowned out over the Channel. "Running

west-southwest will bring you to the cliffs. Perhaps another direction would be wiser."

Did he not understand the mechanisms for flying a kite? "We'll avoid the edge," Abigail promised. "What do you say, Ethan? Shall we give it a go?"

Ethan nodded eagerly. Feeling Linus's gaze on them, she led the boy out from under the trees.

"Do you see where the shadow of the castle crosses the lawn there toward the village?" she asked.

Ethan glanced that direction. "Yes, ma'am."

"Do not cross beyond that line. That should keep you safely away from the cliffs." She held out her hands, her arm offering only a whisper of complaint. "I'll hold the kite. Play out the string, then run as fast as you can toward that shadow."

He nodded again, so fast his head might have been the kite bobbing on the breeze. He twirled the ball of string to unwind a sizeable length, then turned his back on her and sprinted away. She watched the line lengthen, grow taut. She released the kite.

Up it went, into the blue. Her mother started applauding, and Ethan turned to see why.

His father pointed at the kite. "Well done!"

Ethan stared at it a moment, mouth falling open.

Abigail hurried to his side. "Well done indeed. Now, the breeze isn't strong this morning, so you'll have to keep an eye on the kite. See, it's already starting to fall."

He tensed, feet shuffling in the grass. "What do I do?"

"Tug a little on the string. That's right. See, it's climbing again. Don't let it go too high, or you might catch a breeze from a different direction, and who knows what it will do."

His gaze clamped onto the kite. "What if it crashes?"

Fear laced the tone, and she remembered what Linus had said about Ethan's mother. She lay a hand on his shoulder.

"Kites sometimes fall, Ethan. Or crash into trees or chimney pots. They can usually be fixed. But even if they can't, they're only parchment, twig, and rag. No harm done. Do you understand?"

This nod was more solemn. "Yes, ma'am."

Abigail released him. "See how long you can keep it in the air. I'll be with my mother and your father on the blanket. Remember about that shadow."

"Yes, ma'am," he repeated, gaze on the kite.

She moved back to the others.

"Such a clever boy," her mother said. "I knew he'd get the hang of it. Gideon did."

Abigail seated herself beside Linus on the blanket. He was up on one elbow, legs stretched out, and he had relaxed enough that he could send her a smile.

"Your son is serving in India now, I understand," he said to her mother.

Her mother sniffed. "He is. I miss him so."

"We've been hoping for a letter for some time," Abigail explained.

He glanced from her to her mother, and she thought he understood why a letter would not have arrived. From what he'd told her, he knew the sorts of danger Gideon faced.

"Well, I'm glad you could allow Ethan the use of the kite," he said. "I predict I'll need to find material for one of his own shortly."

"Ask Mr. Inchley for a large enough piece of parchment," Abigail suggested. "He keeps paper for wrapping fish. And the Misses Pierce keep string and rags available. Jess sponsors a kite-flying competition at the spa. It's something of a tradition."

"We have a great number of traditions in Grace-by-the-Sea," her mother put in. "Easter celebrations. Christmas festivities. Weddings."

As if he was just as eager to nudge her off that topic,

Linus sat up. "And a very fine castle. I take it the magistrate approved of us using the earl's property."

Abigail tossed her head. "I didn't ask Mr. Howland. He wouldn't refuse in any event. He owes me a favor."

He chuckled. "Are you using your injury to gain unfair advantage again?"

"I must take whatever advantage I'm given," she informed him.

Especially if it kept him at her side.

Linus hadn't been sure what to expect from their picnic. Once again, his heart had overruled his head, and he'd kissed Abigail there in her studio last evening. He had to admit, if only to himself, that he began to have intentions toward her. But a picnic committed neither of them to anything. It was an opportunity to become even better acquainted. He should not see it as a threat.

And he could not remember enjoying a day more. The sun was warm, Abigail's company warmer, and all seemed right with the world. Mrs. Archer opened her hamper and doled out the feast, and Ethan was persuaded to bring the kite safely down and return for some food. They ate, they talked, they laughed.

As if they were a family.

At moments, his mother and father had found such joy—beside a river in India, around a campfire in America. He had never quite managed it with Catriona and Ethan. Always her gaze had shied away, her thoughts gone to something she found more exciting. He and Ethan had never been enough for her.

Yet Abigail seemed content.

The feeling remained as Mrs. Archer took Ethan back out onto the grass for another try with the kite. Abigail sighed, then leaned back, and the sun picked out the gold in her lashes.

"Did you and your family do this often?" he asked.

She sat up as if suddenly uncomfortable and set about putting the remains of their meal back in the hamper. "On occasion, and usually not with my father. He wasn't much for family gatherings. He preferred the company of the inn's public room."

Her tone had grown sharper. Given what Jack Hornswag had told him, Linus thought he understood why.

"My father was sometimes too tired from his day to do more than come home and sleep," Linus told her. "I never understood why my mother insisted on accompanying him on his travels, but perhaps a little time together was better than none."

"I would almost have preferred none, with my father," she murmured, gaze going to Ethan, who was pelting across the grass as the kite climbed behind him. "He was a carter, carrying goods from the mill in Upper Grace to the cove and back. Perhaps the work grew too difficult, and drink seemed easy entertainment. Perhaps he drank to alleviate physical discomfort. Mr. Hornswag and some of the other men said he was just plain mean. Whatever the reason, he drank to excess and took his frustrations out with his fists—other patrons, the barkeep, acquaintances, even the vicar once. Few attended his funeral, I was told. My brother left us to join the army as soon as he turned fifteen."

"You and your mother deserve better," Linus said. "From your father, certainly. Even from your brother. He might have found a way to return."

She sighed. "I cannot blame Gideon. I would have left too, if I had thought I could find employment. Like Ethan, I'd been sketching since I was a child, but Jess's father encouraged me to paint, and I think even he was surprised when I turned out to be good at it. Still, it took me a while to figure out my paintings could help pay our way, then to convince the members of the Spa Corporation board at the time to allow me to open the shop where others could sell their handicrafts. They thought I was too young, too untried. Jess's father supported the idea, so the others agreed to give it a try. Now we support ourselves. We need no one's pity."

But perhaps their respect, their admiration. He could see it in the way her gaze went off across the grass, the proud set of her chin. She had every right for pride. She had made a way for herself and her mother.

His father had been revered by the soldiers he tended. They knew their lives rested in his hands and that he would do all he could to be worthy of their trust. Linus felt the same way about his patients. Abigail had taken on the burden of supporting not only her family but others in the village. She should be commended.

Yet those who were used to leading sometimes found it hard to follow. And she had been raised by a man she could not trust. Would she trust any more easily now?

Mrs. Archer trotted back to the blanket, smile broadening her face. "Such a fine young man, your Ethan. You must be very proud of him, Doctor Bennett."

"I am blessed to have such a son," Linus assured her. "As you are blessed with a remarkable daughter."

Abigail glanced at him, brows up in obvious surprise. Then her gaze traveled past him.

The smile she effected was patently false as she rose. "Someone's watching us from the trees. It could be one of your French assailants. Hurry! Let's catch him!"

# CHAPTER SIXTEEN

A BIGAIL DASHED TOWARD THE TREES, sure that
Linus would follow. The shadow she'd spotted ran,
and she chased him deeper into the green. Brown coat,
brown breeches, brown boots, a cloth cap pulled low. She
couldn't even be sure of the color of his hair as he fled
from sunlight to shade.

"Stop!" she shouted. "In the king's name!"

That only made him run faster.

"Abigail!" Linus's voice pulled her up short, and she
waited for him to reach her side. He put a hand on her
good arm. "Stay here."

"Why?" she asked, but he was already striding past her.
She followed.

They broke from the trees. Like courtiers before their
king, the grass of the Downs bowed in the breeze. A
lone rider was swiftly disappearing on the road to Upper
Grace.

"He had a horse waiting." Abigail threw up her hands,
then winced as her arm gave her a nip.

Linus rounded on her. "He could have had colleagues
waiting. Do you have any idea how dangerous it was to
run after him? You aren't even armed."

"Neither are you," she argued. "And you came along
readily enough."

"To protect you!" He put both hands on her shoulders and peered into her face. "You took a risk, and an unnecessary one. Do you think me incapable of defending myself and my family?"

"Apparently more capable than you think me," Abigail said, pain spreading. "Please remove your hands. You're hurting my arm."

Immediately he stepped back, face paling. "Forgive me. Do you need a sling?"

"No. Nor do I need laudanum or an examination of any sort. I'm going to walk back to my mother now, and I don't require your assistance to do that either." Eyes burning, she turned and marched for the trees. He did not follow.

Abigail slowed her steps and rubbed at her eyes. What, was he no different than the other men she'd known after all? She'd thought more of him. Her father, Mr. Greer, even the vicar didn't deem it a woman's place to support herself or make decisions about life-and-death matters. She wasn't foolish, uneducated, or incapable. Why must she trust that some fellow, who was just as fallible as she was, would come to her rescue in any situation? One never had before.

"Is everything all right?" her mother asked as she rejoined them. Her mother must have called Ethan in, for she sat on the blanket with one arm around the boy, who was once more clutching the kite, face tight.

"Fine, Mother," she said, keeping her voice light for Ethan's sake. "I repacked the hamper. When Doctor Bennett returns, we should go."

Her mother's face fell, and Ethan slumped. Abigail made herself bend to retrieve the parasol so they wouldn't see her own disappointment.

Linus came out of the trees a short time later. Ethan watched him warily.

"What happened, Doctor Bennett?" her mother asked. "You and Abigail left us so suddenly."

"I'm sorry if we concerned you," he said. "There was a stranger in the wood. He rode away. No harm done."

She didn't believe that. Their watcher had escaped, and they had no idea if he had been a passing traveler curious about the castle or a French agent looking to capture Linus again. And the hopes she'd begun to cherish felt as trampled as the grass. Worse, the ache inside her refused to leave, spreading from her arm to her chest.

Linus walked beside his son on the way down the hill. Once again, Abigail brought up the rear. This time it felt lonely.

"If you would remove your items from the hamper," he told her mother as they reached the flat, "I'll take it back to the Mermaid on the way home. Thank you for making the arrangements."

Her mother glanced from him to Abigail and back. "It doesn't seem to have been worth it."

"I'm sure Ethan enjoyed himself," he said, putting an arm about his son.

Ethan took the hint. "Thank you very much for inviting us, Mrs. Archer, Miss Archer."

Her mother's face melted. "You are very, very welcome, dear boy. Any time." She hurried to open the hamper and begin taking out the things that belonged to them.

"Will you still be available tomorrow morning to look after Ethan?" Linus asked her.

It was as if she wasn't there. Abigail rubbed a hand on her arm. That only made him frown.

Her mother frowned as well as she finished sorting through the hamper. "Of course. Why wouldn't I be?"

"No reason at all," Abigail assured her. She met Linus's gaze. "You heard my mother. Ethan is always welcome. And I'll be working in the shop, so you needn't worry you'll have to speak to me."

Her mother gasped. "Abigail, how rude. Apologize."

Not to him, she wouldn't. "I'm sorry, Mother," she said.

Her mother turned to Linus. "I don't know what's gotten into her, Doctor Bennett, but I hope you know you're always welcome as well."

"Until tomorrow," he said, hefting the hamper. Ethan shuffled after him out the door.

Her mother shook her head. "You will end up an old maid if you don't mend your ways."

"What ways are those?" Abigail snapped, tossing the parasol onto the sofa. "Taking care of myself? Having an opinion? Protecting those I love? I can promise you, I will never change there."

Her mother's lips thinned. "I'm not going to live forever, you know. What will you do when I'm gone? You'll be all alone."

"I have friends, acquaintances, the shop customers," Abigail countered. "I don't need a husband, Mother. I didn't particularly want one until…"

Her mother started nodding, white curls bouncing. "Until Doctor Bennett. I knew it. He's the right one for you, Abigail. Give him a chance."

Abigail closed her eyes. "He doesn't want a woman like me, Mother."

Arms came around her, and she leaned into her mother's hug. "Then he isn't the man I took him for," her mother murmured. "Any man would be fortunate beyond words to win a bride like you."

The tears came then. She couldn't stop them. She cried for what might have been, for who she was determined to be, for whatever the future held. Her mother rubbed her back and crooned nonsense words. At length, Abigail pulled back.

"Better?" her mother asked, eyes bright with her own tears.

"Better," Abigail agreed, attempting a smile. "And thank you."

"You may thank me when you are standing at the altar,"

her mother told her, chin coming up. "And I will have a few words to say to Doctor Bennett in the morning."

Dread dropped like a lightning bolt. "Mother, you mustn't say anything to him. This is between him and me."

That chin edged higher. "It most certainly is not. I have a right to see my only daughter happy."

"But not Doctor Bennett miserable," Abigail told her. "Please. Leave this to us."

Her mother eyed her. "You have two days. Then I scold him."

Abigail started laughing despite herself. "Well, I'm sure he wouldn't want that."

She snapped a nod. "No, he wouldn't. So, see that you bring him up to scratch before then."

Up to scratch. Ready to propose. Is that what she wanted?

The wonder and joy of the idea rushed up on her like a wave crashing against the Dragon's Maw. It seemed some part of her very much wanted him to propose.

Yet, what would she say to him that hadn't already been said? He could not value her independence. She could not appreciate his command.

She made sure to be in the shop when he came with Ethan in the morning. But she sent word to Eva via one of Mr. Lawrence's sons to request a moment of the magistrate's time.

James Howland, Eva's husband, arrived in the shop by ten. A tall man, with a head of golden blond hair and a stern face, he listened as Abigail quickly told him about what had been happening in his absence.

"Eva explained that the militia is protecting our physician by night," he said when she finished. "From what you observed, it appears we may have to protect him by day as well."

"That's what I fear," Abigail told him. "We seem to

have a general direction of our adversaries—somewhere between here and Upper Grace. Mr. Greer told the detachment at West Creech about the matter, but I never heard the result."

"A report was waiting for me," he told her. "They located several houses that appeared to have been broken into, but of Doctor Bennett's abductors, there was no sign."

"Then we must look harder," Abigail insisted.

"Perhaps," he allowed. "But there is word of a press gang in the area. Men alone or even in small groups are likely to find themselves heading for a stint in the Royal Navy. I can't send anyone who doesn't own a red coat to mark his office."

Even more than a month after the formation of the Grace-by-the-Sea militia, red coats were few and far between. Mr. Treacle, the tailor, had enlisted the aid of the Misses Pierce at the linens and trimmings shop as well as several talented local seamstresses to help him fill the orders.

"What then?" Abigail demanded. "Are we to sit and wait for the next attempt on his person?"

"For now, that may be our best approach."

Why did no one else see the need to act? It had been the same way when her father had been alive. No one had listened to a frightened little girl then. Well, she was no longer that frightened little girl. She was capable.

Linus was going to receive her help, whether he wanted it or not.

"Are you angry with Miss Archer?" Ethan asked the next morning as he and Linus started toward High Street from the cottage.

Linus kept his gaze out over the blue-grey waters of the cove. "No. I said some things I regret, and I hurt her."

A small hand slipped into his. Linus gripped it, thankful for the touch, the trust it implied.

"You can always say you're sorry," Ethan told him. "That's what Charlie says when Mr. Wingate corrects him."

He looked down at his son and smiled. "You and Charlie are getting along well, it seems."

"He's too bossy," Ethan said with a prim set to his mouth. "But he's very clever too." He cast Linus a look out of the corner of his eyes. "He thinks we should learn to sail."

Fear poked him in the ribs. Linus ignored it. "That might be a good idea living where we do. You should learn to swim too. Perhaps Charlie might suggest a teacher."

"I'll ask him," Ethan said. "I hope Miss Archer forgives you. Mrs. Archer says she knows how to sail. Maybe she could teach us."

Somehow, it didn't surprise him to hear his son confirm that Abigail sailed. There seemed nothing she could not do. Except, maybe, tolerate his foibles.

He could not blame her if she didn't want to talk to him. He'd made a mull of things. When she'd run toward danger, every part of him had frozen. Images of gunshot wounds, bayonet slashes, had filled his mind. Then he'd rushed after her, determined to protect her or die trying.

The depths of his feelings had shocked him, and he'd pushed her away. The whole situation was too much like life with Catriona.

He could not deny the lift of his spirits when she was waiting just inside the door of the flat when he brought Ethan that morning. Gowned in a shade of green that matched her eyes, she stood stiffly as her mother greeted them and took Ethan over to the sofa.

"I alerted the magistrate to what happened at the castle," she said, chin up. "And Charlie Lawrence stopped by a bit ago to let me know Mr. Greer has called the monthly board meeting for tomorrow night. It will be at the Swan at seven. Mother can watch Ethan."

She thought of everything. "Thank you," he said. "Will you be coming to the spa later? I know Mrs. Denby was hoping for help with the Regatta."

"I need to keep the shop open," she said. Then she met his gaze, like the flash of a beacon far out at sea. "As an independent woman, I have responsibilities."

"And your attention to them is admirable," he assured her. She waited. He swallowed. Why was it so hard to speak his mind?

Abigail, forgive me for being a fool.

Abigail, I'm afraid to fall in love.

"Until tomorrow night, then," he said and bowed himself out.

She did not meet him at the door that evening or the following morning, and disappointment rode his shoulders like a black crow on a fence. He was so eager for the board meeting, he arrived before the others. He watched as Greer, Lawrence, Ellison, Mrs. Kirby, and Mrs. Catchpole came in and took up their places, chatting amongst themselves. And he felt as if he truly drew breath when Abigail came in and sat at his right.

Greer convened the meeting then, nodding to each of his board members, then turning to Linus. "Doctor Bennett, tell us how your first few weeks have gone."

He should have thought they'd want an update. "Things are going well," he allowed.

They waited expectantly.

"If I may," Abigail put in, drawing a paper from her reticule. "I helped at the spa while Mrs. Denby was on her honeymoon, so I was privy to some of the activities there. I took the liberty of compiling a few statistics."

She glanced at the parchment. "Since Doctor Bennett arrived, appointments have risen three hundred percent."

Murmurs of appreciation passed around the table. Since there had been no physician and no appointments before Linus had arrived, he could not put much faith in the number.

"Once Mrs. Denby returned, attendance also tripled," she continued, "and those who had planned to stay only a week have lengthened their visits."

"Subscriptions are higher than they've ever been," Mr. Lawrence added with a proud smile. "I project a very healthy dividend for the village if this keeps up."

Mrs. Catchpole started applauding, and the others joined in.

"So we have more than enough money to lease Doctor Bennett a bigger house," Abigail said as the sound faded.

Mrs. Catchpole blinked. Ellison and Lawrence frowned.

Greer sat straighter. "Doctor Bennett has only his son. What need could he have for a larger house?"

"Because he could expand his practice," Abigail answered. She leaned forward. "Imagine—the entire village having access to as fine a doctor as our spa guests."

Mrs. Kirby nodded. Ellison still looked skeptical.

"Only fair," Mrs. Catchpole said. "Doctor Chance helped everyone. He had room at his house on High Street."

Mrs. Kirby glanced to Greer. "There's a fine house just up the street from Shell Cottage available for lease right now."

"The owner?" Mr. Greer asked.

Her smile dimmed a little. "The Earl of Howland."

Greer shook his head. "He'll make us pay dearly. He always has."

Mrs. Catchpole cleared her throat, bringing all gazes her way. "You probably know that the former earl has passed away. You didn't hear it from me, but Mr. Pym, the magistrate's man, came to ask me about staff for the castle. Seems the new earl means to take up residence with us for a while. I hear he's far more accommodating than his father."

Mrs. Kirby beamed. "The earl in residence? He's still relatively young, quite handsome, and a widower who will be in want of a wife. He could be the making of us!"

"I predict subscriptions will soar yet again," Lawrence said, grinning as well.

"It won't be enough," Greer predicted. And Abigail thought Linus was too cautious! "We have already agreed to pay for Mrs. Denby's time without deducting anything from Doctor Bennett's pay."

"And Mrs. Tully's time," Abigail reminded him.

He grimaced. "Exactly so. Earl or no earl, we will be tight on funds for a while."

"I would be willing to take a lower salary," Linus put in. "With the understanding that I could keep what my village patients could afford to pay."

Greer snorted. "Believe me, that's little enough."

"And we could rent out the cottage on the shore," Abigail reminded him. "That should offset some of the cost as well."

Greer cocked his head and studied Linus. "Perhaps if Doctor Bennett would accept a fifty percent cut in pay…"

"Ten percent," Abigail argued before Linus could respond.

Greer narrowed his eyes. "Thirty."

"Fifteen," she countered.

"Twenty-five," Linus said.

"I motion that Doctor Bennett take a twenty percent cut in pay to go toward leasing a larger house for the purpose of treating anyone in the area," Mrs. Kirby rattled off as if she feared interruption. "And that the Spa Corporation pay the lease on said house and lease the cottage he's been using."

"I second," Mr. Ellison barked.

Greer sighed. "All in favor?"

"Aye," they chorused. Greer didn't ask whether any were opposed.

"Thank you," Linus told Abigail when the meeting ended a short while later, after the members had settled some other fees and assessments.

She inclined her head as she rose from the table. "It was a worthwhile proposal. I'm glad the others agreed."

"Because of your championship," Linus assured her. "I want you to know I value that about you, Abigail."

She eyed him as the others filed out. "Be careful, Doctor Bennett. I might think you were encouraging me to take risks."

"Appropriate risks," he hedged. "Risks that don't put you in danger."

"I am afraid we disagree on that," she said as they turned for the door. "There is always a degree of danger when you put the needs of others before your own. It may not be a risk to your life, but to opportunities, your peace of mind. Yet I would live no other way."

And how could he ask her to live any other way? He too believed in putting others first.

"There is also a risk to those we love," he tried. "We may take a chance, but our failing may mean sacrifice for them."

She paused in the doorway, face troubled. "What sacrifice do you see in attempting to learn the identity of our French spies? Surely there are only benefits to the entire village."

"If you were successful in keeping out of their reach. If you were not successful, you could have been killed, Abigail. Think how that would affect the families who rely on your shop. Think how it would affect those who love you."

He dared not say more on the matter. Already she was staring at him as if in wonder.

"I can only admire your determination," he said. "I also admire your artistic eye. Perhaps you'd be willing to advise me on how to furnish this larger house."

It was a peace offering. He had no idea if she would accept it. But oh, how he wanted her to accept it.

She cocked her head as if giving the matter due consideration, and he held his breath.

"Very well," she said. "I would be glad to help. For the good of the village, of course."

Linus bowed. "Of course."

And he left the room feeling lighter than he had in days.

# CHAPTER SEVENTEEN

HE ESCORTED HER HOME, AS if they were court-ing. His bodyguard for the day, Mr. Truant of the Swan, trailed respectfully behind. True, he had to fetch Ethan anyway, but when his fingers brushed hers, she allowed her hand to slip into his. For a moment, that was all she needed.

Their conversation after the meeting could not help but give her pause. She hadn't thought how her actions might frighten him, particularly after his experiences with his late wife. Perhaps he didn't fault her for her independence after all. Surely if he found her unsuitable, he would never had asked her help in setting up his new house. Indeed, some might consider such a request as a prelude to a proposal. Best not to mention the matter to her mother or Jess.

They found out anyway.

"Perhaps one of Mrs. Catchpole's pretty pots for his dressing table," her mother suggested when she came through the shop the next day. "He could store cravat pins in it."

"Who, Mother?" Abigail asked, moving toward the dis-play of painted clay pots the employment agency owner crafted in the evenings.

"Why, Doctor Bennett, dear. Ethan says you'll be help-ing decorate their new house."

Abigail jerked to a stop. "I didn't agree to help with the idea of selling him things from the shop. And I have never seen him use a cravat pin."

Her mother looked thoughtful. "Then perhaps we should furnish him with some of those too. I'll ask Mr. Lawrence what he thinks." She trotted out before Abigail could respond.

Jesslyn was more pointed. "I understand you'll be helping Doctor Bennett set up his house in the village," she said when Abigail ventured up to the spa to assist her with Regatta planning late in the day. "I can tell you what Father preferred."

Abigail shook her head. "Who told you?"

She nodded across the Grand Pump Room, which was as crowded as ever today. "Doctor Bennett, of course. He seems inordinately pleased by the fact."

Abigail looked to where Linus was speaking with Doctor Owens. He glanced up and met her gaze, then excused himself and strode to her side. Suddenly, she wasn't sure what to do with her hands, her face. Her heart.

"Abigail," he greeted her with all politeness even though she caught Jess's pleased smile at the use of her first name. "I know you and Mrs. Denby must have work on the Regatta. Would you have a few moments to talk?"

"Of course." She excused herself from her friend and followed him toward the bronze wall clock. Mrs. Harding, seated in her usual spot by the windows, nodded her approval as they passed.

He leaned closer, and she caught a whiff of mint. "I signed the lease on the house this morning. Mrs. Kirby says I may move in whenever we like. I have only a few furnishings from London—my desk and chair, Ethan's bookcase, and a small table my mother favored."

She had to force her mind to focus. "Mrs. Catchpole will know who's available to help move. The house has beds, a dining table and chairs, glass hutch, and settee,

if I recall. What else would you like? Mrs. Kirby keeps
catalogs from all the major furniture manufacturers and
cabinet makers in Dorset and London. We can order what
we need and have it delivered. What's your budget?"

He grimaced. "Seeing as how I just took a cut in pay,
not as much as I'd like. Besides the basic necessities,
which we appear to have covered, there are the table and
cabinets for the examining room."

"I'll speak to Jesslyn about those," Abigail said. "I believe
she put some of her father's things up in the attic when
she and Lark moved into Shell Cottage. I'm sure she'd
rather they went to good use."

He nodded. "There is one other item," he said, so hes-
itantly she could not imagine what it could be. "I'd like
a painting for over the hearth in the withdrawing room.
One of your paintings."

Warmth pulsed through her. "I'd be honored."

His smile had her leaning closer before she thought
better of it. He was moving to meet her.

Then his head snapped up so fast she felt the rush of air.
"Was there something you needed, sir?" he asked.

Abigail turned to find Doctor Owens standing beside
them, smile amused. "Miss Archer, Doctor Bennett. Forgive the interruption, but a rumor has been brought to
my attention, and I thought to track it to its source."

Had he too heard she was helping Linus with his new
home? Her cheeks heated, but he looked to Linus first.

"Is it true you were abducted by French agents?"

Abigail blew out a breath even as Linus put on a smile.

"Two gentlemen were rather insistent on my help,"
he told the other physician. "We believe they may be
French."

"Some say they come through the castle on the headland," Owens confided. "Secret caves, I believe the story
goes."

Only a few knew the French had been using the caves

beneath the castle as a way to sneak ashore without anyone seeing them. Who had mentioned the matter to a
Newcomer?

"Not much of a secret if rumors are flying," Abigail
told him.

"And I have had no further trouble," Linus added. "I
can only hope they have left the area, perhaps with willing smugglers or a crossing in the night."

Doctor Owens nodded. "Then there's to be no action
by the militia."

"No, worse luck," Abigail said. "Though the soldiers at
West Creech did make a search, I understand. Never fear,
Doctor. We will not allow a French victory in Grace-by-
the-Sea."

Linus merely nodded, but he was regarding her again
as if he very much feared she was about to take a risk too
big for her, and him.

A few miles away, across the Downs, a caravan of
coaches rolled along the road to Grace-by-the-Sea.
Drake, the newly belted Earl of Howland, had driven this
way many a time over his thirty years, but never with so
much riding on his shoulders. His late father had been
a man well known throughout the realm and feared no
little by those who'd understood him best. Three of them
sat in the carriage with him now.

"How much longer, Father?" Miranda asked, swaying
back and forth in her seat as she tried to catch a glimpse
of their new home out the window.

"Will you please stop asking that question?" her grandmother fretted, face the same shade of white as the hair
that peeked out of her tall, feathered bonnet. "We will
reach the castle when we reach it."

"That was the turning from West Creech just a few moments ago," his aunt Marjorie assured Miranda far more kindly. "Not long now."

He had been treated to a full examination of his family tree as the College of Heralds confirmed his right to succeed his father, so he knew the older lady with her grey hair and warm brown eyes was actually his cousin once removed, but he had been calling her aunt since he could remember. Of course, he'd gone by Thorgood, for his father's lesser title, for all that time too. Surprisingly difficult to remember he was Howland now.

Miranda stiffened, eyes widening, and she pointed out the window. "There it is!"

Even his mother pressed her patrician nose to the glass then.

Castle How, the hunting lodge where he'd spent part of every summer, stood tall on its headland, as if it truly guarded the way from the Channel to the Downs. His mother and Aunt Marjorie knew the visit would be of much longer duration this time. When one faced penury, one stayed where one could.

"I want the blue suite," his nine-year-old daughter declared to all and sundry. "The one looking out over the Channel. That way I can keep watch for the French."

His mother shuddered. "The French will not be coming over the water, Miranda. I have the king's word on that."

King George might offer as many promises as he liked. Drake had a feeling Napoleon would do whatever pleased him. The best they could do was pray for unfavorable winds for crossing for the foreseeable future.

"You can watch the Regatta from there too, if you like," he suggested to his daughter as the coach and its two companions, carrying the servants and luggage, trundled down the graveled drive for the wide front doors. "I understand it's only a week away now."

"I'd nearly forgotten," Aunt Marjorie exclaimed. "Now, that's a wonderful time to be in Grace-by-the-Sea."

His mother sniffed. "If there is a good time. The crowds, the noise. And entirely too much celebration." She shuddered again.

"I love it," Miranda said. "I don't want to watch it from the castle this year, Father. Will you take me to the shore?"

Much as he hated to agree with his mother's pessimistic outlook, the Regatta was favored by people his sheltered daughter might never meet otherwise. "I would prefer you stayed at the castle."

Her face darkened under her shiny blond curls even as her jaw hardened, and he readied himself to withstand the storm that was building. His late wife, Felicity, had doted on her daughter, caring for her herself. When she'd died, he hadn't been able to bring himself to hand Miranda over to a governess. But that was when his father had insisted on managing everything about their holdings, leaving Drake with little to do except teach and support his daughter. Now they had far fewer holdings, but he had responsibilities nonetheless. Yet what governess could withstand his daughter's outbursts? Even his aristocratic mother quailed before them.

Aunt Marjorie was no more immune. "Now, then," she said soothingly. "Your father will be expected to open the festivities this year, as earl. I'm sure James will build a fine grandstand on the headland. The four of us, James, and his new wife, Eva, can all sit there."

Miranda's color faded, and she smiled benignly at her great-aunt. "What a splendid suggestion. I can hardly wait."

Linus could only be thankful the next few days passed uneventfully, for him and Abigail, and for the spa. Some Newcomers and Irregulars left, but many more took their places, all coming for the annual Regatta. Every room at the Swan and the Mermaid was full, and Mrs. Kirby told him every house had been let, if only for the next fortnight.

"I'm very glad you took your house when you did, or I wouldn't have been able to let you in until September," she confided.

The difference in the village was appreciable. As he walked Ethan from the Archers up the street to their new house, others strolled in the same direction. Lines formed at the baker's and the grocer's. Mr. Carroll's shop was more stuffed with people than curiosities for once, and Abigail kept her shop open longer hours.

"Though I may have to close if we continue selling as we have," she told him when he stopped to get Ethan one evening.

"Congratulations," he said. "You have excellent wares, and our guests are taking notice."

"But I still have something for you," she said, crooking her finger at him. He followed her to her studio.

They had had little time together since she'd helped him finish the house, a fact he found more frustrating than he'd expected, but somehow, she'd made time to work on a new canvas. The vista looked out from the cove, headlands embracing the calm blue water. Beyond them, the Channel disappeared into the distance. She had yet to finish the foreground, but already the piece called to him.

"Magnificent," he said.

Her cheeks were turning pink, and he had to fist his hands to keep from reaching out to touch them. "Thank you," she said. "Will it do for over the hearth?"

"It would do for hanging in Hampton Court for the

royal family to enjoy," he assured her. "Thank you, Abigail."

She looked up at him, gaze wistful, and it was the work of a moment to bend his head and brush his lips against hers.

He should have known his Abigail would never be content with so small a gesture. As if she had been missing him as much, she wrapped her arms about his neck and kissed him back. When she released him, he had only enough wits about him to catalog his symptoms. Pounding pulse. Blood rushing to his face. A slight dizziness.

Euphoria.

Love?

No, that he wasn't ready to diagnose, even if he recognized the other symptoms: an admiration, a desire to cherish, protect. A hope to be at her side forever. Some part of him demanded he offer her his heart, his life. He settled on something far safer.

"Will you and your mother do me the honor of attending the Regatta with me and Ethan?" he asked.

She peered up at him as if she had hoped for another kind of invitation as well. "We'd be delighted, sir. I already purchased four seats on the eastern grandstand. Will those suffice?"

Linus started laughing. "I should have known you'd be one step ahead of me. I didn't even know there were grandstands."

Indeed there were. The scaffolding became evident the very next day as fishermen, carters, and farmers worked to build the wooden frames. Below the castle, on the rocky arm enclosing the eastern portion of the cove, stacked benches four high held seats for fifty people. Across the cove, on the opposite headland, another set of benches welcomed fifty more. That didn't count those who sat on blankets or the rocks along the cliffs to the east and west or those watching from pleasure craft anchored at either end of the mile-long course that stretched from the castle to where he had been told Lord Peverell's Lodge lay among the trees.

"Either Lord Howland or Lord Peverell opens the race," Abigail explained as she, her mother, he, and Ethan ventured out onto the headland with the others making the trek the morning of the event. Flags flew from every shop, and a red or blue pennant snapped from the upper corners of the grandstands. "This year, Lord Howland has the honor."

"His first time as the new earl," her mother put in with a glance up the hill toward the castle, where a special covered stand had been built.

"Look at all the boats, Father!" Ethan cried, pointing with his free hand. Mrs. Archer held firmly to the other.

It was an impressive sight. So many masts poked up they might have been looking out at a winter forest. Already sailors scrambled from deck to rigging and back, while others worked at raising anchors.

Abigail climbed to the third row of the stand and squeezed past Mr. Lawrence and his family to four vacant spots with numbers painted on the spaces. Ethan was fairly wiggling as he sat. From along the shore came calls from villagers selling sweet pickles, meat pies, and various biscuits and pastries.

"See there?" Abigail asked Ethan, nodding to where two boats stood with tall pennants below the castle. "That is the starting line. There will be three fleets of six boats each. They sail down and back again. The two fastest of each fleet will meet again for a final race to determine the winner."

"And the winner gets a fancy silver cup," her mother put in, "big enough to hold a gallon of cider."

Ethan's eyes widened.

"There, see the sails going up?" Abigail continued, nodding toward the east. "Those will be the first six."

At the cliffside closest to the starting line, James Howland stepped forward, a man who looked very like him at his side. The magistrate held up a speaking trumpet, aiming the bell out over the water.

"Attention! If I may have your attention, good sirs and madams."

Voices grew quiet. Ethan stared up at him. Abigail grinned at Linus and took his hand. The day felt finer.

"I have the pleasure of introducing you to my esteemed cousin, Lord Howland." He handed the other man the speaking trumpet with a bow.

"Ladies and gentlemen," his cousin, the new earl, called out, voice echoing across the water. "Allow me to welcome you to the thirtieth annual Grace-by-the-Sea Regatta."

Cheers and applause echoed from both headlands, with yells of support from the vessels at sea.

"This year," he went on when things had quieted a little, "we have a very fine showing of eighteen vessels from Dorset, Devonshire, Cornwall, and as far away as Kent."

More cheers erupted.

"May the best captain, the fastest ship, win."

He bowed and offered the speaking trumpet back to his cousin, then went to take his seat on the shaded grandstand beside a little girl, two older women, Eva, and Mrs. Tully.

"That girl is his daughter," Abigail told Linus. "He's a widower too."

He felt for the fellow. Yet how much better was life now that Abigail was beside him?

The magistrate's voice boomed out. "In the first fleet, we have the Hind of the Waves with Captain Meadows, the Merry Widow with Captain Grant, the Valiant with Captain Willison, the Importune with Captain Barkins, the Spirit of the Sea with Captain Norris, and the Siren's Call, captained by our own Quillan St. Claire, who joins our Regatta for the first time, with first mate Mr. Alexander Chance, who is no stranger to our event."

"Ooh, the captain." Mrs. Archer craned her neck as if she could see the fellow from her perch. Abigail perked up as well. So, he realized, did every lady near him.

"Gentlemen," the magistrate bellowed. "Prepare your sails."

Canvas unfurled like low-hanging clouds. Bows headed away from the shore.

"On my mark," Mr. Howland shouted. "Away!"

They swept across the waves. The wind before them, they each had to tack back and forth while avoiding the other. Linus caught himself holding his breath as they began the turn past the Lodge. Abigail leaned closer, until the scent of peaches overpowered even the salt of the air.

"Look," Ethan cried, pointing. "Captain St. Claire is in the lead!"

He was indeed. The Siren's Call with its mermaid on the bow and black sides cut through the waves, taking advantage of every ounce of sail. Abigail grinned at Linus. He grinned back.

"But look, the Hind!" someone called.

Another boat narrowed the distance, until the two sliced side by side. Linus wasn't sure who finished first.

Jack Hornswag scrambled up from his perch above the Dragon's Maw to speak to the magistrate, who nodded and raised his speaking trumpet.

"First place, the Hind of the Waves. Second place, the Siren's Call."

A groan went through the onlookers. It seemed to be coming mostly from the ladies.

"But that means he gets to try again," Ethan said with a look to Abigail.

"Indeed it does," she said, giving Linus's hand a squeeze as if to reassure him as well. "Do not count our good captain out yet. I'm sure he has plans."

"Here comes the second fleet," her mother said.

Ethan looked, then frowned. "Why are there seven of them?"

The rest of the onlookers must have seen the other ship at the same time, along with the flag she flew so brazenly, for voices rose in fear.

"The French!"

"The enemy!"

"Invasion!"

"Run!"

# CHAPTER EIGHTEEN

ALL AROUND THEM, PEOPLE CRIED out, scrambled to their feet, shoved their way down the grandstand. Her mother fell over as one of the men above them clambered past. As Abigail bent to help her, she heard a cry from Ethan. Twisting, she found Linus staring at the spot where his son had been.

"He slipped through the opening between the seats!" He started to kneel.

Abigail caught his arm. "Don't! You'll be trampled."

Her mother regained her feet even as another woman was dragged down the grandstand by those higher up. She lay on the ground at the bottom, face white and wrist hanging crookedly.

"Go to her," Abigail told Linus. "We'll find Ethan."

He hesitated only a moment before loping down the seats.

"Are you all right?" Mr. Lawrence asked Abigail and her mother even as he directed his wife and children down the stand. "I can leave Davy to help."

"Go," Abigail told him. "There are others who need more help."

"Ethan," her mother worried as the jeweler followed his family.

Abigail felt it too; fear like a fist squeezed her heart.

"We'll find him, Mother," she promised. "Come with

me."

The crowd had thinned sufficiently that she was able to lead her mother off the bench and assist her down to the ground.

"Stay here," she said, tucking her under the edge of the highest seats. Then she crouched and peered into the shadows below, lip caught between her teeth.

A frightened pair of eyes gazed back, and she nearly sagged with relief.

Instead, she offered him her hand. "Come out, Ethan. It's all right."

He crept toward her, face striped by dust and tears. "I fell," he said.

"I know," she said, sending up a prayer of thanks and brushing dust from his hair as he reached her. "And you were very brave and very clever to stay still until we could find you." She gave him a hug for good measure, then held him out at arm's length. "Were you hurt?"

"Not much," he said, rubbing at his backside. "Not like when I was sick."

She did not want him thinking about his illness at the moment. "Good. Let's collect your father and see what's to be done."

"He's coming," her mother put in, and Abigail turned to find Linus approaching.

"Miss Whitacre's family came for her," he reported. "A sprain only, as far as I can tell. Nothing broken." He put his arm about Ethan's shoulders, peered deep into his eyes. "All right, my boy?"

Ethan nodded. "I knew you and Miss Archer would come for me. And Mother Archer too."

Her mother stretched out her arms as far as they would go and gathered them all close. "Of course I will. We're family."

The dream, the hope, was as warm as her mother's embrace, but now was no time to discuss the possibility of making that dream a reality. As her mother released them, Abigail sent her a smile, then turned to look around. The grandstand was empty. So was the one across from them. The French sloop had taken up a position at the entrance to the cove, as if to stop anyone from escaping by water. Would they fire?

Would they land?

"Quickly, now," Linus said, as if he had the same fears. "We must get off this headland."

Abigail took her mother's hand in one of hers and Ethan's hand in the other, and they all hurried for the village.

But Grace-by-the-Sea was in an uproar. A few must have had time to return home, for they struggled up the hill now, arms laden with clothing, blankets, and family belongings. The militiamen were doing what they could to organize the evacuation, but they were down in numbers. Half of the troop was out on the water as crew or timers for the Regatta.

"Head for the Downs," Mr. Greer was calling as he stood outside his apothecary shop near the shore, waving people up the hill. He had thrown his red coat over his waistcoat and hadn't taken the time to button it. "Bring only what you need."

"I won't leave my best lace for the French," Miss Pierce the younger informed him as she came out of her shop nearby. She clutched a bolt to her chest.

"We will leave nothing for the French," Mr. Greer promised her. "We'll torch every building as soon as we know everyone has escaped."

Abigail gasped. "Surely not!" She hurried up to him, pulling her mother and Ethan with her, Linus right behind. "These are our homes, sir, our livelihoods."

"That is a direct order from the Lord Lieutenant for Dorset," Mr. Greer insisted. "Laid down in the evacuation plan for each village. We must leave nothing that might give the enemy aid or comfort."

"If my linens would comfort a French soldier, I'd rather he had them than burn them," Miss Pierce the elder said before pushing her sister up the hill.

Linus stepped forward. "Right now, we must think of safety first," he told Greer, and she wanted to cling to his calm, reasoned voice the way Miss Pierce the younger clung to her lace. "You're sending them to the Downs. Why? There's nowhere to house them, no way to feed them. There isn't even a source of drinking water from what I've seen. And any troops landing will march up that hill in the same direction, right into them."

"I am merely following the plan of the Lord Lieutenant of Dorset," Mr. Greer said testily. "It is not my place to question it."

"No," Abigail said. "Apparently it's mine." She turned to Linus. "We must send them to Lord Peverell's Lodge. It's hidden among the trees on the far headland, out of the way. The French might not even notice it. There will be water, shelter. Once the French pass, we can fish."

Linus nodded. "Take Ethan. Lead as many as you can in that direction. I'll find the magistrate and Mr. Denby. We'll get the rest."

"Now, see here," Mr. Greer started. "I cannot authorize the confiscation of private property."

"Only if it's to be burned, it seems," Abigail returned. "You, sir, are overruled. Ethan, Mother, come with me. We must turn the tide."

She was amazing. Linus only had a moment to watch Abigail wade into the stream of escaping villagers and visitors and begin to guide them toward the opposite headland. He left Greer sputtering and went to look for

Howland and Denby. Surely they would know how to protect everyone.

He found the magistrate coming down the path from the castle with Eva, Mrs. Tully, and the Denbys. Linus met them and explained the change in plan.

"Excellent notion," Mrs. Denby proclaimed. "I'll gather our Regulars and enlist their aid." She picked up her skirts and hurried for High Street.

"Some will run for the church," Eva said. "We'll send them to the Lodge. Come, Maudie."

"The trolls will be here shortly," she told Linus before following Eva down the lane. And he could not tell if she thought her trolls would be their salvation or their ruin.

"The earl and those with him have already left the castle on my orders," Howland told Linus and Denby as they followed. "They will alert Upper Grace."

A large group was headed in that direction, the remaining militiamen among them. Enough had reached the top of the hill that Linus and the others had to go up and order them around to the Lodge. They discovered another group heading up Church Street for the path to the headland. Eva and Mrs. Tully were directing them.

"Up you go," Eva advised. "Best place to be at the moment."

"Trolls behind you," Mrs. Tully added. "Move right along."

Howland pressed a kiss to his wife's cheek. "Well done, Eva. We'll sweep the village, make sure everyone is out."

"And stop Greer from setting it ablaze," Linus said.

"Be careful," she said before returning to her task.

"The French won't land," Mrs. Tully told him. "The mermaids won't allow it."

Linus wasn't about to rely on mermaids. He, Denby, and the magistrate returned to High Street, then headed down to the apothecary shop.

Greer stood outside, torch in one hand, staring at his

building as if he simply couldn't bear to see it go up in flames.

Denby stepped in front of him. "Put that out."

Greer roused himself. "I take no orders from the Excise Office."

"No," Howland said, moving in next to him. "But as head of the militia for Grace-by-the-Sea and the magistrate for this village, I do have the authority to issue orders. Put that out."

Greer hesitated, sweat beginning to pop out on his high brow. "You approved the plan, Magistrate. You helped compile it."

Linus stared at him. Howland raised his chin. "I did, to my everlasting sorrow. Before my marriage, I had a tendency to follow the law to its last letter. Now I believe it more important to follow its spirit. No village should have to build itself back from the ashes because of our actions, Mr. Greer. Would you condemn Grace-by-the-Sea after one glimpse of a French flag?"

Greer drew in a breath. "No." He set down the torch and rolled it in the dirt of the road to extinguish it.

Linus wanted to cheer, but there was too much more to be done. "The others are gathering at the Lodge. Perhaps you should join them."

Greer nodded and headed in that direction. Howland, Denby, and Linus started back up High Street.

They met Mrs. Denby coming from the spa, along with Lord Featherstone, Mrs. Harding, Mr. Crabapple, the Admiral, and Doctor Owens.

"Mrs. Rand, Miss Turnpeth, the others?" Linus asked her.

"Most are on their way to the Lodge," she reported. "I couldn't find Mr. Donner or Mr. George. I hope they had the sense to follow."

"How might we be of assistance, Magistrate?" Lord Featherstone asked.

"We'll quarter the village," Howland said. "Knock on every door."

"And once this is over," Linus added, "we must review the evacuation plan. Who decided we should fire the village?"

"Standard practice," Howland said over the cries of protest from Mrs. Harding and the Admiral. "Fire the village, kill any livestock that might be of use. Destroy any food, supplies."

"Draconian," Lord Featherstone pronounced.

"Indeed," Owens agreed, brows up. "Won't the population have to return at some point?"

"My thoughts exactly," Linus said.

"We should move," Denby said. "They'll come ashore any moment now."

They all turned toward the water. The cove sat empty, quiet. Beyond the entrance, the Channel rippled in the sunlight.

Just as empty.

Howland stepped forward. "Where are they? If they intended to land, they'd have to come through the cove. There's no other low bank for miles."

Denby squared his shoulders. "You all canvas the village, get everyone out, just in case. I'll head for the castle, see if I can find a better vantage point."

"Go," Howland said. "Jesslyn, divide your troops. Two to Church Street and Castle Walk, two to each side of High Street. You have a half hour, then I want you climbing for the Lodge."

"The Lodge?" Owens asked Linus as Jesslyn began partnering the others.

"A property hidden on the west headland," Linus explained. "The villagers and our guests are heading there rather than out on the Downs."

"More strategic value," he said with a nod. "Do you need my help?"

"Yes," Mrs. Denby put in. "Take the west side of High Street with Doctor Bennett. It's mostly shops, but some have flats above or behind, and it's possible others took shelter there."

"On our way," Linus said.

It was a mad half hour. He and Owens knocked and shouted as Lord Featherstone and the Admiral canvassed the opposite side. In the distance, other voices shouted on Church Street and Castle Walk.

"Remarkably obedient, your villagers and guests," Owens mused as they headed back up the street, having found no one.

"Remarkably fortunate," Linus told him. "It was utter chaos for a time."

"And so it might have remained," Owens assured him, "but for you, the magistrate, and Mr. Denby."

Linus wasn't so sure about that. Abigail had been the one to think of the Lodge, Jesslyn to rally the Regulars. Eva and Mrs. Tully had proven more effective at leading the villagers and guests than he and the other men had been. Abigail had also rescued Ethan so he could help others.

He nearly stopped in his tracks as the realization hit. The very traits that had concerned him had proven their salvation—her quick action, her fearlessness, her willingness to take risks where others hesitated.

How could any man fail to admire such a woman?

They regrouped a few moments later at the crossroads between Castle Walk and Church Street.

"The French have vanished," Denby reported, breathing hard from his run in both directions. "Most of the boats in the Regatta took sail too."

"Perhaps they went to mount an attack," Owens suggested. "You have such captains designated, do you not? Sea Fencibles, I believe they're called."

"We do," the magistrate allowed. "But their purpose

is to go out and meet the French in the middle of the Channel. Most of the ships in the Regatta wouldn't have been carrying cannons. And there's no time to mount a defense when the French arrive from nowhere."

Linus cocked his head. "An excellent observation, Magistrate. How did a French sloop appear in the middle of the Regatta? One might think it designed to sow panic."

Howland stared at him. "They were testing us!"

Denby glanced out over the water. "And I fear to think what they just learned."

# CHAPTER NINETEEN

L ORD PEVERELL'S LODGE WAS A sprawling place built of brick imported from outside Dorset. It boasted three withdrawing rooms and a dozen bedchambers, but it had not been designed to hold most of the inhabitants of Grace-by-the-Sea and all those who had come up for the Regatta.

"And the Spa Corporation will pay for any damage?" Mrs. Kirby had asked as she had unlocked the door for Abigail.

"Mr. Greer is aware of the change in plan," Abigail had replied, hoping the Spa Corporation president would agree to supply whatever was needed in the end.

Now families and friends clustered in each bedchamber, the spa guests who were not still in the village were congregated in one of the withdrawing rooms, the other Regatta attendees made up the other two withdrawing rooms, and the shopkeepers and workers of Grace-by-the-Sea ranged from the kitchen to the dining room. Children huddled with their parents. Husbands and wives held hands. And everyone listened for the dull boom of cannon fire, the tramp of soldier's feet.

Both Abigail and Mr. Wingate, the vicar, moved from room to room, checking on everyone.

"What are we to do, Miss Archer?" Mrs. Evans asked, holding her new baby close as her daughters clung to her skirts. They had come up the headland alone. Abigail assumed her husband was out on one of the boats.

"We'll wait here for word from the magistrate," Abigail told her, smiling at the baby, who drowsed in his mother's arms as if he was the only one content with the world. "In the meantime, if you brought food or drink, it would be good if you could share it with others."

Mrs. Greer, seated nearby, hugged the bag she'd brought tighter. Lean and angular, the wife of the Spa Corporation president generally liked announcing his position to all and sundry, even those who had voted him into office multiple years now. Abigail generally did not engage with her, but if the woman had food to share, Abigail would make sure the others knew it.

A door slammed somewhere, and everyone tensed. She hurried out to find that Linus had arrived, bringing Lark, the magistrate, Eva, Mrs. Tully, Dr. Owens, Jesslyn, and her Regulars with him. Abigail ran to him, and he caught her close. Breath came easily for the first time since she'd seen the French sloop on the waters.

"How are we faring?" Mr. Howland asked as she disengaged. Linus kept one arm about her waist as if he could not let her go. She couldn't mind.

"The Lodge is filled to the rafters," Abigail reported. "I'm beginning to wonder if there's enough food even for dinner tonight. And the French?"

"Gone," Linus assured her, giving her a squeeze. If the others noticed, they were wise enough not to mention it.

"Gone, at least for now," the magistrate amended. Then he raised his head and his voice.

"Citizens of Grace-by-the Sea and esteemed guests." The words echoed against the wood paneling of the entry hall, filled the house, which went silent as if listening as well. "Give thanks! We have been delivered this day. The French sailed on without landing. It is safe to return to your lodgings."

Huzzahs and praise rang from beyond them, around them, until she thought the very roof would lift from the house.

Her mother and Ethan peered around the corner from the dining room, then came to meet Abigail and Linus.

"What about the ships?" Ethan asked. "The races."

"Our gallant crews are even now sweeping the coast," Mr. Howland told the house as other people began trickling out of the various rooms and down the stairs. "Once they return this evening and assure us our enemies continued to run home to France, we will resume the Regatta."

More huzzahs sounded.

Mrs. Greer approached, bag clutched in her grip. She blinked brown eyes at the magistrate. "Is that wise? Should we not evacuate inland just to be safe?"

Jesslyn met her gaze. "I refuse to let fear rule me."

"Nor me," Abigail said with a nod to her friend.

Ethan slipped his hand into hers. "Me either."

Linus stared at his son in obvious wonder before taking his other hand. "I stand with Grace-by-the-Sea."

"So do I," Eva declared.

"And me!"

"I stand!"

"Never surrender!"

The calls rang from the house, until Abigail couldn't tell where one started and another ended.

"Well done," Mrs. Tully said. "The fairies will be very pleased to hear it."

"In the meantime," Mr. Howland put in smoothly, "you are all free to go. But if you're a militiaman, meet me on the drive in front of the Lodge. I have assignments for you."

Abigail shepherded Linus, Ethan, and her mother off to the side of the entry hall as people began to stream out.

"I'll stay to help Mrs. Kirby make sure the house is

secure," she told them. "You can go back to the village."

Ethan glanced up at his father. "Can we stay? I want to help too."

"Certainly," Linus said.

"We'll all help," her mother agreed.

In the end, Jesslyn and her Regulars stayed too, and teams took each floor and each wing to ensure nothing and no one had been left behind, no damage had been done to Lord Peverell's home, and the holland covers had been replaced over the furnishings. Abigail worked with Linus while her mother and Ethan partnered on the other side of the corridor.

As soon as they were alone in the bedchamber, Linus pulled her close and held her gently. His chest rose in a deep breath, as if he would inhale her. If only she could stay in his embrace, but she knew her duty.

"Why, Doctor Bennett," she made herself tease. "How have I earned such attentions?"

He leaned back enough to meet her gaze. The grey in his eyes flickered with silver. "By being the most amazing woman of my acquaintance. I cannot tell you how grateful I am for your leadership today."

Abigail cocked her head. "You could try."

He laughed, releasing her. "It would take hours, and I would like us all to return home sooner than that. But I promise a full accounting later."

"I will look forward to it." She glanced around the room. "Not too bad here. Tug those covers in place, and we'll see about the others."

They went to work. Some of the rooms needed minor repairs—paintings hanging crooked where a shoulder had pressed too close, corners of carpets flipped up by a careless foot.

"I can see we'll need to fund Mrs. Catchpole's cleaning crew to go through," Abigail said as she picked a rock off the carpet in one of the bedchambers.

"And perhaps set up a display at the spa where people can claim what they lost," Linus added, cloth doll tucked under one arm. "Unless you think some of this was left in the house from previous use."

She joined him in the center of the room to regard the items he'd found. "That tortoiseshell hair comb, possibly, though it might belong to one of the visitors. The rest likely isn't fine enough for the Peverells."

"It was very clever of you to think of sheltering people here," he said as they started for the door.

"It seemed the logical choice," Abigail said. "The castle is larger, but more visible, and we know the French are aware of it. But the Lodge wouldn't have worked for long. We must think of a more viable evacuation plan."

"And apparently have it approved by the Lord Lieutenant for Dorset."

Abigail smiled as they headed down the corridor for the stairs. "He must know his plan is aspirational at best. By the time word reached him that we'd evacuated, it would be too late for him to send help. Grace-by-the-Sea must fend for itself."

He paused at the top of the stairs. "I sense that is your preferred approach to any challenge—to go it alone."

Abigail frowned at him. "Do you find fault with self-sufficiency?"

"No," he assured her. "I admire self-sufficiency. However, now I'm finding partnership a far more useful and satisfying alternative."

As if her heart agreed with him, it started beating faster. "I am listening, sir."

"There you are," her mother sang out from the entry hall below. "Ethan and I finished ages ago."

"May we go home now?" Ethan asked plaintively.

Linus drew in a breath as if reorienting himself. "Go ahead and start back. We'll speak to Mrs. Kirby and be right behind."

Resigned, Abigail put a hand to the newel. He juggled the things in his arms to take her other hand in his. "We must talk, Abigail. Perhaps on the way back to the village."

His touch was warm, his grip sheltering. Buoyed, she nodded. "I'd like that."

Together, they continued down the stairs to check in with Mrs. Kirby. They had survived the first French incursion, but Abigail could only wonder what the future held—for Grace-by-the-Sea and for her and Linus.

Linus escorted Abigail out of the Lodge at last. Most of the villagers and their guests had already left. There should be no one to interrupt his conversation with Abigail as they walked home. Once again, he was all too aware of his symptoms: dry mouth, sweaty palms, trouble breathing. Likely somewhat normal when contemplating marriage, especially when he was unsure of his reception.

But a group was waiting on the drive: Mrs. Rand, Miss Turnpeth, and Doctor Owens. The physician hurried to meet him.

"I have never been gladder to see a colleague," he said with a nod to Abigail as well. "The lady is complaining of chest pains, and she will not heed my advice."

"I'll speak to her," Linus promised. He looked to Abigail, and she nodded. Together, they moved closer.

Mrs. Rand sat on a boulder at the edge of the drive, soft blue skirts pooled about her. Linus could not like her pallor under her feathered bonnet, nor the way her breath came in sharp pants.

He put a hand on her back and bent closer. "Quite a bit of excitement today."

"Too much," she agreed, rubbing at her ribs. "The race,

the French, the flight up the hill. I came to Grace-by-the-Sea for peace!"

"Ah, but a lady of your stamina generally rebounds from such excitement," Linus told her. "If I may, would you allow me to listen to your heart?"

"Certainly, sir. I trust you implicitly, unlike some." She narrowed her eyes at Owens.

Her companion smiled apologetically at the other physician. Owens was watching Linus. So was Abigail.

He pulled back Mrs. Rand's glove to expose her wrist, then rested two fingers against the base of her thumb, counting the beats to himself. The pulse was a little faster than might be expected, but steady. He smiled at the elderly widow, who was watching him as avidly.

"And now your lungs," he said.

She shifted on the boulder to give him her back. He pressed his ear to her gown. The others stilled as if trying to make as little noise as possible. A shame it was difficult to be sure with all the layers between him and her lungs, but he thought he heard a wheeze.

Linus raised his head. "I believe you've had enough exertion for today. Doctor Owens, may I trouble you to take a message to the village? I'd like Mrs. Rand's coachman to come for her and Miss Turnpeth."

"He left us," her companion put in before Owens could answer. "Mr. Greer, the apothecary, ordered all coaches out of the village so the French could not make use of them or the horses."

Linus shook his head as he straightened. Plan or no plan, Greer had a lot to answer for.

"Perhaps Lord Featherstone could carry me," Mrs. Rand ventured, eyes bright.

"I believe his lordship has already returned to the village," Linus said. "And I could not ask such a feat, even from our gallant Lord Featherstone. Excuse me for a moment. Miss Archer? Doctor Owens?"

Abigail and the physician stepped aside with him.

"You heard it too, I take it," Linus said to his colleague.

Owens nodded. "Her heart. Terrible thing, but only to be expected in a woman her age."

Linus frowned, but Abigail spoke up. "If it's a carriage you need, Eva has one. I doubt very much she would have allowed Mr. Greer to order it away. She and the magistrate live just at the bottom of the headland, near St. Andrew's. It will only take me a few moments to go down and ask."

"Does she have that long?" Owens asked Linus.

"We can contrive," Linus said. "Go, Abigail, and ask. And thank you for your quick thinking, as always."

She gave him a smile, then picked up her skirts and hurried for the path down the headland.

"Stay with our patient," Linus told Owens. "Mrs. Kirby is still inside. I'll bespeak some water."

Owens nodded.

Linus managed to occupy Mrs. Rand as they waited, asking about family, friends, their plans when they left Grace-by-the-Sea. Owens kept wandering to the edge of the headland, as if he could spy Abigail and the carriage coming, but Linus couldn't help noticing that his gaze strayed as often out over the Channel. Well, who could blame him? It wasn't every day the French showed up so boldly outside an English village only to disappear.

Testing them, the magistrate had said. Why? Did the French truly plan to land at Grace-by-the-Sea?

At length, the rumble of hooves heralded the arrival of the carriage, which rolled to a stop on the graveled drive.

"Miss Archer said you might need some assistance, Doctor," the coachman said, saluting Linus with his whip.

"Glad to accept it," Linus assured him. He and Owens helped Mrs. Rand up into a seat, then assisted Miss Turnpeth before climbing in themselves.

"Take us to the spa," Linus called up. As the coach set

out, he turned to his patient. "I can make a poultice that should help set things to rights."

"Oh," she said, pausing to suck in a breath. "Thank you."

Owens patted her shoulder. "Such things are easily remedied, I find, with the right exercise, diet, and medication."

Linus merely smiled.

Dusk was falling when he finally made his way to Abigail's flat. She answered his knock. Just the sight of her made the world a better place. She stepped aside to let him in.

"Mrs. Rand?" she asked.

"Resting in her room at the inn with a poultice on her side. Pleurisy. She will bear watching. Ethan?"

"Fell asleep on the sofa. Mother is watching over him. Would you like dinner, tea?"

All at once, he wanted to drop. "Tea would be most welcome."

"Come into the dining room, and I'll bring you a cup."

He wandered into the room where Ethan spent so much time. Indeed, some of his sketches were spread out on the table. Linus sank onto a chair and looked them over. A fantastical castle with a dragon circling overhead. The front of the spa with a more fanciful pediment over the door showing trolls on the march. The cove with a sea serpent arching through the waters. The French ship, colors flying. And only three men as crew. It seemed his son still had some things to learn about sailing.

Abigail returned with a cup of tea in each hand and set one down before him, then took the chair next to his.

Linus sipped the amber brew.

"Milk and honey," she said. "That's the way you always take it at the spa."

"Perfect," he said, shoulders coming down. "And very observant. Only what I would expect from you."

She contented herself with her tea. Somewhere a clock ticked off the time.

He'd wanted a private conversation with her, but he found himself all at sea. He set down his cup. "Help me, Abigail. I am coming to care for you, and I'm not sure what to do."

She lowered her cup as well, but the tea sloshed. "I'm no more sure what you're asking of me. I'll never be the demure miss who flutters her lashes and gazes up at you adoringly while you tell her of your adventures. I'm coming to care for you as well, but I wish to stand beside you, sir, not walk behind in your shadow."

It seemed he had a chance. "I want you beside me as well," he assured her. "Raising Ethan together, encouraging each other in our work, helping the village. Would you ever consider marrying?"

Both hands gripped her cup, and she gazed into the liquid as if his answer lay at the bottom. "For much of my life, I didn't think so. And no man stirred my heart sufficiently to cause me to change my mind." She glanced up, met his gaze, and touched his heart. "Until I met you. So, if you're asking me to marry you, Linus, to be your partner in all things, then the answer is yes."

# CHAPTER TWENTY

WITH ONE WORD, SHE WAS betrothed. Linus surged to his feet, and she met him. His proposal may have been hesitant, but his kiss said he knew his own mind.

And her heart.

Her mother, of course, was overjoyed. "Oh, wonderful!" she cried when they exited the dining room together and told her the good news. She clasped her hands together. Ethan, lying with his head on her lap, woke up sufficiently that they could explain to him too.

"So, you'll be my mother," he said to Abigail, face solemn.

Abigail couldn't hold back her smile. "Yes. Do you mind?"

"No," he said. "You like me."

She gathered him close. "I love you, Ethan, and I love your father as well. We'll all be a family."

Linus put his arms around them both, and her mother leaned in as well. Warmth spread. Hope with it.

"A little squishy," Ethan said, wiggling in the middle.

"Get used to it, my boy," her mother said, releasing them to wipe away a tear.

They were only the first to congratulate her.

"Wishing you and Doctor Bennett all the best," Mr. Ellison said when she went for bread early the next morning after sending Linus up to the spa.

"How did you know?" she asked, accepting the loaf from him.

"Your mother mentioned it to Jack Hornswag, who told his cook, whose son is sweet on my Jenny," he told her. "The Misses Pierce were in before you. I let them know as well. They promised to order whatever you like."

So did the Inchleys when she dropped by to purchase tea and sugar before opening her shop.

"How big a wedding breakfast do you want?" Mrs. Inchley asked as Abigail debated bohea or green tea. "I imagine the church will be full—he is the physician after all, and every lady in this village owes you a debt. But you likely won't want to feed everyone."

"I haven't given it any thought," Abigail told her. "But I'll let you know as soon as I have plans."

"How did you do it?" she asked Jesslyn when she went up to the spa that afternoon to make sure her friend had heard the news about the Regatta. Most of the ships had returned to their moorings, but the Siren's Call was still missing, so the magistrate had delayed the running of the races until Monday.

"Do what?" Jesslyn asked, holding a crystal glass under the sparkling water of the fountain as her guests continued to buzz about the sighting of the French ship the previous day.

"Plan a wedding while working," Abigail clarified. "And one of the most-attended weddings in Grace-by-the-Sea. I don't know where to begin."

Jess peered closer. "Is that Abigail Archer speaking? You built a business that supports most of the families in the area; create works of art that grace the finest homes. Planning a wedding should be nothing."

Abigail dropped her gaze. "Perhaps it would be nothing, if it wasn't my wedding."

A crystal glass edged into her line of sight.

"Drink," Jess said. "It will make you feel better."

Abigail accepted the glass. "Even your famous spa water won't cure what ails me. I said yes, Jess. Me."

She looked up to find her friend smiling. "You. It happens to the best of us. He's a fine man."

Abigail turned the glass in her hand. "I want to believe that. I must believe that. But how did you know, Jess, that Lark was the right one for you? He left you behind once. What made you trust him again?"

Jess cocked her head as if remembering. "I didn't trust him, not at first. He hadn't been content to stay before. Why would I think he would stay now? I was born in Grace-by-the-Sea. I didn't know anything beyond its borders. I had to look inside my heart and realize I could love him—here, there, wherever he went, so long as we were together."

Abigail nodded. "You took a chance on him." She raised her glass. "Here's to risking all for love." She drank deep of the warm, effervescent waters, then set down the glass. "Oh, but I don't know how you suffer this every day."

Jess laughed. "I don't. I just fill glasses so others can drink."

Linus came out of the examining room then. Meeting Abigail's gaze, he smiled, and something far better than mineral water bubbled up inside her. He crossed to her side.

"More water, I see," he said with a nod to the empty glass. "Everything all right?"

"Everything is perfect," she assured him.

Jess excused herself with a smile. Abigail shook her head. What, did her friend think they would exchange words of love in the middle of the spa?

Where nearly everyone was now watching.

She turned her back on the guests. "Is your day going well?"

"Well enough," he said. "I sent a note by post this morning. A friend of my father is serving in India. I asked him to look up your brother, encourage him to write home."

Tears threatened. "Oh, Linus. How thoughtful."

He took her hand, pressed a kiss against the back. "Do not thank me yet. India is a vast nation. Doctor Petry may not be where I last heard from him. He may not be able to find your brother."

"It is far more than we had," she said, clinging to his hand a moment. Mrs. Rand trotted past, surprisingly spry after yesterday. In fact, she made a show of heading for the examining room. Abigail released him so he could attend to his duties.

"I cannot focus on anything," she told Eva when her friend came to congratulate her as she was working in the shop later that afternoon. She didn't ask how Eva knew. The story was obviously flying all over the village.

"I remember," Eva commiserated, leaning against the counter. "I've only been married a month, after all, and two of those weeks James was in London. I'd be delighted to help, whatever you need."

They strategized details between customers, and Abigail had a better idea of what might suit her and Linus by the time she closed the shop that evening. She even had a list of questions to ask him. Did he prefer beef or fish? Dancing or merely fellowship? It generally fell on the lady's family to organize a wedding, but she and Linus were to be partners, after all.

On the way back down the corridor, she stopped in her studio. The painting she'd started for him sat on its easel, waiting.

She eyed it. As a youth, she'd started painting the sea because it was big and complicated, and its many moods matched the tumult inside her. Seascapes had been so popular with their visitors that she'd continued to paint them. She rarely included people in the scene. Someone might look like someone, and they wouldn't be flattered. Or someone else might be hurt that she hadn't chosen them as her subject instead. But there, in the foreground of this painting, she could almost picture people, gazing toward the horizon and the future. She reached for her smock.

Her mother found her there a short time later. "I expect Linus here any moment. Don't you want to see him?"

Linus. Even her mother felt comfortable using his first name now. Abigail smiled as she stepped back. Three people—a man, a woman, and a boy—gazed into the blue. "Certainly I want to see him. I'll just be a bit longer."

Her mother didn't move.

Abigail turned to find her face slumped, tears gathering. She set down her brush and pallet. "What's wrong?"

Her mother's voice trembled. "You blame me, for your father."

Abigail reared back. "What? Of course not."

Her mother nodded, lower lip starting to tremble as well. "You do. I knew it. I see it. You don't trust me to take care of you."

Abigail wiped her hands on her rag. "It's not a question of trust, Mother. I had skills I could use to benefit us."

"Where I was useless."

She bit her lip to keep from responding immediately. Thanks to her father, her mother still doubted her abilities. When he'd died, she'd been willing to exist on whatever village charity provided, all the while thinking she hadn't deserved even that.

"You were never useless, Mother," she said. "You took care of me and Gideon. You keep our home now. You make sure I'm fed. You teach and care for Ethan."

Her mother sniffed. "All activities you despise."

"All activities at which I don't excel," Abigail corrected her. "You do. And I am thankful. Because of what you do,

I can do what I do."

She nodded toward the canvas. "Then why did you leave me out?"

Abigail stared at the scene. "You're absolutely right. I knew it wasn't done yet. Give me a moment." She switched to charcoal and sketched in another person on the other side of Ethan.

"There," she said, stepping back. "I'll paint it tomorrow." Turning, she found her mother frowning at the piece.

"What?" she asked.

"I'm sure I'm not that broad in the hips," her mother said.

"Oh, Mother!" Abigail enfolded her in a hug. "I will paint you as thin as a sylph or with a mermaid's tail, if that pleases you. Just know that I love you, and you will always be part of my life."

"Even when you leave me alone to live with Linus and Ethan?" she asked.

Abigail leaned back. "I thought you'd like having the place to yourself. Would you prefer to live with us?"

Her mother's tremulous nod made her hug her again.

"There are four bedchambers in the new house," Abigail told her. "I'm certain you'd be welcome to one of them. Please know I am not leaving you behind. You're my family."

"And please know I am tremendously proud of you," her mother murmured, pulling back to wipe a cheek. "I have no idea why God blessed me with such a clever, talented, beautiful daughter, but I thank Him every night."

"And I have not thanked Him enough for giving me such a caring mother," Abigail told her. "Nor have I told you enough how much I appreciate you. I will do better in the future."

"So will I," her mother vowed. "Now, let's go get your hair combed before Linus arrives."

Abigail Archer was going to be his wife. Linus couldn't help the height of his head, the strut in his step as he escorted her, her mother, and Ethan to services on Sunday. It seemed the entire village and all its guests knew, for he and Abigail were congratulated time and again before and after Mr. Wingate preached a fine sermon on being thankful for the Lord's deliverance. Linus would have been the happiest man in England but for the cloud that hung over his head.

Suspicion. Doubt.

It didn't help that the man crowding his thoughts did not attend services.

"Has no one seen Mr. Donner?" Abigail asked as they walked back down Church Street with others returning home or to the spa.

"I'll ask Mr. George to look in on him," Linus promised. "He was staying at the Swan last I heard."

As if putting a good face on it, Donner appeared at the spa later that afternoon. He and Mr. George made a point of rejoining the Widow Harding's set, where they were welcomed warmly and teased about their disappearance during the chaos on Saturday. Doctor Owens, in particular, gave them a jibe.

"Young men like you should be leading the charge against the French," he insisted.

Mr. Crabapple drew himself up. "No, indeed. Wiser and older heads must lead in these uncertain times."

Mrs. Harding took his arm. "Well said, Warfield. You are my rock."

Linus had never seen such color rise in the fellow's cheeks.

Yet he could not throw off his suspicions. They dragged

at his shoulders like a sodden cloak, tugging at him throughout the day. Was he being overly protective of his spa, his village, Abigail and Ethan? If he expressed his doubts to the wrong person, he would be branding a man with treason.

But his conscience would not be silenced, so he excused himself early Sunday afternoon to speak to the magistrate.

He found Howland at his home near the church. The garden in front of the house was crowded with flowers. Some seemed to be moving. Linus blinked as he let himself in the gate, then smiled as a butterfly flitted past his face. So that was why the magistrate's home was called Butterfly Manor.

"How might I be of assistance?" Howland asked after his secretary had shown Linus into a well-organized study with glass-fronted bookcases, a claw-footed desk, and a view down toward the cove.

No reason for roundaboutation. "I may know the identity of one of the French spies," he said as he seated himself in the chair opposite the desk.

Howland sat straighter. "Indeed. Did you spot one of your abductors in the village?"

Linus shook his head. "Worse. I suspect he's been hiding in plain sight at the spa." He took a deep breath. "Allow me to sketch out my reasoning. Abigail was shot the night of July ninth. You and the militia were lying in wait for at least three fellows, who we suspect arrived on our shores shortly before then."

James nodded. "Correct. We captured Harris, the French sympathizer, that night. By his confession, we thought there were three or four of them in the area."

"Four," Linus said. "The two who kidnapped me, the man who was injured, and their leader at the spa. Before I tell you who I suspect, I must know. What are the consequences if I'm wrong, and he's innocent?"

"We can keep the matter quiet for now," Howland said.
Linus raised his brow. "In Grace-by-the-Sea?"

Howland smiled. "I didn't say it would be easy. But
I occasionally visit the spa, as you know. A quiet conversation among three gentlemen may not be remarked
upon."

"And if he's guilty?"

His face darkened. "Then he will be questioned and
remanded into the custody of the War Office on charges
of treason."

The sodden cloak he had felt about his shoulders tightened around his neck. "Then come with me," Linus said,
"I'll explain on the way."

Mrs. Denby was serving tea when Linus and the magistrate reached the spa. Most of the guests smiled or
nodded a welcome their way. As if she alone suspected
their purpose, Mrs. Tully began a military march on the
harpsichord.

Mr. Donner looked up as they approached, and Linus
nodded with a pleasant smile. He led Howland to where
Doctor Owens was listening to Mrs. Greer, who had
apparently joined them that afternoon.

"And my eyes," the slender blonde was complaining.
"They twitch every time I go out in the sunlight. Our
previous physician, Doctor Chance, told me to wear a
broad-brimmed hat. Is there not a more appropriate
treatment?"

"No doubt Doctor Bennett will know," Owens said,
seizing Linus's arm and drawing him closer as if he feared
to drown.

Mrs. Greer brightened. "Doctor Bennett, Magistrate.
How nice that our spa has such distinguished gentlemen

in attendance. I do hope we'll have the pleasure of the earl's company soon."

"At his earliest convenience," Howland assured her. "But I believe Mrs. Denby has the particulars. I'm sure she would be delighted to share them with you."

"I will ask this very moment." She hurried off to intercept the spa hostess.

"I pity Mrs. Denby," Owens said, "but I appreciate your efforts to extract me from that conversation. Being a spa physician is never easy, eh, Bennett?"

"Indeed," Linus said.

"Which is why we are here," the magistrate said, voice and look pleasant. "There appears to be reason to believe you are not a spa physician or even English."

Something flashed across his face, but he glanced from Howland to Linus, brows up. "What's this? I'm English through and through."

"But not, I think, a physician," Linus said. "Your employment agreement at Scarborough would have to be generous indeed to allow you to be away so long, particularly during this busy season. And yesterday, you were concerned about Mrs. Rand's heart when it was clearly her lungs involved."

He waved a hand. "I cannot be expected to issue accurate diagnoses under such primitive conditions as the middle of a crisis, sir. And if I were not a spa physician, why would I take up so much of your time?"

"I'd like to know the answer to that question as well," Howland said. "Were you trying to determine the defenses of Grace-by-the-Sea or merely using the spa to hide? Or attempting to identify Doctor Bennett's capabilities so you could kidnap him to tend your cohorts?"

"Tend my cohorts?" Once more he glanced from Howland to Linus, and this time his face reddened. "See here, sir. One might think you were accusing me of being a French agent."

"If you are not one," Howland said, "I suggest you compose yourself. I would not wish to blacken the reputation of a good Englishman."

Owens glanced around. So did Linus. A few curious gazes were aimed their way. Lord Featherstone was frowning.

"I see your point," Owens allowed, tugging at his cravat. "But I promise you, I am no Frenchie." He leaned closer and lowered his voice. "However, I believe I may have crossed paths with one in the melee yesterday. He was watching the evacuation from the shadow of the church tower before I caught up with Doctor Bennett here. I, of course, encouraged him to escape with the rest of us. He refused to address me. At the time, his manners appalled me. Now I wonder—would his accent have given him away?"

"Possibly," Linus allowed. "The men who abducted me refused to speak as well." He looked to the magistrate.

Howland was watching Owens, as if he could see guilt or innocence emblazoned on his face. "Do you know where this man went?"

Owens nodded. "He walked up the hill and disappeared beyond the spa."

"The same direction I was carried," Linus noted.

Owens cleared his throat. "If I may, I was told by another traveler of a public house in that direction, between here and Upper Grace. The fellow seemed to think I might enjoy the less savory company there, though I have no idea why." He shuddered.

"The Grey Wolf," Howland put in. "I've had more than one complaint about the place."

"If I were seeking your Frenchmen," Owens said, "I'd try there. And soon. They must know you're searching for them. They may already have been rescued by the ship we saw. But if you go, watch how you dress. You will easily mark yourself as a gentleman, and they will be alerted."

Howland inclined his head. "Thank you for the information, Doctor. We will take it under advisement. I'm sorry to have troubled you."

"No harm done," Owens assured him. "There's not much I wouldn't do for my native land."

Howland's smile was brief and tart. "Doctor Bennett, a word?"

With a nod to Owens, Linus followed him toward the door. "You believe him then," he said as soon as a potted palm hid them from Owens's view.

"Not necessarily," the magistrate said. "But he certainly wants us to visit the Wolf, and I'm inclined to oblige him."

Linus frowned. "If he is aligned with the French, wouldn't he be sending you into a trap?"

"Very likely," he said. "That's why I'm taking you and Denby with me."

# CHAPTER TWENTY-ONE

LINUS WALKED SLOWLY HOME FROM the spa that evening. Owens had gone out of his way to assure him he was no traitor, alternating between entreaty and righteous indignation. It was very much how another physician might react to such an implication. Yet Linus still had doubts.

And even more doubts about what to tell Abigail.

She would demand to come, and he could not allow it. Even if they discovered nothing nefarious, the very location endangered her reputation. The situation could well endanger her life. And he could not see French spies unburdening themselves to three men and a lady. He'd tried to dissuade Howland from including him.

"If these are the men who abducted me, they'll know me on sight," he'd protested as he'd walked the magistrate clear of the spa.

"And if one of them is the man you treated, only you can identify him," Howland countered.

"Then perhaps we should bring the militia," Linus reasoned.

Howland had regarded him. "You've seen my troop in action. They are improving and acquitted themselves better than I might have expected during the evacuation, but would you trust them on a mission of this delicacy?"

He would not. But he had to trust Abigail or what

chance did they have in their marriage?

Her mother met him at the door. "Linus." Her face puckered. "I may use your given name, may I not? You are going to be my son-in-law."

"Of course," Linus told her. "Would it please you to have me call you Mother Archer?"

The pink of her cheeks attested as much. "That would please me very much indeed. And Ethan can call me Nana."

Some of the weight on his shoulders lifted. He followed her to where his son was packing up his things.

"Another book, I see," Linus mused with a smile.

"From the vicar. Tales of chivalry." Ethan glanced up. "That means gentlemen who brave great things."

"Often in the name of love," Abigail agreed, coming down the corridor. "Like your father."

Ethan leaned back. "What did you brave, Father?"

"Nothing as impressive as what Abigail braved," Linus assured him. He turned to Mother Archer. "I wonder, would you mind keeping Ethan overnight? I have some work that might last longer than his bedtime."

Ethan raised his chin. "My bedtime is too early. Charlie says he often stays up until dawn."

Linus should not smile at the argument, yet he found it difficult to maintain a stern look. It was one of the few times Ethan had held his ground since his mother had died.

"I suspect Charlie might be bragging a bit," Abigail said, coming to join them.

"Regardless, Ethan is always welcome," her mother insisted. "And we can determine the appropriate bedtime for a young man of his age."

Ethan beamed at her, and Linus resigned himself to another discussion of what was best for a growing child.

As Ethan set down his things, Abigail moved closer to Linus. "Work?" she murmured.

"I'll explain," he said. He nodded toward the corridor, and they walked down toward her studio.

To his surprise, she put her back to the closed door as if refusing him entrance. "What's happened?"

"Mr. Howland may have an opportunity to capture the French agents tonight," he told her. "He's asked Mr. Denby and me to accompany him so I can identify them."

She pushed off the door. "I'll get my cloak."

He moved to block her. "Abigail, you cannot come."

She scowled at him. "I thought we'd settled that, sir."

"We have," he promised. "You are my partner, in all things. But this isn't my choice to make. Howland and Denby don't intend to bring their wives."

"That shows how little you know Eva and Jesslyn," she retorted, hands going to her hips.

"The location is not one for a lady," he tried explaining. "Just having one with us will raise suspicions."

She shook her head. "So, you ask me to stay behind, wait and wonder and worry."

"It is the most I could ask of you, but yes. I trust you to care for our family. Do you trust me to do the same?"

She hesitated, and his heart sank. Then she dropped her hands and looked up at him, green eyes solemn. "Yes, Linus. I do. I'll wait." She thrust up a finger. "But you had better come home to me, sir, hale and hearty."

"Madam, I would have it no other way." He bent and kissed her. The sweet pressure, the scent of her, the feel of her was nearly his undoing.

"Partners," he murmured against her lips. "Whatever may come our way."

"Partners," she whispered back before sealing the agreement with another kiss.

Later that evening, he, Howland, and Denby reined in under the sign of the Grey Wolf. The half-timbered building leaned to the east, as if barely holding its own against westerly winds, and the white-washed sides were crumbling. Still, light glowed behind grimy windows, and the open-fronted stable to one side looked nearly full. Howland and Denby had their own horses; Linus rode one he had borrowed from Mr. Josephs at the livery stable. A stable boy came to take charge of them.

"Will you be needing beds, good sirs?" he asked, hands wrapped around the reins.

"We're passing through," Howland told him. "There will be silver for you if you take good care of our horses."

The boy nodded. "They'll be ready to ride when you are."

Very likely many of the men visiting the public house had the same arrangement.

They entered through the battered door. He and Howland had to duck their heads to avoid hitting the low, beamed ceiling. A stout oak table, the benches already filled, sat before a stone hearth. Chairs here and there offered seating to others. A smaller table near the back of the room was piled with the remains of someone's dinner, but the chairs stood empty. Howland made for it.

A woman with a low-cut gown bustled over to drop three tankards on the table. "What else can I get you, gents?" Her smile to Denby showed two missing teeth.

"Just the drink," Howland said, handing her a coin. She also beamed at him, then scooped up an armful of the dishes and trotted off to the counter between the kitchen and the main room.

Linus glanced around. He could see why Owens had suggested they reconsider their usual dress. The rough coat and breeches he'd borrowed from Mr. Inchley made him fit right in with the other occupants. Faces bronzed by the sun, frames bent by labor, they hunkered over their ale. Some laughed and talked with acquaintances. Others kept their heads down and gazes averted, minding their own business.

"I see no one familiar," he reported to Denby and Howland.

Denby leaned back in his chair. "Give them an hour or so. If they've been coming here for food, they should show up soon, or this lot may clean out the larder."

"We may have to wait until after dark," Howland advised. "Safer for them if they come then. The public room at the Swan may close at nine, but Hornswag keeps the Mermaid open until after midnight."

He certainly hoped it wouldn't take that long.

But the hours lengthened. Howland fended off offers of more drinks even though theirs remained untouched. Other patrons came and went, but everyone who arrived was greeted by friends. Linus, Howland, and Denby were the only strangers, and the curious or belligerent glances being aimed their way confirmed as much.

"We might as well give up," Denby said as the clock struck ten. "Best we can do is question the publican."

Just then, the door banged open, and a half dozen men crowded through to block the exit. Each was armed with a black truncheon, and a long knife hung at their belts. Howland shook his head ever the slightest. Right. Best not to move and draw attention to themselves.

One man stepped to the front, broad face leering. He smacked his truncheon into his meaty paw, as if they might have missed the weapon.

"Greetings, gents," he called. "His Majesty has issued an invitation for you to join his Royal Navy. We've a quota to fill, and I've been told there's a surgeon among you. Hand him over, and we might allow a few of you to go home tonight."

Abigail settled Ethan to sleep in one bed and her mother in the other. Both slumbered easily enough. Impossible for her. Just as impossible to perch on the settee and wait. She headed for her studio.

Her first task was to adjust the hips on the figure she'd sketched earlier. That brought a smile, but it quickly faded. She'd never been good at waiting. She began mixing her paints. Soon, azure and emerald dotted the expanse, but her mind was not calmed by the cool colors. Instead, her thoughts tumbled over each other, like waves cresting the shore.

Linus had asked for her trust.

Jess had said she had had to trust in a future with Lark.

Her mother claimed Abigail did not trust her.

When had she become so determined to be an island? No, a fortress, proof against any calamity. If Linus could come to appreciate partnership, after all he'd been through in his first marriage, so could she.

She drew in a breath and set down her pallet. The scene before her was serene, and so, for the first time in years, were her emotions. That is, until she went to check the time. Nearly midnight? Where was he?

As if in answer, someone tapped at the door. Abigail hurried to answer before the sound woke her mother or Ethan.

But instead of Linus, Jess and Eva stood on her doorstep, both covered in long cloaks.

"Have you seen them?" Eva demanded, and Abigail did not have to ask who she meant. She stepped outside and shut the door behind her.

"No," she told her friends. "Shouldn't they be back by now?"

Though the lights were long out in the village, enough

of a moon had risen that she could see Eva make a face. "James never told me where they were going, so I cannot be sure. And Jesslyn says Lark didn't tell her either."

"Protecting us," Abigail told them. "And endangering themselves in the process. Well, we are not without resources. What do we know?"

"The location isn't within walking distance," Jess reasoned. "Lark took Valkyrie, his horse."

"And James took Majestic," Eva agreed.

"Which means Linus required transportation. We can check with Mr. Josephs. What else?"

"They plainly thought it too dangerous for us," Eva complained with a sniff.

"And someplace that would endanger our reputation," Abigail remembered.

"Possibly a public house or an inn, then," Jess said. "There's one between here and West Creech, another on the way to Upper Grace, and two more in that village."

Abigail nodded. "Nate, Mr. Josephs' son, may have seen which direction they turned at the crossroads."

He had indeed, they discovered when they roused him and his father from their beds a short time later.

"West, ma'am," he told Abigail, pushing tousled blond hair off his forehead. "And the magistrate and Mr. Denby were with him. Only they were dressed like common folk, not gentlemen."

"Thank you," Abigail told him.

"Would you be so good as to harness Lord Howland's traveling coach?" Eva asked the livery stable owner. "I understand he had to store it here as the carriage house at the castle would only hold the other two he brought with him."

Mr. Josephs frowned. A burly blacksmith, his frowns were as impressive as they were rare.

"Did his lordship authorize that?" he asked.

Eva smiled. "My husband, as you know, is steward of all

the earl's properties. I authorize it on his behalf. I'd use my own carriage, but, alas, it's not large enough to suit our needs." She turned for his son. "And Nate, there's a silver piece for you if you run to Butterfly Manor and wake Mr. Connors and Kip in the coaching house. Tell them to bring the musket and pistols as well as Mr. Yeager and Mr. Pym."

At a nod from his father, he ran off.

"You don't do anything by halves," Abigail said admiringly.

"Never," Eva vowed.

Jesslyn smiled sweetly at Mr. Josephs. "Might I borrow a few things from your charming wife?"

A half hour later, as darkness wrapped around the village, Mr. Connors was driving them along the road leading west toward Upper Grace. The three men and Kip rode on top of the coach, with Abigail, Jess, and Eva inside.

"They won't be pleased to see us," Abigail told her confederates.

"Certainly not," Jess agreed. "But they'll be alive, and right now that's all that matters to me."

Mr. Connors could only go as fast as the horses could see by lantern, but it didn't take long to reach the closest public house. It was a shabby place under the sign of the Grey Wolf. Even with the late hour, lights gleamed.

"Ready?" Abigail asked, tucking her hair up under the cap Mrs. Josephs had provided. "As we agreed."

Jess effected a weary look, eyes and shoulders sagging. "Ready."

"Me too." Eva rubbed her palms against her cheeks to redden them. Pym, a spry older man, jumped down as the lanky dark-haired Yeager helped them alight.

"Stand ready for my call," Eva told them. "And if I don't call within a quarter hour, come in anyway."

"Yes, ma'am," Yeager agreed, sharp nose pointing

toward the inn.

Pym went before them and opened the door, his wizened face at odds with his quick movements. As he hurried to the counter, Eva followed, leaning heavily on Abigail on one side and Jess on the other. Abigail caught sight of a few men around a big center table, a barmaid sweeping up behind. They all stopped talking to watch.

"My mistress needs your best room," Pym said, short nose appropriately in the air as if he found even the smell of the place offensive. "And the closest physician."

The man behind the bar was nearly as short as Eva's servant, with thick brown hair and a nose that was crooked enough to have been broken a time or two.

"You're in luck," he said, thumbs in the tie of his dirty apron. "I was full up, but the press gang came through and cleaned out half my customers not an hour ago. I can't help you with a physician, though. The only one in the area is down in Grace-by-the-Sea at their fancy spa."

Abigail leaned closer to Eva. "They can't have been here, then."

"These fellows may not have known Linus for a physician," Eva whispered back. Jess nodded.

One of the older men nearer the stone hearth barked a laugh. "Too bad your mistress wasn't here sooner. The press gang came looking for a physician too."

Abigail and Jess frowned at each other.

Eva broke away from them to straighten, chin up and eyes flashing. "Where did they go, this press gang?"

The proprietor frowned at her, even as Pym sighed and stepped back, hand going to the pistol at his hip.

"Answer her immediately," Abigail ordered.

"Or face the magistrate's justice," Jess threatened.

Even as the proprietor held up his hands, the old man started laughing again. "You're too late, I tell you. I didn't know the two fellows with him, but I recognized our magistrate, even if he chose to dress like common folk. All that shining gold hair. He tried to put on airs, but they'd have none of it. Last time I saw him and his friends, the press gang was marching them for Weymouth. They'll be sailing for the south this time tomorrow."

# CHAPTER TWENTY-TWO

"JUST KEEP WALKING, SAILOR," THE press gang leader ordered. "This is your last evening on land for some time. Enjoy it."

Hands bound behind his back, Linus stumbled on the rocky road and righted himself. Already, two of the other men captured with them had fallen. The members of the press gang had used their truncheons to force them to their feet again. He had no desire to feel the blow himself. An ill-placed truncheon could break bones, crush skulls. He'd seen it firsthand working beside his father on soldiers injured that way.

"All I need is one person to recognize me," Howland murmured at his side. "A magistrate cannot be impressed."

"Neither can an Excise Officer," Denby tossed back from his place ahead of them. "Not that it matters to this lot."

"Quiet!" A truncheon fell, striking Denby on the shoulder. He buckled, and Howland surged forward to prop him up.

Linus wracked his brain for a way out. It had been a trap, just as he'd feared. He had been right about Owens, but the knowledge brought little comfort. Howland and Denby might escape service as agents of the king. A physician was far too great a prize to be released so easily. They might not realize which of their captives had such skills yet, but once Denby's and Howland's professions became known, the physician would be obvious.

"Yes, you lot should be honored," the press gang leader said, strolling along as if he hadn't a care in the world. "We normally don't work at night. But we were told of a prime group just itching to serve on the high seas." He laughed, and his men joined in, until the sound circled them like a cage.

Behind them came the thunder of hooves. A coach, out so late? The press gang herded them to one side of the road and waited until it passed.

"That's a Howland coach," the magistrate murmured. "Someone's out looking for us."

"Would they recognize us in this group?" Linus asked.

"Quiet, I said!" The truncheon fell again, but Howland shoved himself between Linus and Denby and took the blow himself.

"Oh, a fellow what likes playing the hero," the gang leader sneered. "Looking to rise in the ranks, no doubt. What you need is a little humility. Walk at the rear, and eat my dust." He pushed Howland back as the others shambled forward again.

Linus found himself walking with Denby on one side and a press gang sailor on the other. No chance to talk without risk of injury. Denby was nursing his arm as it was.

Ahead, the road wound past a copse of trees, like black fingers pointing at the sky in the predawn light. As they approached, a figure stepped into view, physique obscured by a cloak, face by a hood. But there was no mistaking the pistol aimed their way.

"Stand and deliver."

The voice was husky, but…female?

The press gang leader held up his truncheon to stop the group.

"You're outmatched, my friend," he told the would-be

robber. "You've got one ball; we've got six clubs." He smacked his into his hand again for emphasis.

"And I," the figure countered, "have friends."

Five more, cloaked like their leader, moved from the trees. One aimed a musket at the press gang.

"Well, you've picked a poor group to rob," the press gang leader declared, holding his ground. "You might find six pence among us, but I doubt it."

"Free them," the robber ordered. "Now."

"You think they'll join you?" The press gang leader shook his head. "They'll run, every last one of them."

The pistol edged higher. "I'm counting on it."

"Run!" Linus shouted, and men scattered in every direction, shoving past their captors to stumble out across the Downs and disappear among the grass. Linus made for the trees, Denby right beside. Behind him, he heard a pistol bark.

He whirled, but no one had fallen. Indeed, the press gang was knotted together.

"Don't just stand there," the leader ordered. "After them!"

Linus ducked into the cover of the trees.

"Howland?" Denby asked, keeping low.

Linus shook his head.

A wizened little man materialized out of the darkness, and, for a daft moment, Linus wondered whether Mrs. Tully's fairies had found them.

"Mr. Denby, Doctor Bennett," he said with a bow. "This way."

Bemused, Linus followed with Denby.

On the other side of the grove, the Howland coach waited, their would-be highway robber at its side.

"All accounted for," the little man reported.

"Good," she said. "Climb aboard, Mr. Pym."

He knew that voice, even hoarse from dissembling. "Abigail!"

She pulled back her hood, ginger hair catching the first rays of dawn. "Yes. Quickly now. I doubt that press gang would be so hesitant if they knew three of their attackers were women."

Glancing around, he found Mrs. Denby and Eva approaching the coach as well, dressed in long cloaks like Abigail. Their chins were up, their faces resolute.

"Then they are fools," he said.

Another man with a pointed nose came forward to cut the bonds on Linus and Denby, and they all piled into the coach, where Howland was waiting, hand pressed to one arm. Blood seeped through his fingers.

"I very much fear your betrothed shot me," he told Linus. "I suppose turnabout is fair play."

They were safe.

Abigail breathed out a prayer of thanksgiving as the coach started for the village. She wanted to hold Linus close, not let go. She contented herself with sitting as close to him as she could.

It wasn't a difficult feat. Besides the staff on the roof, the interior, designed to hold four in comfort, now squeezed in six. Jesslyn perched herself on Lark's lap. Eva looked as if she would have liked to do the same with her husband, but the magistrate was pale, and blood continued to leak past his fingers. After they'd put a little distance between them and the press gang, Linus insisted that they stop so he could tend the wound.

"I was aiming for just in front of your captor's foot," Abigail told the magistrate. "Perhaps I should participate in musket drills myself."

Howland gamely smiled. "A dueling pistol wasn't intended for long-distance shots. I'm surprised you hit anything."

"At least it was a glancing blow," Linus said as he tied it up with his own cravat. "We'll want to remove any impurities when we reach the village to make sure it doesn't fester."

"Thank you," Eva said as he shifted across the coach so she could sit beside her husband and he could sit next to Abigail. Then she thumped on the roof of the carriage. "Take us home, Mr. Connors. We'll return the coach and horses in the morning."

Lark peered out the window. "I think it's already morning."

Indeed, a golden light spread across the eastern horizon. It brightened tree and grass, set the Channel to sparkling like a gem. Abigail could just envision the painting. Perhaps she could start it tomorrow.

For now, she leaned her head against Linus's shoulder. "I could sleep for a week."

"Not me," Eva declared. "I want to know what happened."

Abigail raised her head to meet Linus's gaze. "Yes, Linus. You went to capture a French agent, and you ended up captured instead."

"It was a trap," the magistrate put in. "Bennett feared as much, but I thought we'd be a match for them."

"And so we would have been," Lark said, "if they had actually shown their faces."

"Instead, they showed their hand," Mr. Howland said.

"We had heard a press gang was in the area," Linus reminded Abigail. "Someone alerted them to a prime catch at the public house tonight."

"Including a physician," Lark put in. "They couldn't pass that up."

She felt the shudder go through Linus. To think she might have lost him to the sea, for years. She scooted closer still.

"It was Doctor Owens," Mr. Howland said, the name like a curse on his lips. "Bennett suggested as much. He must be their leader, the one from whom Harris received orders."

"Then you must bring him to justice," Jesslyn said, normally sweet voice surprisingly hard.

"This very day," the magistrate vowed.

Abigail lay her head back on Linus's shoulder. His hand cradled hers. Once they had Owens, surely they could find the others, and all this would be over.

Mr. Connors dropped Eva, her husband, and most of her staff off first at Butterfly Manor, and Eva promised to treat the magistrate's wound exactly as Linus ordered.

"I'll come by later this morning to check on him," he told her.

"We'll let you know when Owens is in custody," Mr. Howland put in before allowing Eva and Mr. Pym to help him into the house.

The coachman stopped at Shell Cottage, the Denby home, next.

"I'll open the spa at eight," Jess told Linus as Lark helped her to alight. "Sleep if you can."

"I should be the one telling you that," Linus said, "but I am learning that the women of Grace-by-the-Sea are a fearsome lot."

"Indeed we are," Jess said with her usual smile before Lark closed the carriage door.

"Where to, Miss Archer?" Mr. Connors asked.

"The shop called All the Colors of the Sea on High Street," Abigail told him, and he clucked to the horses once more.

"You are redoubtable," Linus said, slipping an arm about her shoulders and pressing a kiss against her temple. "I begin to understand why you rush to help. It's impossible to ignore when someone you love is in danger."

"Of any kind," she assured him. "And I do love you,

Linus. Make no mistake about it."

His hand trailed along her cheek, leaving her trembling. "I love you too, Abigail. You risked much tonight, but you saved my life."

"So you are willing to admit that having an unconventional bride might come in handy," she teased, hope brightening with the day.

"I would change nothing about you," he insisted. "Except perhaps one thing."

Abigail frowned. "What?"

"Your seating position at the moment." He pulled her onto his lap and kissed her, and she could not find the least fault with him either.

# CHAPTER TWENTY-THREE

LINUS HAD NEVER FELT MORE thankful. He and the others were safe, and he was set to marry the most remarkable woman of his acquaintance. Together, there was nothing they could not do.

Including capture a French agent.

Mother Archer was awake when they returned, and she encouraged Linus to sleep a few hours in her bed. Abigail took to her own bed. She woke him at nine.

"Sorry," she said as he sat up, still fully clothed in the rough shirt and breeches he'd borrowed. She had changed into a green sprigged-muslin gown, the sort the ladies favored these days, and her ginger hair was curled about her face.

"Did you sleep?" he asked, rising.

"A little." She leaned in and pressed a kiss to his cheek. He held her close a moment, breathing in the scent of peaches. He would never think of the fruit the same way again.

Then he released her to run a hand back through his hair. "I'm in poor shape to be manning the spa today, but I don't want our guests to be concerned. How many will have heard about our adventures last night?"

"This is Grace-by-the-Sea, sir," she reminded him, sparkle in her green eyes. "Everyone will have heard about our adventures last night."

She was right. Mother Archer had gone to his house with Ethan, after asking Mrs. Kirby to let them in, and brought him back clean clothes, so at least he looked like a competent spa physician when he walked in an hour later, Abigail at his side.

The guests stood and applauded. Lord Featherstone offered him a bow. The Admiral stumped over to shake his hand. The rest of Mrs. Harding's set surrounded him with congratulations. Even tiny Mrs. Rand joined them.

"I had no idea you could perform such manly feats," she said admiringly.

Linus looked to Abigail. "Thank you for your kind words, but it wasn't manly in the slightest. I don't know how I might have fared if Miss Archer hadn't intervened."

Mrs. Rand raised her silvery brows, but Miss Turnpeth beamed at Abigail.

"I only wish that scurrilous Doctor Owens had been found," Mr. Crabapple said. "Imagine having the temerity to impersonate a physician." He positively trembled with indignation.

"Unforgiveable," Mrs. Harding agreed.

Mrs. Rand sniffed. "I knew he was a charlatan. He never once asked me to cough."

"I told you he was a troll," Mrs. Tully reminded them.

Mrs. Denby took pity on him. "Perhaps a glass of our marvelous waters is called for," she suggested, and they obediently turned for the fountain.

"Then the magistrate wasn't successful?" Linus asked her before she could move away as well.

"Eva ordered the militia out first thing," she told them. "But there was no sign of that Owens fellow at the Swan this morning. Lark was disappointed at the result as well. The magistrate sent word he is delaying the races one more day, but I don't know how many will remain."

Abigail frowned at her. "Surely we can determine where Owens went. Did Mr. Truant at the Swan see him leave?"

"No," she admitted. "Nor did the stable hands."

"The maids, then," Abigail said. "Stay with the spa, Linus. We'll sort this out."

Linus caught her hand and tucked it in his arm. "Mrs. Denby, please reschedule my appointments this morning. I'll be assisting my beloved, though I doubt she'll need it."

Mrs. Denby smiled. "Of course. And good luck!"

Abigail waited only until they had left the spa before giving his arm a squeeze. "Sorry. I'll do better at remembering we are partners. I promise."

"You've learned to trust only yourself," Linus allowed as they started up the hill for the coaching inn. "I understand. I fell into the same trap. But we aren't alone, Abigail. We can rely on each other. I hope you know I would never let you down."

"I do, Linus," she said. "I love you, and I trust you to do what's best for us both."

Love. He had feared to feel the emotion again, doubted his ability to truly recognize it. Looking into her face, feeling her touch, he knew he had made the right choice this time.

He took her hand and kissed it. "I love you, Abigail Archer. Let's catch a spy."

He loved her. She could feel it in his touch, hear it in his voice. She could almost see it shining in the brine-scented air. Though they were tracking danger, she wanted to skip up the hill, throw flower petals into the sky.

They would think her as whimsical as Mrs. Tully.

She didn't care.

But she did care about locating the French spy calling himself Doctor Owens. She would not allow him to endanger the man she loved again.

Nancy Haughsby at the Swan offered the first clue. The chambermaid nodded as Abigail asked her about the morning.

"Yeah, I seen him," she said, hands on her ample hips. "Bag in hand and strutting out the door, bold as you please. I wondered at the time if he'd paid his shot, but it's not my place to question a fine fellow like him."

"Did he turn left or right out the door?" Abigail asked.

She wiggled her lips a moment before answering. "Left. Down toward the village."

Abigail thanked her, then led Linus out onto High Street.

"Mr. Ellison is up early to make his bread," he mused. "Perhaps he saw someone."

"And if he didn't, we might be able to rule out the shore," Abigail agreed.

Mr. Ellison had been working, but his son had been out in front of the shop, watching for early customers. He could vouch for the fact that Doctor Owens had not passed that way.

"But I'd like a word with the good doctor," the baker said, rolling up the sleeves on his burly arms. "Mrs. Archer told me what happened last night. No one accosts our magistrate, our Riding Surveyor, or our physician."

He insisted on following them back up the street, leaving his son in charge of the bakery.

One by one, here and there, they gathered more clues. Mr. Carroll had not seen Owens, though he had been up as well, preparing to accept a shipment from London. He too joined their train. Mrs. Kirby had seen Owens after returning from Linus's new home with the key and had noticed him heading toward Castle Walk. Mr. Lawrence had recently taken a house on that street. His wife had come upon the sham physician passing when she'd gone out to her garden to snip chives to go on the eggs. The jeweler was at work, but his son, the militia drummer, ran to fetch the magistrate at Abigail's request.

"He's making for the castle," she told Linus and their followers as they waited at the end of Castle Walk. "The French boat was still in the caves beneath the headland, last time I heard. Perhaps he'll attempt to sail it himself."

"But the earl already took up residence," Mr. Ellison protested. "He can't just wander into the castle and expect a welcome."

"A fine physician from Scarborough?" Abigail countered. "He may not receive an audience with the earl, but he could request a tour. Visitors often do that at the great houses. Mrs. Kirby will tell you how many times she's had to fend off requests to visit the Lodge."

"We should wait for the magistrate," Mr. Carroll said with a glance up the headland. "He'll know what to do."

"We can't wait," Mr. Ellison argued. "We have to catch him now. They might not grant tours to the likes of us, Carroll, but we could come in through the kitchen. My Jenny has a job there now. She'd let us in."

Linus shook his head. "We must do nothing to make him feel threatened. We don't know whether he's armed. And we cannot allow him to take the earl or his daughter hostage."

"Then perhaps," Abigail said with a look to him, "we should request a tour too. Surely the earl could spare a moment for the physician who treated his father."

Linus smiled. "He might at that."

In the end, they divided to conquer. Mr. Ellison and Mr. Carroll went to the back of the castle and the kitchen door; Abigail and Linus knocked at the front. She had hoped the earl had requested help from Mrs. Catchpole and she would recognize the staff, but the tall, slender footman who answered the door was a stranger to her.

"Doctor Bennett and Miss Archer, calling to welcome the earl to the area," Linus told him. "I had the honor of attending his father, the late earl. I believe you came with him when he was last with us."

The dark-haired footman colored. "I did, sir. Thank you for remembering me. We're a bit busy at present. The earl refused to see the other fellow who called this morning."

"Slight fellow, ingratiating smile?" Abigail guessed.

"Yes, miss," he said.

"Did you send him away then?" Linus asked.

"No. He asked to wait. Mr. Jonas, our butler, put him in the downstairs withdrawing room. Is he a friend?"

"An acquaintance," Abigail hedged. "Perhaps we could wait as well?"

He shifted. "Mr. Jonas will have my hide, but I do think his lordship will want to speak to you." He opened the door wider. "Welcome to Castle How."

They ventured in.

Things had certainly changed since the last time Abigail had visited. Then, holland covers had obscured most of the furnishings. Now all the woodwork—from the dark flooring to the stairway climbing one of the tall walls—gleamed with a fresh coat of polish, and the twin stone statues flanking the hearth were visible, the graceful ladies balancing baskets on their heads.

The biggest difference, however, was in the amount of noise. From every quarter, doors slammed, and voices called.

"Miranda!"

"Lady Miranda!"

"Has the earl's daughter gone missing?" Linus asked, and Abigail was likely the only one who knew the reason for the sudden tension in his voice.

The footman grimaced. "She likes to play her games, she does. It wasn't difficult to find her in the London

house, where everyone knew her hidey-holes. But here?"
He spread his hands.

"Perhaps we could help," Abigail ventured.

"After we speak to Doctor Owens," Linus put in.

Of course. The French spy could not be allowed to escape again.

But when the footman led them to the withdrawing room off the grand entry hall, they discovered that the earl's daughter wasn't the only one missing.

Owens had vanished as well.

# CHAPTER TWENTY-FOUR

"WE MUST ALERT MR. ELLISON and Mr. Carroll," Abigail told Linus before dashing past the footman.

The fellow looked from her to Linus.

"Miss Archer thinks quickly," Linus explained, edging after her. "You'll become accustomed to it and be glad for it. I'll assist her. You'll want to help find Lady Miranda."

He slumped. "Yes, sir. And thank you." He hurried off.

Linus followed Abigail.

He had been in the castle before to tend the previous earl, but he wasn't entirely sure of the location of the kitchen. Both the scent of something savory and the sound of more raised voices led him down a corridor on the opposite side of the grand entry hall, where he found Abigail in the midst of turmoil.

Mr. Carroll was apparently attempting to calm an agitated cook, while Abigail tried to make sense of a younger assistant. Both women were talking loudly and over each other.

"I've never had such doings in my kitchen," the cook blustered.

"Of course I let my da in," the younger woman protested.

"That other fellow went past me like I wasn't standing right there," the cook complained.

"And what does he do but go thundering down the stairs?" Jenny Ellison asked Abigail.

"I hadn't even noticed that door before Lady Miranda went traipsing through it the other day," the cook insisted.

"Why are they so eager to reach the caves?" Jenny demanded.

Abigail met Linus's gaze over Jenny's blond head, and he knew she had come to the same conclusion. This was as bad as he'd feared. Both Lady Miranda and Owens must have headed for the caves below the headland, the girl from curiosity and Owens to escape capture. Small wonder Ellison had given chase. Lady Miranda could well stand between Owens and freedom. She had unknowingly put herself in harm's way.

Linus knew the pain of almost losing a child. He didn't wait to sort things out in the kitchen. He plunged after Ellison, knowing Abigail would follow.

The stone steps turned down and down, and only a few yards below the kitchen, the light faded. Linus put one hand to the rough stone wall and slowed his movements. Below, a glimmer of light beckoned. He made his way toward it.

Soon voices drifted up. How many were in the caves? Had the French landed after all? No, it seemed only one or two voices, repeating. An echo, perhaps?

The glimmer grew until he stepped down into a cavern that stretched into the distance. A lantern sat crookedly on the rocks fallen from the ceiling that lay somewhere in the darkness above him. Ahead, Ellison stood, hands outstretched, with Owens before him, back against the lapping sea and one arm around the neck of a dark-haired girl about Ethan's age. The so-called doctor was short enough, Lady Miranda tall enough, that the crown of her blond head reached his chin.

"There's nowhere you can go," Ellison was saying. "especially if you take the daughter of an earl with you.

Give up, and let her free."

The girl tilted back her head, curls swinging, as if to try to see how her captor was taking all this.

Owens' gaze went past the baker to Linus, then narrowed. "You? It seems you're more clever than I thought to escape the press gang. But it matters not. I have my ticket out of this wretched little village. What Navy vessel will fire on me with the daughter of the mighty Earl of Howland at my side?"

"I don't want to go anywhere with you," Lady Miranda said. Her voice was petulant, but it had a catch to it, as if she held back tears with difficulty.

"Leave her," Linus urged. "Take me instead. Even the French army needs another physician."

He hesitated, and Linus eased forward. Owens tightened his grip on the girl, and her face began to turn red.

Linus held up his hands. "I am no threat to you. Let her go."

"You," he said with a nod to Ellison. "Remove your boots."

Ellison stiffened. "My boots?"

"Do it!" Owens shouted.

The echo mocked them.

Ellison glanced to Linus, who nodded. Very likely the Frenchman thought the baker wouldn't be able to run after him over the rocks in his stocking feet. Ellison sat on one of the larger stones and began pulling off his boots. Owens was watching, so Linus inched another step closer, then another. He could not like the girl's color.

A clatter behind him spoke of someone else entering the cavern, but he didn't dare turn his head to look. Every step closer was a step toward freeing Lady Miranda. Still, he wasn't surprised when he heard Abigail's voice not far behind him.

"You're choking your prize," she warned the Frenchman. "She's no good to you dead."

Owens glanced down.

Lady Miranda reared back her head and struck him in the lips. As he staggered, Linus lunged.

"Here, Lady Miranda!" Abigail shouted, and the cave cheered the girl on as she dashed out of reach. Linus bowled Owens over, grappling for purchase as the waves splashed against them, frigid. Owens hands reached for him now, struggled to clasp his neck. Even as he shook the fellow off, Owens fingers jabbed toward his eyes.

Lady Miranda darted back in and dropped a stone on Owens's head. His flinch was enough for Linus to gain the upper hand. He pressed the Frenchman's shoulders down into the rocks and held him still.

"Nicely done," Abigail said, coming to put her arm around the girl. Lady Miranda hid her face against Abigail's chest.

Suddenly, the cavern boomed with noise as more people spilled from the stairway—Mr. Carroll, the staff of Castle How, and its earl. Lady Miranda broke from Abigail to run for her father.

Linus hauled Owens to his feet.

"Look, Father!" Lady Miranda declared, pointing back toward them. "I captured Napoleon."

Ellison moved to help Linus with their captive. Salt water dripped from his trousers, his fine coat was askew, and a lump the size of a goose egg was growing on his forehead. Abigail shook her head at him.

"Not quite Napoleon," Linus said as the others came to meet them. "But one of his agents. My lord, does your castle have a dungeon where we might house this villain until the magistrate takes charge of him?"

"I'll be happy to carry the word," Ellison offered, giving Owens a nudge.

"No dungeon," the earl said, one arm about his daughter and blue gaze like steel. "But I have a storeroom with a stout lock on it. Tell my cousin I wish to be present when he questions the fellow. I would like to know what else the French have planned for my castle."

"Mr. Ellison, Mr. Carroll, if you would do the honors?" Linus handed the spy to them, and they led him toward the stairs.

"It seems I owe you a great debt," Lord Howland told Linus. "You saved my daughter's life."

"Actually, my lord, Lady Miranda was beyond brave. She may well have saved my life." He put his arm around Abigail. "But then, I have come to expect such valor of the women of Grace-by-the-Sea."

She ought to be dragging her feet with weariness, but Abigail marched with Linus back down to the village. James Howland had arrived shortly after they'd climbed out of the cavern. He'd begun questioning Owens immediately. While the fellow refused to tell the whereabouts of his cohorts or their number, he admitted to being an agent of France. He had stopped in the village after Harris had been captured to determine why Grace-by-the-Sea seemed to thwart their every move.

"You must tell me," he had urged Howland in the thick-walled storeroom, as Linus, Abigail, and the earl stood in the background. "I thought you, Bennett, and Denby were the leaders. If I removed you, I cleared the way. There must be another. St. Claire? Greer?"

"My wife, Mrs. Denby, and Miss Archer have been one step ahead of you at every turn," the magistrate answered with a grim smile. "You see, it isn't just the men of England you should fear. Every man, woman, and child will come out to fight for our land. A shame you cannot tell your emperor that."

"I will tell the emperor everything," he threatened.

"My men will come for me."

"I don't think they will," Linus put in. "If I'm not mistaken, your men are on their way to France and have no idea you've even been captured."

"Indeed," Mr. Howland said with a look to Linus. "Captain St. Claire returned this morning to tell me as much. He chased that French ship nearly to France. How did you know, Bennett?"

"Ethan saw something the day of the Regatta the rest of us missed," Linus explained. "He sketched the French vessel with only three men aboard, a precarious crew at best. Put the word out up and down the coast, and I think you'll find someone's pleasure sloop has been stolen."

"Lord Waverly's," Howland had agreed. "The word came through yesterday. He sent his regrets that he could not join the Regatta, which will run tomorrow without French interference."

And it did. Abigail, her mother, Ethan, and Linus joined the rest of the village and their guests to cheer for the Siren's Call.

"Second," Ethan lamented as they walked home that evening. "I wanted him to win."

"I have a feeling he could have won," Abigail told him. "Perhaps he doesn't want the French to know how fast he can truly sail."

They returned to a fine fish stew courtesy of Jack Hornswag at the Mermaid. As her mother and Ethan finished clearing the table, Abigail led Linus down the corridor for her studio.

"I want to show you something," she said as she opened the door and let him in. "Something for our home. What do you think of this?" She stepped aside to let him view her seascape.

Four figures—grandmother, father, mother, and son—stood with their backs to the viewer and their gazes trained out over the boundless waters. The sun broke through clouds to gleam about them, as if anointing them from above.

He stared at it, and the wonder and awe on his face called to her more surely than the sea itself.

"I love it," he said. He turned to her. "And I love you, Abigail."

He gathered her close, her love, her healer, and she knew the future would be as bright and boundless as the waves she had painted.

DEAR READER

    Thank you for choosing Linus and Abigail's story. I knew Abigail required the right man to heal her heart. And Linus needed a little healing himself. A special thank you to my Facebook fans, especially Karen Visnosky, who suggested the title for the book. One tiny confession: grand stand was two words in the Regency period, but I used one word here for clarity. If you missed how Jesslyn and Lark fell in love anew, see The Matchmaker's Rogue. Eva and James found each other in The Heiress's Convenient Husband.

    If you enjoyed this book, there are several things you could do now:

    Sign up here *https://subscribe.reginascott.com* for a free email alert so you'll be the first to know when a new book is out or on sale. I offer exclusive free short stories and giveaways to my subscribers from time to time. Don't miss out.

    Connect with me on Facebook or Pinterest.

    Post a review on a bookseller site or Goodreads to help others find the book.

    Discover my many other books on my website here *www.reginascott.com*.

    Turn the page for a peek of the fourth book in the Grace-by-the-Sea series, The Governess's Earl. Rejected by the man she loved, quick-witted bluestocking Rosemary Denby is determined to win the position of governess to the temperamental Lady Miranda, daughter of the Earl of Howland. But is it the widowed earl who truly needs a lesson, in love?

    Blessings!

*Regina Scott*

# SNEAK PEEK:
# The Governess's Earl,

## BOOK 4 IN THE GRACE-BY-THE-SEA SERIES

by
Regina Scott

# CHAPTER ONE

*Castle How, Grace-by-the-Sea, Dorset, England,*
*August 1804*

HE MIGHT BE EARL, BUT he would never be his father.

Standing in a dressing room of the castle his father had used as a hunting lodge, Drake, Earl of Howland, pulled away from the well-meaning attentions of his new valet. Pierson had been, until recently, a moderately successful under-footman, but Drake's former valet had refused to leave London for the wilds of Dorset, and promoting Pierson had meant one less servant he would have to discharge.

If his cravat looked as if it had been trod upon by a herd of angry hippopotami, that was a small price to pay for household harmony.

Somewhere a door slammed, and Drake flinched, imagining the fit Miranda was likely throwing with some unfortunate maid.

"Too tight, my lord?" Pierson asked, pale blue eyes liquid with anxiety as he gazed at the ruined cravat.

"It's fine," he assured the manservant yet again as he regarded himself in the standing mirror. Pierson had combed his blond hair back from his face and trimmed the ends to rest neatly above his ears on the sides and collar at the back. Likely few would notice that one side-burn was slightly shorter than the other. Then too, few here in the little spa village of Grace-by-the-Sea would notice that he was wearing the same waistcoat he'd worn the day before and the day before that. Did Pierson have some sort of affinity for the striped wine-colored silk? He would have to remind the fellow he possessed several waistcoats, in different colors and textures, as well as more than the brown breeches and coat he persisted in pairing it with. At least his wardrobe hadn't had to be sold off at auction like their townhouse and country estate. Then again, what did it matter what he wore? It wasn't as if he had anyone left to impress.

A knock sounded at the dressing room door. Pierson froze, eyes wide in indecision. A footman answered doors. But a valet? "Should I...?" he started.

"Please," Drake said.

As soon as the servant turned, he snatched a different coat off the hook and shrugged himself into it.

Pierson opened the door, then scuttled back like a crab on the shore so that Jonas, the family butler, might enter. Now, there was a fellow any servant might wish to copy. Black hair pomaded in place around an impassive face, the butler advanced into the room with stately tread. He was the third fellow in the position that Drake remembered, the other two having been discharged by his father for not representing the House of Howland with sufficient aplomb. No one would ever level such an accusation at Jonas. He stood just behind Drake, his head only slightly higher, and kept his gaze respectfully in the middle distance until Drake recognized his presence.

"What is it, Jonas?" he dutifully asked.

"The next candidate has arrived for her interview, my lord."

Another one? Already he was regretting putting the advertisement in the local newspaper for a governess for

Miranda. She had pouted for hours when she'd learned he intended to locate someone to care for her. And he'd sat through four interviews so far, finding any number of reasons why none of the women were clever enough, devoted enough, and kind enough to see to his daughter's needs.

He eyed the butler. "I don't recall scheduling an interview for this morning."

Jonas kept his gaze over Drake's left shoulder. Why did he still feel a touch of impatience? "Nevertheless, Miss Denby is waiting downstairs in the library."

"Perhaps a cravat pin, my lord?" Pierson fussed. "Or a different coat?"

Drake waved him back. "I am sufficient, thank you. Jonas, you may tell Miss Denby I will be right down."

Now that regal face hinted of disapproval, dark brows gathering over his long nose. "I'm sure Miss Denby will be willing to wait until you are pleased to see her, my lord." He paused; Drake nodded. He inclined his head and left.

Very likely this Miss Denby would have had to wait on his father's pleasure. How he had relished any display of power—making the staff wait, making callers wait. Making Drake wait. He would never be his father—the fact had been drummed into him since birth.

And he couldn't mind in the least.

"Boots, perhaps?" he suggested to Pierson, who immediately went to fetch the shiny black pair.

He found Miss Denby seated in one of the heavy-armed chairs in the library. Felicity had laughed at the pretentious red and black dragons entwined on the satin seat, but then again, his late wife had had a way of making the darkest day seem bright. Would there ever come a time he didn't yearn to have her at his side again?

He made himself smile at the waiting lady. "Miss Denby. Forgive me for keeping you."

"Punctuality is a prize few capture," she replied, and he had to stop himself from apologizing yet again. Odd. She wasn't particularly large or stern-faced. Indeed, her gown of sea-green wool was tailored to a neat figure, and the patterned shawl over her shoulders might have graced any young miss in London. The only things about her that were the least intimidating was the way her warm brown hair was pulled back into a severe bun behind her head and how her clear blue eyes narrowed as if trying to determine his character.

But he was the master here, the one intent on hiring a governess. He would be the one asking the questions.

"Indeed," he said, taking the seat opposite her. "Is punctuality a lesson you generally impart to your charges?"

She regarded him. "I have no need to impart it, my lord. My charges are seldom late."

Slippery. He kept the smile on his face. He'd learned a few tricks from his father, after all. Never let your guard down. Never let them see your deliberation unless it puts you at an advantage. "I see. I assume you brought references from your previous employers."

She clucked her tongue. "I would never advise making assumptions on such short acquaintance."

Drake opened his mouth, then shut it again. What was it about this woman that put him in so defensive a position?

He gathered his dignity with difficulty, raising his chin and squaring his shoulders. "Exactly how much experience do you have as a governess?"

She glanced up at the ceiling as if calculating the beams that crossed it. "Six years, three months, and eighteen days."

Well, that was something, both the amount and the precision. Though she must have started rather young. She could not be much beyond six and twenty. "And how many charges have you schooled during that time?"

"One."

Drake raised his brows. "One?"

She cocked her head. "Yes. I distinctly said as much. Have you a difficulty with hearing or recall?"

Neither, but he somehow thought she would turn aside any response he tried. "One child is not sufficient experience for this position."

Her eyes widened. "But you only have one child. Why would you need a governess with experience schooling more? Besides, I started the dame school in Upper Grace and developed its curriculum before leaving it in my older sister's good hands."

So she hadn't actually taught there either? He felt as if the bookshelf-lined walls were closing in around him. "Miss Denby, I do not wish to appear rude, but you do seem unsuited for the role of caring for my daughter. She has been through a great deal for having only attained nine years. She requires encouragement, nurturing."

"Precisely why I applied," she insisted. "Lady Miranda and I have much in common. She lost her dear mother a year ago, I understand. I lost my father when I was eight."

The memory of his own loss was still too sharp. He would not have wished the pain on any child. "My condolences."

She did not pause to acknowledge his comment. "Furthermore, through a change in circumstances, Lady Miranda finds herself in a new home in a new location. I too had to leave Kent for Dorset to live with my uncle after my father's death."

Perhaps she had something to teach after all. He leaned forward. "How did you manage?"

She spread her hands. "As you can see, I grew into an educated woman capable of securing her own future. I would like to help Lady Miranda reach a similar happy state."

Felicity would like that. She had refused to hire a nanny

or governess, preferring to care for Miranda herself. He had never seen such love and devotion. He had been desperately trying to mimic it for the last year. Now that he was earl, he no longer had the luxury of spending all his time with his daughter. He must find a way out of the financial chasm his father had dug for them all, support his mother in her grieving, do his duty in Parliament when it started up again in the fall, and help his cousin James safeguard the village from the impending French invasion. Why, a French ship rested in the caverns below the castle even now, waiting for someone. Therefore, he needed another to step in and care for Miranda.

Could Miss Denby be exactly what he needed?

Rosemary Denby counted off the seconds. The new earl of Howland must grant her the position. Truly, what other recourse did she have near Grace-by-the-Sea? She hadn't the ever-pleasant aspect of a spa hostess to serve in the Grand Pump Room in the village, and her highly competent sister-in-law Jesslyn held that position in any event. The local fathers were distressingly uneasy with a young, single woman teaching their sons, so she had yielded her place at the dame school in Upper Grace to her older, widowed sister, Hester. And she would never have the patience to work in a shop.

"I don't understand why you must work at all," her mother had lamented only that morning when Rosemary had begged the gig to drive herself to the castle. "Your uncle left us with enough income that we need never worry."

"It isn't the income, Mother," Rosemary had tried to explain. "Hester has the school and little Rebecca; you have uncle's properties to manage. I just want something of my own."

Her mother's face had bunched. "And a husband won't do?"

The words were like a lash across her back. As if she hadn't paraded herself at nearly every assembly the last four years, accepted the attentions of any number of shopkeepers and farmers in Upper Grace, the young officers stationed at West Creech. The one man she'd hoped, prayed, might be interested had made it abundantly plain she was not the woman for him.

"I'm not certain I wish to be a wife, Mother," she'd said. "And there are few gentlemen here interested in taking a bluestocking for a bride."

But perhaps a governess.

And so she had brazened her way into this interview, claiming an appointment the earl had never made. So what if she'd only ever cared for her niece, Rebecca? She remembered what it was like to be a girl whose world had suddenly upended. Her uncle had encouraged and supported her dreams of learning. She could pass that along to another.

"I can see you are passionate about your profession, Miss Denby," the earl said. He looked so much like their magistrate, Mr. Howland—same golden blond hair waving from a strong-jawed face, the same piercing blue eyes. But the magistrate was all cool logic and determination. If she had been forced to find one word to describe his cousin, the earl, it would be...

Lost.

"I live to serve, my lord," she assured him, leaning forward.

By the set of those impressive shoulders as he too leaned into the conversation, he was not convinced. "But Lady Miranda, I have been informed, can be a challenge."

"A challenge I welcome," she promised.

They were nearly nose to nose, and she caught herself

holding her breath. Still he studied her. Would he see more than the fathers who had rejected her as teacher? Would he see more than Captain St. Claire when he'd refused to consider her as wife?

The click of the door sent them both upright in their seats. A blond-haired girl flounced into the room, ruffled pink muslin skirts dancing about her matching kid-leather slippers.

"There you are, Father," she declared as if he were late for some state function. "You said we could visit Mr. Carroll's Curiosities today and pick a new book. I'm ready."

"So I see," her father said with a fond smile. "I will take you when I finish my interview with Miss Denby."

Lady Miranda glanced her way. Rosemary knew that set to her chin, that light in her eyes. On any given day, she might have seen such a look in her own mirror.

"But I want to go now," Lady Miranda said.

Lord Howland looked to Rosemary. She did not so much as straighten a finger. This was a test. She had never failed one yet.

"Certainly you should go now," Rosemary said. "All your father has to do is agree to hire me as your new governess."

Her father frowned.

So did the little girl. "But I don't need a governess."

"Now, Miranda," her father started.

She turned to put both hands on his arm and gaze at him beseechingly. At least Rosemary had never stooped so low, but then, she'd seldom had to do more than argue with her uncle. He had been one to appreciate logic.

"But Father," Lady Miranda wheedled, "I only want to be with you. I love you."

His face melted. Truly, it was an extraordinary sight. Any resemblance to their stern magistrate vanished. In his place was a man who cared: deeply, desperately. A man who would have done anything to see his daughter smile.

And the little wretch knew it.

"I love you too, Miranda," he murmured. "And I want you to grow up into the accomplished woman your mother hoped for. That's why I'm searching for the perfect governess."

Such a creature did not exist. No one was perfect. But Rosemary knew she could do good in this house. Er, castle.

"I don't need a governess," Miranda repeated, and now her tone was mulish.

"Ah," Rosemary interjected. "Then you know the difference between elephas and plesiosaurus."

The girl turned her way. "No. I don't know what they are."

And didn't like that. Good.

The earl was watching her. Rosemary tried to focus on Lady Miranda.

"I'd be delighted to teach you," Rosemary told her. "My uncle, Flavius Montgomery, the famous geologist, taught me everything he knew. I can tell you why fossils appear in clays and where the ancient elephants lived in this area." She leaned closer to the girl and lowered her voice. "I can even lead you to their last remains."

Hazel eyes met hers, calculating, curious. "I'd like that. What about mathematics?"

"The square root of twenty and four is approximately four point eight nine eight nine eight."

She swung her gaze to her father once more. "You didn't teach me to do square roots. Is she right?"

"Yes," he said, lips hinting of a smile. "And square roots might be a bit beyond your skills at this point."

"Nonsense," Rosemary and Lady Miranda said at the same time.

Lady Miranda beamed at her. "I like her. Hire her, Father, so we can go."

"There's a bit more to hiring than merely giving my

word," he explained to his daughter. "We must agree on when she starts, her salary, half days off, and requirements for room and board."

"I'll start tomorrow," Rosemary said as fast as she could. "I'll accept twenty-five pounds per quarter. Sunday afternoons off, and a bedchamber and sitting room here at the castle with meals with the family most days. And I dress as I like. No uniforms."

"Done," Lady Miranda said. She grabbed her father's hand and gave it a tug. "Now, come along, Father."

He rose slowly, but his gaze was on Rosemary. "Ask Jonas to fetch you a bonnet, Miranda," he said, and she released him to scamper from the room.

He waited for Rosemary to rise, then closed the distance, and she had to stop herself from falling into the blue of his eyes.

"I am devoted to my daughter, Miss Denby," he said, as if she could have had any doubts on the matter. "As you can see, I deny her little. So, I will agree to your terms, but only for the next fortnight. You will have to prove to me you can do this job. And I won't be nearly as easy on you as I am on my daughter."

Learn more at
*www.reginascott.com/governessearl.html*

# OTHER BOOKS BY REGINA SCOTT

## Grace-by-the-Sea Series
*The Matchmaker's Rogue*
*The Heiress's Convenient Husband*
*The Artist's Healer*

## Fortune's Brides Series
*Never Doubt a Duke*
*Never Borrow a Baronet*
*Never Envy an Earl*
*Never Vie for a Viscount*
*Never Kneel to a Knight*
*Never Marry a Marquess*

## Uncommon Courtships Series
*The Unflappable Miss Fairchild*
*The Incomparable Miss Compton*
*The Irredeemable Miss Renfield*
*The Unwilling Miss Watkin*
*An Uncommon Christmas*

## Lady Emily Capers
*Secrets and Sensibilities*
*Art and Artifice*
*Ballrooms and Blackmail*
*Eloquence and Espionage*
*Love and Larceny*

## Marvelous Munroes Series
*My True Love Gave to Me*
*Catch of the Season*

*The Marquis' Kiss*
*Sweeter Than Candy*

**Spy Matchmaker Series**
*The Husband Mission*
*The June Bride Conspiracy*
*The Heiress Objective*

*Perfection*

And other books for Revell, Love Inspired Historical,
and Timeless Regency collections.

# ABOUT THE AUTHOR

REGINA SCOTT STARTED WRITING NOVELS in the third grade. Thankfully for literature as we know it, she didn't sell her first novel until she learned a bit more about writing. Since her first book was published, her stories have traveled the globe, with translations in many languages, including Dutch, German, Italian, and Portuguese. This book marks her fiftieth published work of warm, witty romance.

She loves everything about England, so it was only a matter of time before she started her own village. Where more perfect than the gorgeous Dorset Coast? She can imagine herself sailing along the chalk cliffs, racing her horse across the Downs, dancing at the assembly, and even drinking the spa waters. She drank the waters in Bath, after all!

Regina Scott and her husband of 30 years reside in the Puget Sound area of Washington State on the way to Mt. Rainier. She has dressed as a Regency dandy, learned to fence, driven four-in-hand, and sailed on a tall ship, all in the name of research, of course. Learn more about her at her website here *www.reginascott.com*.

CPSIA information can be obtained
at www.ICGtesting.com
Printed in the USA
LVHW021607070820
662642LV00013B/1069